"Why so coy, sweetheart?"

The man's smile widened, revealing even, white teeth. The grin did not reassure; nor did the unashamed gleam in his dark eyes.

"There's no need for playacting with me. Your charms are well worth displaying, as you are very well aware."

Before she could respond, his left arm gathered her efficiently against his bare chest and he kissed her.

FRANCESCA SHAW

A COMPROMISED

Lady

HARLEQUIN®

TORONTO • NEW YORK • LONDON
AMSTERDAM • PARIS • SYDNEY • HAMBURG
STOCKHOLM • ATHENS • TOKYO • MILAN • MADRID
PRAGUE • WARSAW • BUDAPEST • AUCKLAND

ISBN 0-373-30326-2

A COMPROMISED LADY

First North American Publication 1999

Printed in U.S.A.

FRANCESCA SHAW

is not one but two authors working together under the same name. Both are librarians by profession, working in Hertfordshire, but living virtually side by side in a village in Bedfordshire. They first began writing ten years ago under a tree in a Burgundian vineyard, but although they have published other romances, they have only recently come to historical novels. Their shared interests include travel, good food, reading and, of course, writing.

Chapter One

The guns had ceased their incessant booming, but the sound was still echoing in her head with the clamour of battle and the screams of men and horses.

The girl shifted restlessly and pain shot down the column of her neck, bringing her awake with a jolt. As she opened her eyes, the sensation of noise faded away leaving a silence almost as deafening. A sparrow flew across the dusty space above her, flitting in and out of the shafts of sunlight which streamed through the rickety timbers of what she could now descry to be a barn.

She stared up at the cobwebbed beams. A barn? She had no recollection of coming here. Nor was she alone: as she blinked in bewilderment her eyes met the baleful brown stare of quite the ugliest horse she had ever seen. Its iron grey flanks were streaked with mud and it stood awkwardly, favouring its left hind leg which was scabbed with blood. It soon lost interest in her, dropping its head and blowing heavily at the pile of hay at its feet. The sound was loud in the dusty space as it pulled disconsolately at a mouthful.

Disconcerted, she put up her fingers and pushed the tangled black curls off her forehead. She winced, then her fingers moved more cautiously, exploring the egg-shaped bump on the back of her head. That explained the headache which made it so hard to think…but where was she, and where had that horse come from?

Now that she was fully awake the barn no longer seemed silent: the corners were full of scufflings and more sparrows chattered overhead. The hay on which she was lying scratched and tickled her shoulders and a spider scuttled across her bare ankle. Bare? Where were her clothes? She straightened up on the make-shift bed, realising she was dressed in only her shift and covered by a thick black cloak.

Something large moved the straw beside her. All pain forgotten, she twisted round and stared, open-mouthed, at a man—unconscious, totally unknown. Her horrified gaze took in the tousled chestnut hair, the lean tanned face smudged with dirt and sweat, the mouth and chin masked with reddish stubble.

He was deeply asleep, yet there was nothing vulnerable or unguarded in that face. His restless movements had dragged the cloak from his shoulders revealing muscular shoulders and chest, paler than his face, one upper arm wrapped in a stained, clumsy bandage.

With a gasp of horror, the girl sat up, drawing back against the rough boards of the manger behind them. The movement was enough to rouse the fourth occupant of the barn, a large shaggy hound which, she could now see, lay guarding its master's flank.

The young woman began to edge cautiously away from the man, then froze as the action was met by a low, blood-curdling snarl from the dog, its lip curling over threatening canines.

"Good...dog," she whispered, but the result was not encouraging. The hound's head came up and its ears pricked.

"Quiet, Percy." The man spoke without opening his eyes as if he were used to such behaviour. In response, the hound put two enormous forepaws on his chest and licked his master's face with gusto. "Down, sir! Detestable animal!" He pushed at the big hairy body with both hands, then swore viciously at the effect on his wounded arm.

The girl gasped at the oath and both dog and master turned as one to stare at her. "Hell and damnation, I'd forgotten you were here," the man remarked amiably, his eyes openly admiring the soft swell of breast above her scanty chemise.

"Sir!" she protested, scandalised at the frankness of his admiration. Her hands shot up to pull the cloak up to her bare throat, but the heavy garment was wrapped around the man's legs and came up no higher than her waist.

Her hands tried in vain to cover herself and she felt beneath her fingers the hot blush spreading up to the tips of her ears.

The man's smile widened, revealing even, white teeth. The grin did not reassure; nor did the unashamed gleam in his dark eyes. "Why so coy, sweetheart? There's no need for play-acting with me; your charms are well worth displaying, as you are very well aware."

Before she could respond, his left arm gathered her efficiently against his bare chest and he kissed her. Hard lips explored hers, stubble rasped her cheek and, where her bare skin met his, she was shockingly aware of the warmth of him and his strength.

As unceremoniously as he had taken her, he released her. Outraged blue eyes blazed into his, her slight frame aquiver with fury. His obvious amusement only inflamed her more.

"Sir! How dare you! I... I..." She fought to express her shock and said the first thing that came into her head. "We have not been introduced. I do not even know your name!"

The man threw back his head and laughed, startling the horse. It was some moments before he composed himself, scrubbing a dirty, bruised hand across his face as if to straighten it. He made her a mocking half-bow from his reclined position. "Ma'am, I do beg your pardon. I have obviously misjudged your...status. Permit me to introduce myself: Captain Jervais Barnard, Eleventh Light Dragoons, your humble servant." He picked up one of her hands in his and raised it to his lips. "And whom do I have the honour of addressing?"

She flushed angrily at the heavy irony in his tone. "I am..." She shut her mouth as words failed her, then tried again as thoughts ran incoherently through her brain, a jumble of names, one of which must be hers, none of which sounded familiar.

He saw the panic in her eyes and was serious at once. "Can't you remember?" he prompted gently, all the mockery gone.

"No," she whispered in horror. "I cannot remember who I am, how I came here... Please, help me!"

As she started to shiver in reaction, he sat up and pulled the cloak round her shoulders, gathering her against him. She stiffened, then relaxed: in a frightening, unfamiliar world this big man was the only rock to cling to.

She held him, feeling his unkempt hair tickling her brow, his breathing steady and reassuring under her cheek. It felt right, familiar, to be held against a man like this. But the strong young man in her memory had no face, no name.

When the officer spoke the words echoed under her ear, although they were soft and thoughtful. ''I have seen this happen before after a blow to the head or the shock of battle. Your memory will come back in time, you must not strain for recollection. But we can deduce something.'' He gently sat her back against the manger and picked up her right hand. ''Your name, for example.'' There was a ring of coloured stones on her middle finger and he pointed to each gem in turn. ''Coral, amber, ruby and opal spells CARO. Does that seem familiar to you? Could you perhaps be called Caroline?''

Could she? The name was not unfamiliar, yet…the mists swirled in her brain again… No, the name meant no more than any other. She shook her head, then winced. ''I cannot say, I have no remembrance.''

''No? No matter, it will do for now and I must call you something.''

''Very well. It is strangely comforting to have a name, even if it may not be my own.''

He looked into her face consideringly. ''It suits you. What else can we surmise? No wedding ring, nor trace of any mark on your finger.''

He turned her hand over so it lay in his big brown one. ''Your hands are white and soft, and your face under the paint…'' Jervais smiled and ran one finger down the smooth, unlined skin of her cheek. "Your face is that of a beautiful woman, no more than perhaps eighteen."

Caro raised her eyes to his and felt her heart contract with a sensation she knew instinctively was new to her. She didn't understand it, had no name for it, but the warmth of it filled her and for the first time since she'd woken, she felt a stirring of happiness and trust.

"As for how you came to be here," Jervais continued, "that is simple to recount. I found you near midnight on a track off the Brussels road lying senseless in a rut full of water. I surmise you had fallen from a cart, although what one was doing off the main highway I do not know. And at the time I did not greatly care—it was dark, Caesar was almost on his knees and I was still losing blood." He tossed aside the blanket and she saw his overall trousers were torn and soaked with blood.

Caro rubbed her forehead as if the action would call back her memory. "Then there was a battle? I remember the guns and the ground shaking and I was searching...searching."

"Yes, there was a battle." Jervais laughed, but without humour.

"Who won?"

"We did, the Allies—if you can call such a slaughter victory."

"Wellington..." Caro said hesitantly "...the Duke and Napoleon...and there was fighting at Quatre Bras. Why do I remember that?" she demanded angrily, "when I cannot remember who I am, or why I came to be close to a battle?"

"Quatre Bras, that was Thursday the fifteenth. Of

June, 1815,'' he added, glancing at her to see how much was familiar. When she shook her head he shrugged and went on, ''This is Monday the nineteenth and we routed the French at Mont St Jean last night. Wellington and the Staff are probably at their HQ at Waterloo. Which is where,'' he added ruefully, ''I should be.''

His obvious concern for his own duty was lost on Caro, deep in her own preoccupation. ''But how came I to be so near a battle? And why are we here?''

''It was the nearest shelter I could find. It's a farm of sorts, although the house must have taken a direct hit. The inhabitants—if they are alive—will be out there cutting the throats of any Frenchmen they come across.''

She shuddered and pulled the cloak more closely round her shoulders. ''Why so delicate?'' Jervais was suddenly hard. ''As a soldier's woman you must have seen a battlefield before. You know what follows after.''

''As a soldier's woman?'' Caro echoed incredulously. ''Sir, you are offensive!''

''My apologies.'' The mocking tone was back. ''An officer's woman I should have said, from your obvious quality. But what other explanation can you offer? The only Englishwomen on that road were campfollowers or members of the muslin company sent back to Brussels for their safety and to clear the lines. You have paint on your face, no wedding band on your finger, and as for your clothes…''

He gave the hound an unceremonious shove and pulled a crumpled garment from the floor where the dog had made a bed of it.

Caro spread out the carmine silk gauze of the dress upon the hay. The bodice was the merest wisp of fabric, expressly designed to display not conceal. The skirts were cut to cling to the wearer's limbs and would scarcely need damping to become totally transparent. "Where are the petticoats?"

"You were wearing none," he said drily. "I have to say I have the greatest admiration for the taste of your...protector."

Could it be true? Caro sat and thought over what he had said. She could not recognise herself in his description, yet she knew that campfollowers existed, that officers would offer protection to young women—the muslin company—some of them of good birth, as she felt herself to be. Captain Barnard must be correct, for some instinct told her that sheltered young ladies would know nothing of such things as she was discovering she did.

There was a very long silence, both Caro and Jervais deep in their own thoughts, then they both spoke at once.

"I must get back to my regiment..."

"I cannot stay here..."

The Captain looked at her consideringly, then said, "I can take you to the Brussels road, put you on the first wagon we come across. Once you are back in Brussels someone will recognise you."

"Will you not come with me?" Caro felt a sudden panic at the thought of losing him, which was not entirely fear for her own safety.

"I must find my men, there will have been orders to rally. I should go to HQ and find out what is happening."

Jervais was getting to his feet as he spoke, but as

he put his weight on his left leg, it gave way and he fell back to his knees in the hay. ''Hell and damnation!'' Sweat stood out on his brow and he grimaced in pain. The big hound pushed him with his muzzle, whimpering softly. ''Get off, Percy! Damn this leg, it must have been a deeper thrust than I thought.''

''Let me see.'' Caro kneeled beside him, pulling aside the torn fabric of his grey overalls to expose a raw, jagged cut. She winced, but managed to say with composure, ''It needs cleaning and binding. Lie still,'' she added sharply as he tried to sit up. ''You will set it bleeding again.'' Suddenly there was a familiarity in this role of ministering to a man...

Caro scrambled to her feet, heedless of displaying her bare limbs in the scanty shift, and pulled on the red dress without a second thought. A pair of insubstantial satin slippers were under it and she thrust her feet into them. ''There must be a well outside. We need water—I will look for a bucket.''

''Take care!'' Jervais tried to get up, then fell back with a gasp. ''Percy: Guard!'' The dog trotted obediently after Caro, his great head pressed against her thigh.

With caution she pulled open the door a crack and peered out. The farmyard was deserted, the house indeed a smouldering ruin. The smell of burning was rank in the warm sunshine, yet incongruously the skylarks were filling the sky with song. She jumped at the sharp crack of a rifle, but it was some distance away.

In the centre of the yard was a well, mercifully with bucket and rope still intact. With an effort Caro winched up a half-full bucket, sniffing suspiciously at the water before realising that the unpleasant smell in her nostrils was being blown from the body of a horse lying dead across the gate.

Back in the barn she set the bucket down by Jervais. "Here, you must drink or you will take a fever. I think the water is clean. Do you have a saddle bag?"

He nodded towards the great horse, still standing patiently in the shadows. "Over there, by the saddle. Is there still water for Caesar in the trough?"

The charger moved over obediently as she slapped his shoulder and Caro realised she was used to horses and not afraid of them. It was a small thing but she was coming to treasure every scrap of self-knowledge.

The saddle-bags yielded a pair of clean shirts and a neckcloth, a hunk of dry bread, a greasy bundle which proved to contain a piece of bacon and, right at the bottom, a silver flask.

After a brief struggle she managed to tear one of the shirts into strips. "I had better look to your arm as well," she said firmly, steeling herself to remove the grimy bandage. At the sight of the torn flesh she quailed momentarily, feeling slightly sick, then forced herself to continue. This was no occasion for a fit of the vapours.

"Here." Captain Barnard pulled a knife from the top of his boot. "Cut the cloth with this."

She worked quickly and with grim determination, cleaning the wounds and bandaging them tightly. As her hands moved deftly over his body, she acknowledged that this close familiarity with the male form must confirm what Jervais had told her about herself.

That she had touched a man's skin, was familiar with the feel of leg muscles, of the weight of a man supported against her shoulder...all proved that indeed she was some man's mistress.

She looked up from tying the bandage tight around his thigh, her blue eyes puzzled. "I think my...protector must be an older man than you. His skin is not so..." She broke off, finding to her confusion her fingers were skimming his bare chest, sensing the hard muscles beneath the supple surface.

Captain Barnard smiled laconically. "Hell's teeth, don't tell me I've spent the night with a general's mistress. Not the way for an ambitious officer to gain promotion."

He narrowed his eyes and scrutinised her more closely as she bent to her task again. She was an enigma to him... No unmarried lady of breeding would handle a semi-naked stranger with such calm efficiency, yet her voice, her bearing, her obvious education shrieked "Quality".

The orphaned daughter of an officer, perhaps, he mused. Fallen on hard times and choosing to put herself under the protection of a man rather than starve. A sad, but not uncommon state of affairs after years of war.

She was a piquant little thing, too: that slender, almost virginal figure in that outrageous dress, her blushes and indignation when he'd kissed her had seemed real enough but must be artifice. Perhaps her protector liked that appearance of girlish innocence.

"Here, put this on." She had finished bandaging his leg and was holding out the second clean shirt. "You need a good wash and a shave, but this will have to suffice." Her hands were gentle as she eased his bad arm into the sleeve and buttoned up the garment.

Captain Barnard looked down at the tousled dark head, dismissed all prudent thoughts of irritable senior officers and tipped up her chin. "Thank you, sweetheart." This time his kiss was welcomed and answered with soft lips that parted under his and arms that snaked round to encircle his neck.

The feel of his mouth on hers felt strange, frightening, yet Caro had no urge to pull away from the warmth and pleasure of the embrace. She had no recollection of kisses in the past, yet she knew she had never been kissed like this before. Jervais was responding to her willingness, bending her back over his good arm so that she arched against his chest, their hearts beating together.

He moaned huskily, his mouth trailing hot kisses down her temple, teasing her earlobe with his teeth, then nuzzling through the soft cloud of her hair to her bare shoulders.

Caro closed her eyes and felt reality begin to float away on a tide of sensation; her entire body was suffused with warmth, where his lips touched her skin burned and her fingers tightened involuntarily in the clean linen of his shirt.

She was laying back on the hay now, breathless as his weight shifted above her. Part of her knew this should not be happening, although she could not remember why that should be so. But she trusted, desired, this man she did not know...

Jervais gasped in pain and fell back against the hay. "I'm sorry, sweetheart, but I do not think I can acquit myself with any distinction with these damned wounds! I must have lost more blood than I knew."

Indeed, he did look dreadful. Pinched and white

around the mouth, the lines tight around his eyes as he struggled with the pain.

"I should never have behaved so..." she stammered, suddenly overcome with guilt and shame, mixed with fear for Jervais.

He opened one eye and managed a slight grin. "Indeed we should not have, it might upset the general."

"Oh, never mind the general!" Caro would have stamped her foot had she been standing. Why she was suddenly angry with him she did not know, but the irritation was helpful.

They could not stay in this barn much longer. As if to underline the thought, the sharp crack of a rifle sounded, much closer than before.

Jervais pulled himself painfully to his feet. "They are probably just shooting looters and wounded horses, but we cannot be sure. I've no intention of surviving the battle only to be shot by a French sniper. Come on, my lovely, we must be on our way."

Between them they got Caesar saddled. Jervais led him round in circles, scrutinising the wounded leg, but after a few stiff steps the big horse loosened up and pricked its ears eagerly. Jervais slapped its dusty flank with affection. "Come on, old lad. One last pull and it's a stable and oats for you."

He limped back to the makeshift bed and found his uniform jacket, shrugging it on with a grimace. The dark blue cloth was stained and dirty, the silver lace tattered. Jervais smoothed down the buff facings and fastened the buttons, then began to buckle on his sword belt, tugging the sabretache to hang beside the curving scabbard of his sabre.

Caro was watching him when he looked up, her blue eyes fierce with the effort of memory as she stared.

"Is this uniform familiar?" he asked.

"No..." She shook her head doubtfully. "No, his is a red jacket, gold lace." There was no face to the figure she was remembering so hazily. Jervais stooped and picked up his shako. The plume was missing from the black, peaked hat and the silver cords were tangled. "And the shako is wrong, it should be more like a helmet."

"First Dragoon Guards, I think." He was tying his scarlet and gold sash around his waist, his face unguarded as he thought back to the battle. "They were in the centre, to our right." He didn't add that they had taken heavy losses; this girl watching him with troubled eyes might be more alone now than she knew.

"Come, take the cloak. That dress is not fit for riding in."

Caro could only agree with him as they emerged cautiously into the farmyard and the strong sunlight rendered the flimsy silk almost transparent. She was suddenly self-conscious, although if what Captain Barnard had suggested of her calling were true, why she should be so shy was a mystery.

Captain Barnard hoisted himself painfully into the saddle and surveyed the chaotic yard until he saw the mounting block. Caro found herself sitting behind him on Caesar's broad back with little trouble and her body responded easily to the steady walk.

"I have ridden before," she remarked, tightening her fingers in Jervais's sash.

They rode on in silence down the rutted cart track,

away from the farm and through scrubby woodland. Caro was aware of her companion's vigilance as his head turned to scan the trees, wary of every sound. It was a relief to emerge into the open and they stopped for a moment, looking north towards Brussels.

What had been standing fields of rye and wheat only days before were now muddy trampled wastes, across which limping figures made their way to the road. The highway was congested with a stream of wagons bearing the wounded back to the city, and mounted officers rode up and down shouting orders to try and speed the flow.

Jervais kept Caesar to the fields to make better progress, but he was watching the officers as they went and Caro guessed he was looking for someone of his own regiment to ask for news.

They were almost within sight of the city when he reined in and shouted "Harding!" A captain in the same buff and blue wheeled his horse away from a mired wagon and cantered over, his face breaking into a broad grin as soon as he saw who had hailed him.

"Barnard, my dear fellow! I thought you were dead!" Peeping round Jervais's back, Caro saw a stocky figure with a cheerful, plain face.

"What news of the brigade?" Jervais demanded urgently. "What losses did we suffer?"

"Less than you might think. Perhaps a half-dozen officers gone, including poor Stewart, and under a hundred men. When I think of that charge up to the French guns: we must have been insane!"

"Couldn't stop more like," Jervais remarked grimly.

"Anyway, I've been detailed to try and order this shambles, the rest are mustering at Nivelles, in case Bony tries a counter-move. Unlikely in my opinion: the French were done for the moment the Old Guard turned and ran."

"Captain Harding, get back to your duty, sir, and stop gossiping like a schoolroom miss!"

A bellow from an approaching rider caused the captain to wheel his horse, getting a sight of Caro as he did so. "By God, Barnard, you lucky dog! What a little sweetheart!"

"Damn you, watch your mouth," Jervais snarled with a sudden ferocity which alarmed Caro and obviously surprised Harding.

"No offence, old chap! Take care..." Harding cantered off, giving a wide berth to the approaching officer, who nodded curtly in acknowledgement of Jervais's salute.

"Good to see you, Barnard. Wounded, I see."

"Yes, Major. I'll get it dressed and return to the regiment. We are mustering at Nivelles, Harding said..."

"You will do no such thing. That leg's bleeding badly and you have hurt your arm by the look of it. Your brigade's in good enough shape: they don't need you slowing 'em down. Get into the city and find a surgeon, then you might be of some use later."

The Major nodded curtly and tightened his reins. "At least you still seem to have your wits about you. The quality of your battlefield souvenirs appears to be improving."

Before Jervais could respond, he had ridden off back to the road. "What did he mean?" Caro demanded.

"You. I have the reputation of collecting odd things from battlefields. Caesar from Salamanca, Percy from a nameless skirmish outside Lisbon. Neither of them, you must agree, a very beautiful sight."

For a moment Caro felt a little flicker of pleasure at the somewhat backhanded compliment. Then she felt anger. So she was just some battlefield memento, was she? To be compared with an old war horse and a scruffy mongrel? Whatever else she might be, she was no man's just to take, she knew that! Irritably, she poked him in the ribs. "Well, don't just sit there! Your leg has begun to bleed again and I cannot pick you up if you fall off…"

He nudged his heels into Caesar's side and the horse walked on. "I have every intention of getting us both safe back to Brussels and into bed."

Caro flushed at the mocking warmth in his words. "You are most certainly going back to bed, Captain Barnard! You have no strength to do anything else, as I recall."

"Touché," he murmured and fell silent as they entered the city gates.

The streets were chaotic, a mass of overturned carts and tumbled furniture, abandoned as panic-stricken residents had tried to flee in the face of the French onslaught they believed was coming. The relief was plain on every face they passed and many people waved and called out to the Allied troops straggling in.

Caro twisted and turned to try and see a familiar landmark, but nothing struck a chord. Surely she would remember something: a street, a shop, a church? After all, the army had been billeted in Brussels since Wellington had arrived in April in response to Napoleon's escape from Elba. There was another piece of intelligence she knew, another confirmation that her protector had been a military man.

Sighing, she sat patiently as Caesar made his way through back streets and across a small square, its market stalls deserted, through an arch and into a respectable street of modest houses.

They halted before a door and almost as they did so, a skinny youth ran out calling, "Tante Elise, Tante Elise! Le Capitaine Barnard!"

Jervais dismounted stiffly and helped Caro slide down to the cobbles. "Here." He tossed the reins to the lad. "Take Caesar and Percy, make sure they are both fed and comfortable and put a poultice on that hind leg." The youth nodded eagerly and led the horse away, Percy trotting behind.

"Monsieur, you are hurt!" A plump, respectable-looking woman was hurrying down the steps towards them, wiping her hands on her apron. Her expression of concern froze as she took in Caro who hastily wrapped the cloak around her all-too-revealing dress.

"This is Mademoiselle Caroline who has suffered a severe blow to the head and has lost her memory. I am relying on you, Madame, to help her." Jervais smiled warmly at the bristling Belgian landlady. "I told her that we could depend upon your kindness."

He turned to Caro, adding, "Madame Briquet has made a home from home for several lonely British officers and we all look upon her as a favourite aunt."

The look Madame returned was hardly that of a favourite aunt and Caro registered how very effective Jervais's charm could be. At the same time, she was very conscious of the reason for Madame's coolness.

Young women such as she herself appeared to be were not welcome in respectable homes. Why she was not hardened to such a response she did not understand; perhaps her military protector had sheltered her from the censorious world.

Humiliated, Caro followed Madame Briquet into the house and waited while a manservant helped Jervais up the stairs. Now that he had got them safely back, the sheer strength of will that had sustained him deserted him, and Caro realised with a sudden pang of fear how seriously he was hurt.

"I will call my own physician," Madame announced, firmly shutting the bedroom door on the two men. "You may have this room, Mademoiselle. I will send my maid up with hot water and some more...suitable clothes."

Left alone, Caro sat on the bed, hands clenched in her lap, fighting down the tears that threatened to overcome her. In a barn on a battlefield, anyone might be excused for feeling confused and uncertain. Now that she was sitting in a placid, bourgeois home surrounded by all the trappings of everyday life, her lack of memory became even more frightening.

What would be the fate of a young woman in a foreign country with no money, no past, no connexions? Her only friend was Jervais and he was seriously ill. Men died from wounds such as that, she knew. Loss of blood, infection, shock—all could be fatal.

But her fear for him was not purely selfish. True, he believed her to be a woman who sold her favours in return for a man's protection—it seemed it must be so, for there was no other explanation—but if she were to lose Jervais, she would have lost far more than a protector.

Caro shivered and realised she was touching her lips lightly with her fingertips: whatever else she had forgotten, or would forget, the memory of Jervais's mouth hard and sure on hers would never leave her.

There was a tap on the door and a maidservant slipped in, a bowl and ewer in her hands, a plain dark gown over her arm. The look she gave Caro was not unfriendly, but held a wealth of curiosity that made her flush.

Caro spent the rest of the day closeted in her room. The bustle of the doctor's arrival brought her to the door, urgent questions on her lips, only to be shooed back inside by Madame.

In the late afternoon the widow came in briefly. "He is sleeping now," she said, not unkindly. "The wounds are bad, but Doctor Degrelle is hopeful that with rest and good nursing, he will make a full recovery. And he is strong," she added with a sly glance that brought a flush to Caro's cheeks.

"I must help nurse him…" she began, getting to her feet.

"I do not think that is wise." Madame was firm. "You must be discreet and remain in your room: there are several other officers billeted in this house. The maid will bring you your supper within the hour. I bid you good evening, mademoiselle."

Rebuffed, Caro moved restlessly to the window and pushed at the shutters. The room looked out over the courtyard at the rear of the house where long shadows cast by the late evening sunshine patterned the cobbles. Percy was lying in a last pool of warmth, his great shaggy head on his paws, one eye cocked at the yard cat who slunk insolently around just out of reach.

The whole house was quiet and still. At long last the echo of the guns had gone from her brain, but no helpful thoughts came to fill the space left by the sounds of the battlefield. She was tired it was true, she tried to console herself, and worried about the man who had snatched her from danger...

It was quiet now; perhaps she could slip across the landing and just look at him. He was bound to be asleep, the doctor would have given him a sleeping draught, so she must take care not to disturb him.

Gathering up the skirts of the drab gown Madame had given her, Caro eased open the door and peeped out. Up above her a door banged. As she glanced up, startled, she caught a glimpse of scarlet uniform and the jingle of spurs as someone ran down the stairs. Caro drew back and the man was past without noticing the door standing ajar. One of the other officers billeted here, no doubt.

Once more the house was silent. Caro counted sixty under her breath then crept across the corridor, slipping into Jervais's chamber, holding her breath for fear of discovery.

She need not have worried: he was alone and asleep. The room was shuttered and dark, save for a shaft of light from the gap between the wooden slats which slanted across his face. Caro moved softly to the bedside and stood looking down.

Under the tan his skin was pale from loss of blood, the bone structure of his face honed by pain, dark shadows under his closed eyes. They had made no attempt to shave him and the light caught red glints from the stubble that was now almost a beard.

Caroline put out tentative fingers and gently pushed back a wayward strand of hair that had fallen onto his forehead. His skin was hot and dry to her touch and her heart quickened with anxiety. He was running a fever—perhaps one of his wounds was infected...

She was looking round for a water jug to bathe his face when Madame's voice floated up the stairs, sending her hurrying back to her room. ''Sit with Monsieur Barnard tonight, Henri. You know what to do, and call me immediately if there is any change.''

Reassured that Jervais would not be alone, Caro undressed and climbed wearily into the narrow bed. The bolster was firm, and as her head touched it a sharp pain lanced through her neck. Cautiously she massaged the large lump on the back of her head: no wonder she had no memory, it was a wonder she had any wits left after that blow! If it felt no better tomorrow, she would ask Madame if she might consult her doctor.

She had expected to lie awake worrying half the night, but as soon as she settled herself sleep swept her into deep oblivion.

Chapter Two

He was drunk again, Caroline realised with disgust, as she stood regarding him from the top of the sweeping staircase. His scarlet face, lined and jowly, stared up at her, the weak blue eyes struggling to focus.

Moved by exasperated pity, she ran down to assist the valet who was supporting his master and urging him to mount the stairs. Caroline put his arm around her shoulder, slipping her own across his back. Mercifully he was not a corpulent man, but the drink had made him clumsy and the two of them could hardly manage him between them.

The scene blurred and shifted in her sleeping mind and Caro tossed restlessly. Now he was sprawled on the big half-tester bed and she was tugging the nightshirt over his head while the valet pulled off his master's boots.

"Darling Caro...my dear girl," he was muttering drunkenly. "What would I do without you? You're a good girl to put up with an old man like me...had a drop too much...make it up to you...pretty necklace, eh?"

The incoherent ramblings faded away as Caro's head moved restlessly from side to side on the unyielding bolster. But as she slipped back into deep, dreaming sleep again, the face that came to her was no longer old.

The soldier standing framed in the doorway was young, handsome, glowing with pride in his new uniform. She ran to him, running her fingers over the gold lace, the gold and crimson braid, proudly adjusting the sash round his slim waist.

He put his arms round her and held her close as she kissed him, trying not to show her fear for him and spoil his moment of pride in his commission.

"Do not be fearful, darling," he murmured into her hair. "I will be back soon, safe and sound. And if something should happen, well, you'll be taken care of…"

"No, no… I do not care about that…" Caro said out loud in her sleep, but the young man had gone leaving only a name on her lips. "Vivian? Vivian?"

He came back into her dream as though called. This time they were both happy, drinking champagne, the bubbles fizzing up her nose, the taste sharp on her tongue. He held up his glass. "To us, Caro!" and she knew she was happy.

She fought to see the details of the room, but it was a blur of candlelight on fine crystal, of panelling hung with paintings and long windows swagged with damasks.

"Vivian?" she murmured again, but he had gone and in his place was a lovely woman, her face painted artfully, her hair teased into locks which tumbled enticingly over her voluptuous shoulders and daringly exposed bosom.

Her own voice echoed through the dream, confused, questioning. "But what of love?"

"Love?" The other woman laughed shortly. "Oh no, my dear, we may not love. That is not part of the bargain. We sell ourselves for protection and security for as long as it lasts. Women in our trade guard only two things: the money we gain and our innermost feelings." The carmine lips twisted slightly. "Fall in love and you regret it forever, for they never truly love you in return."

Caro woke with a start to find her cheeks wet. She rubbed the back of her hand over her eyes as she fought to keep hold of the dream, but it had faded leaving only the name "Vivian" and the sickening certainty that Jervais had been right about her profession.

At the window she breathed deeply, struggling with the feelings her dream had evoked. It seemed she had been the mistress of at least two men, two very different men. Why then was she so shamed by the knowledge?

Servants were moving about the yard. As she watched Percy walked out of the shed, stretching each leg out with a great effort then trotting purposefully off to the kitchen door. Conscious of her nightgown, Caro pulled the shutters closed and washed rapidly in cold water from the ewer before scrambling into her borrowed dress.

Her hair was knotted and tangled from her restless night and it took several painful minutes before the glass to tame it into some semblance of order.

For the first time since she had regained consciousness she was able to regard herself in a mirror. Caro's first thought was how dreadful she looked in bottle green, how the shade did nothing for her pale complexion and black hair. It even succeeded in drowning the blue intensity of her eyes.

Her glance strayed to the crimson gown tossed on the end of the bed. No, she thought regretfully, she would never be allowed to visit Jervais wearing that!

Twisting her hair back into a severe knot that made her look positively dowdy, Caro ventured out in search of Madame. If she looked demure enough, perhaps the widow would relent and let her move about the house.

Downstairs, all was activity. A hubbub arose from the dining salon where Caro could see officers crowded around the table, talking non-stop while they demolished the first good meal most of them had seen in days.

She slipped past into the kitchen and almost collided with a maid carrying a jug of porter in one hand and a platter of ham in the other. Madame was in the centre of the kitchen, sleeves rolled up, apron swathing her gown, giving orders.

"Ah, mademoiselle—take care! That hot water upstairs for Lieutenant Hargraves, Henri, then back here for the Colonel's shirts, he rejoins Lord Wellington's staff this morning."

Taking refuge behind a chair as the servants scurried around her, Caro asked tentatively, "May I help, Madame?"

The widow seemed about to refuse when a maid enquired, "Am I to take up Monsieur Barnard's breakfast, Madame?"

"I will take it," Caro said eagerly, reaching for the tray.

Madame sighed, then nodded her assent. "Better

that than you remaining down here with so many officers in the house.''

Caroline was stung by the implication that she could not be trusted, but was mollified when the widow added, ''Perhaps I was mistaken in my opinion last night. I would not wish you to receive any unwanted attentions from these gentlemen.''

The other manservant put his head round the door and reported, ''The army surgeon has been and dressed Monsieur's wounds, Madame. He seems quite satisfied that the crisis is over, but he wishes a word with you in the parlour.''

Caroline seized the opportunity—and the tray—and hurried upstairs. Jervais was propped up in bed looking, if anything paler than he had the night before. When he recognised her, his face broke into a smile that lightened her heart like magic until he spoke.

''Caro! Where did you get that dress?''

''Madame felt it to be suitable,'' she said stiffly, placing the tray beside the bed and shaking out the napkin. She was suddenly shy with him, and tried to cover it with light conversation. ''Do you not care for it?''

''If I were looking for a governess, no doubt I would. No, give me the bowl,'' he ordered as she lifted a spoon. ''I am quite capable of feeding myself. What is this?''

''Gruel, I think. And bread and warm milk.''

Jervais gazed into the bowls with horror. ''And there was I thinking that the morning held no worse terrors than the gentle ministrations of Surgeon-Major Fortescue.''

''Was it very bad?'' Caro busied herself at the

shutters, not meeting his eyes. What had seemed natural yesterday in the enforced intimacy of the barn was discommoding now. To be alone in a man's chamber, to be alone with a man who was to all intents and purposes a stranger, was embarrassing. She did not want to look at him, to remember as she saw the clean white bandages against his bare skin the feel of that body against hers.

"Well..." Jervais was laconic "...after he decided he was not going to cut my leg off, things improved, but on balance I think I would rather fight the battle again."

"Eat your breakfast," Caro urged, steeling herself to turn from the window and not think about what he had had to endure. "You need to eat to restore your health."

"This will do nothing to help," he grimaced, spooning the pap up distastefully. "I need good red meat and a bottle of claret."

"Eat it," Caro wheedled, forgetting her self-consciousness in her concern for him, "and I will see what can be done for luncheon, but red wine and red meat will only inflame the wounds."

"Quite the little nurse," he mocked her. "You speak as if you have a knowledge of sick-rooms."

"I believe I have," she said slowly, stung by his harshness, but the memory of the older man from the dream refused to clarify into anything more substantial.

"Do not you remember anything more? I should have asked, how are you this morning?"

"My head is sore if I touch it, but it no longer aches. I had a dream last night..." her voice trailed off.

"A dream? That is promising." She had caught his interest. "Here, take this thing—" he pushed the tray aside "—and come sit by me."

Caro hesitated for a moment, then sat right on the edge of the bed, as far as possible from him.

"What do you recall?" he urged.

"An elderly man, I believe...he was drunk or ill...drunk, I think. I helped him to bed. No, it is gone again." She shook her head helplessly.

"Your general, no doubt." Jervais was tart. "Come on, what else?"

Caro rubbed her forehead. "A young man, in uniform. Younger than me, I think. He was so proud, and alive—vital. So handsome."

Jervais pulled himself more upright on the pillows. "When you have quite finished eulogising this paragon, try and remember something more to the point. After all, the army is full of young cubs you would no doubt regard as well-favoured. I can hardly be expected to identify him from that!"

She looked at him with hurt in her eyes and he felt a momentary irritation at her, sitting there so nun-like in that dreadful gown, confidently expecting him to deliver her back to some young puppy. Damn and blast the pain that was making him so short.

"Look, Caro," he said more gently. "I'm trying to help, but let us be frank with each other. Which of these two was your most recent...protector? Returning you to the wrong one would hardly be tactful."

Caro sat pleating the coverlet between her fingers. She didn't want to be returned to anyone. All she wanted was to remember who she was.

She lifted her eyes to the lean, laconic face. She

did not know him well enough to interpret his expression or the wry twist to his lips as she said, "Vivian. That's all I recollect."

"Vivian?" His eyes were narrowed in thought. "Surely you cannot mean Major-General Sir George Vivian? I would not have thought you were in his style."

"No, the younger man is called Vivian, of that I am sure."

"That is a source of some relief," Jervais said drily. "The thought of enquiring tactfully of Sir George whether he has mislaid his mistress makes my blood run cold."

"I do not feel like anyone's mistress." The beautiful, unsettling blue eyes were raised to his again.

"Well, at the moment you are not, are you?" He saw her flush and wondered at himself for his restraint. She really was a piquant little thing. Even dressed in that frightful gown her slender figure was alluring... Why he was so reluctant to offer her his protection he was uncertain. Despite what he had said to her, the thought of dealing with an enraged senior officer gave him no qualms, and he had recently parted company with a charming Portuguese mistress with no hard feelings on either side.

As he thought, Jervais rubbed his hand across his jaw, grimacing at the scrape of stubble. "Damn it, I feel like a hedgehog. I cannot recall when I was last shaved."

"I can do it for you." The words were out before she could stop them.

"Can you indeed?" His eyebrows rose. "I am very attached to my ears and I have a fancy to keep them."

"I have done it before, quite often, I believe..."
That wretched, elusive, memory! Caro shook herself
and stood up briskly. "I will go and get some hot
water." She was already regretting her unthinking
offer which would necessitate such enforced intimacy, but to change her mind now would seem mis-
sish.

When she returned with hot water and a towel,
Jervais gestured at his saddle-bags, still propped
against the wall. "My kit is in there." He watched
as she opened the canvas roll and pulled out one of
the pair of ivory-handled razors. "Take care for the
edge..."

Even as he cautioned her, she was testing the edge
of the blade competently with her thumb. "Good, it
is very sharp, I never could strop them properly, it
is quite an art." Caro was aware of Jervais watching
as she moved purposefully about to hide her apprehension, setting the basin by the bed, whisking up a
lather and draping the towel around his shoulders.

She had to perch on the edge of the bed, close
against him, forcing herself to concentrate on her
task, a trace of delicate colour mantling her cheeks.

With resolution Caro dipped the badger-hair brush
in the soap and began to lather his face. Jervais sat
very still, and she strove to seem quite unconscious
of his eyes watching her.

Her fingers were firm and cool as she pulled the
skin tight over his cheekbone and began to run the
razor with apparent confidence down through the
stubble. Jervais saw the concentration in her eyes,
the way her teeth caught the fullness of her underlip
as she wiped the blade on the towel and began on
his chin.

Caro twisted round as she tried to reach his right cheek. The height of the bed and the size of the man in it made getting the correct angle difficult. She hesitated. She could hardly leave him half-shaved... Without giving herself time to think what she was doing, she kneeled up on the bed and leaned over him. She worked steadily and silently, the only sounds in the room the scrape of the blade, his breathing and the occasional creak as Caro shifted her balance on the mattress.

"There!" She sat back on her heels, rather breathless, and wiped the razor for the last time. "Just a last bit of soap here..." She reached across him and dabbed with the edge of the towel at the point of his jaw.

Their eyes met and the towel fell unheeded from her fingers. They were as close as they had been when she had woken in the barn, but now he was no longer a stranger. This was Jervais...

Caro's breath caught in her throat and her heart drummed in her ears until she felt dizzy. She was caught by the intensity of his gaze, trying to fathom the question his eyes were asking her.

Jervais reached up and cupped the softness of her cheek with one hand, his fingers moving round to pull her gently down into his embrace. She went with no resistance, almost fatalistically. Caught against his chest, held in the circle of his unwounded arm, Caro raised her face trustingly to his.

The kiss was gentle, slow, almost leisurely, yet the warmth and tenderness was insidious. Caro's very bones felt formless, her body was weightless, floating as Jervais deepened the kiss. She responded without artifice, knowing she had never been kissed like this before.

The very artlessness of her response was a provocation. Jervais groaned, deep in his throat, his mouth moving on hers, the pain in his wounded arm as if nothing as he tightened his hold on the slim body. Caro's trust, her air of innocence, was intensely erotic: he was damned if he was giving her up to any other man.

He freed her mouth, murmuring into the softness of her throat, "Take off your gown for me, damn this arm—I cannot do it for you."

"Your wounds!" His voice recalled her part way to reality. "We should not…"

"I doubt I can," he said ruefully, "but come back to bed, my darling Caro, and let me give you pleasure."

Her hands moved obediently to the fastenings of her gown, yet even as they did so, she was conscious through the turmoil he had aroused in her body that in one corner of her mind a small voice said coldly, clearly, "No".

Caro stared at Jervais as he smiled back at her, his mouth warm, promising tenderness and delight. "Jervais… I…." She sprang from the bed and ran.

In her own room she slammed the door and turned the key in the lock, resting her flushed cheeks against the wood. Fighting down the clamouring of her body, she forced herself to think. Ever since she had woken in the barn she had been doing things she could not remember having knowledge of. She could ride a horse, dress her own hair, shave a man. Yet when Jervais invited her to his bed, there was no knowledge there—and never had been. She had never known a man: and if that were so, then everything else she had come to believe about herself in the last two days was untrue.

Caro sat down on the bed, her legs suddenly weak. She gazed round the small room seeking something, some clue as to who—or what—she was. She was frightened: it had been bad enough before, having no memory, but at least Jervais had offered her some explanation that she could hold on to. Now she knew nothing.

The room yielded no inspiration. A gloomy print of Daniel conversing with a number of cross-looking lions did nothing to raise her spirits. Voices floated up from the courtyard and suddenly Caro needed sunshine, warmth, people.

Snatching up a pelisse, she hurried downstairs. There was no one about in the hall. Should she leave Madame a note? No, she had to get outside and the widow might try and stop her. Caro slipped through the front door and looked up and down the street. Nothing seemed familiar, she could recognise no landmarks. After a moment's hesitation she turned left and followed where most of the passers-by seemed to be heading.

Ten minutes of brisk walking brought her to a wide market square, hedged with tall gabled buildings, its centre a bustling mass of servants with baskets amid the stalls.

''The Grand Place!'' she exclaimed out loud, causing several people to turn and stare at her. Excited, Caro looked round, realising she could name the King's House, the Town Hall, that the masses of statues decorating the house fronts were familiar. She hurried across the square looking for more landmarks, hoping against hope she might see a face in the crowd she knew.

At the edge of the pavement she paused. If she could remember this place, perhaps she could remember her name. But it would not come. Tears of frustration welled in her eyes, she clenched her fists in a physical effort... As she turned from the road a voice rang out, shrill with excitement across the hubbub.

"Caroline!"

Caro spun on her heel, searching for the source of the voice. Her shoe slipped off the kerbstone, vainly she flailed her arms for balance, then fell. A sharp, familiar pain lanced through her head, then darkness enveloped her.

She came to, lying across the seats of a barouche, her head pillowed in the lap of a slender woman in her late twenties.

"Flora!" Caroline gasped.

Her aunt smiled with relief, stroking Caroline's cheek with a hand that shook slightly. "Darling girl, we have been frantic with worry for you! Where have you been? What has become of you?"

Caroline struggled to sit up, wincing at the pain in her head. "What has happened? Where am I?"

Her aunt took in the gathering crowd of gawping bystanders. "Drive home, Jacques!" She delved into her reticule and produced a bottle. "Here, sniff this, the fall has shaken you out of your senses."

Caroline waved away the sal volatile, wrinkling her nose. "Flora, please, it makes me feel dizzy." She closed her eyes, seeing lights dance against the lids as she fought against nausea. After a moment she blinked and sat up slowly against her aunt's supporting arm. "This is the Grand Place, isn't it? But I don't remember coming out today. And why," she demanded, catching sight of her skirts, "am I wearing this dowdy gown? It is not mine."

Lady Grey glanced at the back of the driver and gestured to Caroline for discretion. "You have had a dreadful bump on the head, dear, just lie back and close your eyes until we get home."

The elegant town house in the quiet square was familiar and welcoming as Jacques helped Caroline down from the carriage. Her aunt wanted her to lie down, but she was too confused and full of questions to rest.

Flora insisted on bathing the lump on the back of Caroline's head. "It looks as though you struck your head twice when you fell," she commented, gently parting the black curls. "There are two nasty bumps here."

"Ouch!" Caroline protested. "Oh, please let it alone, Flora, and tell me what is happening! I cannot even recall going out this morning."

"This morning!" Her father's only sister sat down abruptly on the end of the bed and stared at her aghast. "My dear girl, you have been gone since Saturday noon and it is now Tuesday morning!"

"I have been missing for three days?" Caroline was equally aghast. "But where have I been?"

"But I do not know! You took your horse and went to ask Colonel Jones, the Military Commandant, if we should leave, do not you recall? I became concerned because of the rumours that our army was retreating and you said we should stay because of Vivian…"

"Vivian! How could I have forgotten him!" Caroline was half off the bed in her agitation. "Is the battle over? Is he safe?"

"Your brother is quite unscathed," her aunt assured her, her calm tone belying the tired, drawn cast of her face. "Tired, filthy and very hungry, but without a scratch, thank God. He called by for an hour this morning. He was half-mad with worry about you, but he had to go back to his regiment."

"At Nivelles?"

"Yes, but how could you know that?"

Caroline looked at her bleakly. "I do not know, I just do not know. I cannot recall leaving the house or where I have been these past three nights..." She could feel the colour ebbing from her cheeks. Nivelles...there was something about Nivelles. Then it came back with a clarity that shocked her: her arms around Jervais's waist, the movement of Caesar beneath her, the voice of the other officer giving Jervais the news of victory and of the troops reassembling at Nivelles.

"Oh, my dear, you have gone such a strange colour!" Flora cried in distress. "I must send for the physician—I fear you are succumbing to a brain fever."

"No...no, please do not. It is simply that it is so distressing being unable to recollect what has occurred." It was the exact opposite of the truth: at that moment Caroline felt she would give almost anything to be in ignorance once again, to consign to oblivion the remembrance of waking in the barn, in the straw with a man beside her!

And how had she come to be there? There was still Saturday noon to Monday morning to be accounted for; that part of her memory was still hidden behind a closed door in her mind and, struggle as she may, she could not open it.

Her aunt came and sat beside her on the bed, a slight flush staining her cheeks. "Caroline, my dear." She took her niece's hand and sat smoothing the skin over her knuckles. "I hardly know how to put this into words for fear of offending you...but you are not even wearing the clothes you left in. Did anything occur...are you... I mean to say..." She looked away, her flush deepening. "Are you unhurt?"

"My head aches." Then Caroline caught her aunt's meaning and blushed scarlet, the question striking home to the most mortifying memories of her experience. "I am quite unharmed! Nothing is amiss. I am certain I would know...if..." She, too, could not continue: the thought of her forward behaviour, of her willing surrender to Jervais's kisses in the barn and later, of that moment in his bedroom when she so nearly capitulated to his passion, was too searing to face. How could she begin to explain to Flora how she had abandoned every tenet of modest behaviour? How could she begin to explain to herself?

"Of course...forgive me, you understand why I had to ask." Her aunt smoothed her gown in her agitation. "Now, we will not refer to it again. I am sure the solution to this conundrum is quite simple: you must have had an accident and been cared for by a respectable Belgian family. That would explain the modesty of your gown and how you came to be in the city."

Flora seemed quite satisfied at her explanation and Caroline grasped at such an innocent theorem. She hated the thought of lying to her aunt but the outcome of revealing the truth was beyond contemplation.

There was a tap at the door and a maidservant came in with hot water. ''I will leave you to rest, dear, and go to write some notes. I must let Vivian know you are safe, and Colonel Jones, also. Since I reported you missing he has set people to look for you.'' She paused, her brow furrowed. ''Perhaps it were best we say you were stunned as a result of a fall, and unable to give the family who found you your name and direction.'' She closed the door behind her with a worried backward glance at her niece.

Caroline fidgeted about the bedroom as the maid tidied up after her bath. She had replied very confidently to her aunt's delicate probing, but how could she ever rest easy in her own mind until she discovered how she had spent those missing two nights and a day before Jervais had found her, and why she was clothed in that indecorous gown?

She smoothed the peignoir at her throat, and with the touch of her fingers on the bare skin a sudden flash of memory transfixed her again. His lips on her throat, grazing, caressing the softness...

Jervais! Jervais kissing her so intimately. No, she must not think about him! If only she could believe that the blow on the head was causing her to hallucinate... No man other than her brother or father had ever done more than kiss her hand in a respectful salute until Jervais.

She stared into the mirror, expecting to find she had changed, but the face that looked back at her was indubitably that of Miss Caroline Franklin: twenty years old, single and likely to stay so. The example of her parents' mismatched union and her own notorious discrimination—which some had chosen to characterise as over-particularity—had kept her from accepting the many flattering proposals which had come her way in three Seasons.

Miss Franklin might be warm, vivacious and friendly, but none of her suitors, however ardent, had made the mistake of presuming that she was fast. If the slightest whisper reached the ears of Society that she had spent the night unchaperoned with Captain Barnard, she was ruined beyond redemption. Her fingers strayed over her throat again as though seeking to recapture his touch. The only comfort was that this would remain forever her secret, for he did not know who she was and never would.

All this time the maid Evangeline had been patiently waiting, a simple lawn day-dress over her arm. Its fresh sprig pattern was in sharp contrast to the dull stuff of the gown she had just discarded. Flora had at least been correct in her assumption that some respectable Belgian had come to her aid: she regretted her inability to send word to the widow that she was safe. Despite Madame's censorious demeanour, she had been kinder than Caroline could have expected.

At dinner that evening Caroline forgot her own intimate worries in hearing news of what had occurred in the city whilst the battle had been raging.

"It was chaos, Caroline, and so frightening." Her young aunt shivered at the memory. "We knew not what to do for the best. Rumour was rife…we had won…we had lost…the Corsican Monster was at the gate…the Guard was defeated… I could not leave because I expected your return at every moment. I kept telling myself the crush was so great in the streets you could not get through, but all the time I was reproaching myself for ever having let you go.''

Her aunt's distress was so apparent that Caroline pushed back her chair and came to comfort her. More like an elder sister than an aunt, her father's widowed sister was a scant eight years older than herself.

When her elderly husband Lord Grey had died, two years after the wedding, Flora had pressed her niece hard to come and live with her. But Caroline could not bring herself to leave her father. His behaviour, always rakish, had been increasingly dissolute since the death of his wife, the only restraining force upon him.

''It must have been intolerable for you, Flora.'' She bent to kiss her cheek. ''My disappearance on top of all our worries for Vivian! Oh—I had quite forgot to ask after Major Gresham! Is he safe?''

Flora coloured, the smile in her eyes making her seem eighteen again at the mention of her suitor's name. ''Quite safe, just a scratch on the cheek. And so tired and worried for his men as all the officers are.'' She was suddenly serious. ''He says there was no glory in the victory, the carnage was terrible on both sides: I fear we have lost many friends and acquaintances.''

Flora returned her embrace and Caroline returned silently to her place. There was no need for words, they knew each other too well. It seemed selfish to be happy, but at least her brother and Flora's suitor were not counted among the dead or the wounded.

They had made many acquaintances in the three months they had been in Belgium, lured—as so many of the *ton* were—by the prospect of safe travel on the Continent again after so many turbulent years of conflict.

It was half past nine and the butler had just brought in the tea tray when the two women heard the knocker bang on the front door. Booted feet clattered on the tiled floor of the entrance hall and spurs jangled as the wearer ran upstairs.

Caroline sprang to her feet as the double doors flew open and her brother strode across the room to gather her into his arms.

"Vivian... Vivian..." was all she could say, so overcome was she to see him. They clung together and she could sense he was as affected as she at the reunion.

At last he broke the embrace and held her at arm's length. "Let me look at you. Caro, wherever have you been? I could make no sense at all of Flora's note, although never have I been so thankful to receive a billet!"

Caroline made much of settling her brother in a chair and pouring him a cup of tea while she collected her thoughts and schooled her face. Vivian would never believe she could lie to him; if only she could reassure him, all would be well. If he discovered the smallest part of the truth he would call Captain Barnard out, of that she was certain.

"I must have been thrown from my horse," she confessed, after explaining how she came to leave the house. "And after that I know nothing." She saw the consternation on his face and hurried to reassure him. "Flora and I have settled between us that I was rescued by a respectable Belgian family. Except for the blow to my head I am quite unharmed and I was

wearing the most dowdily respectable gown you
have ever beheld!''

"Quite frightful,'' Flora interjected, laughing for
the first time that day. "We can rest assured that
whoever was looking after your sister had the most
decorous taste!''

"You make it sound like an insult,'' Caroline
teased, forcing herself to keep the conversation light.

"I would not dream of putting even a governess
into that gown,'' her aunt countered.

"Flora, that is the second time you have said I
looked like a governess in that gown: there is no need
to remind me what a dowd I looked!''

"No, it is not,'' her aunt insisted.

Caroline rubbed her forehead. "I was certain...''
No, the voice that echoed in her brain was not her
aunt's light tone, it was Jervais's: masculine, deep
and sardonic.

"Caroline?'' She realised her brother had been
speaking to her. She must guard her tongue, her
thoughts, every moment or she would betray herself.
It was hard to be dishonest with the two people she
cared most for in the world.

"I am sorry, Vivian,'' she apologised. "I keep
having these unsettling moments of abstraction.''

They talked long into the evening, hardly noticing
as the servants came in to light the candles and set
a taper to the fire.

Tired as she was, Caroline was reluctant to go to
bed. She was happy and secure, home at last, Vivian
was safe... She smiled hazily at him as the firelight
flickered on the gold lace of his uniform.

The room tilted around her and she clutched the
arm of the sofa to steady herself. The figure of her

brother in scarlet and gold was overlain by another in blue and silver. The images shifted and merged and she threw up her hands to cover her eyes.

"Caroline!" Her aunt was by her side and Vivian was bending over her. "I thought you were about to faint. It was foolish of me to let you stay up so late. You should feel the bump on her head, Vivian!"

Caroline fell asleep as soon as Flora blew out the candles and left her room. And with the sleep came the memories and the dreams of Jervais. His arms were tangible as he held her to him, his mouth hard and demanding on her yielding lips, and she was drowning, drowning in sensation.

In the velvety darkness her lips parted and she murmured, "Jervais, Jervais." But there was no one there to hear her.

Chapter Three

It had been one of those unexpectedly warm days England often experienced in early October, but now the sun was sinking and a vicious breeze was getting up.

Looking down from the drawing-room window on the first floor of the house in Brook Street, Caroline watched as the under-footman struggled to gather up the fallen leaves he was attempting to clear from the front steps.

"Is there any sign of him?" Flora was sitting beside the fire, a tambour frame in her hands. "We cannot wait tea much longer."

"You mean, is there any sign of them?" Caroline teased, turning away to smile at the blush mounting to her aunt's cheeks. Ever since Vivian and Major Gresham had arrived back in England for a month's furlough, the senior officer had been a frequent visitor to the widow's London residence.

Anthony Gresham had been very good to Lieutenant Sir Vivian Franklin, introducing him to his club and taking him about Town. Flora maintained stoutly that this was merely the kindness of an older man for a promising young officer in his regiment. "He has simply taken him under his wing," she would protest to Caroline's teasing.

"I think it has more to do with the fact that Vivian is under your roof," Caroline had replied. Although Vivian and she frequently twitted Flora about her suitor, they were both very glad that, after over five years of widowhood, she was finding happiness at last. She had dutifully married her elderly husband at twenty: although no words of complaint had ever escaped her lips, Caroline guessed it had not been an entirely happy marriage.

"It seems an age since we were in Belgium," Flora mused as she held up a tangle of green silks to the light. "Despite all the horrors of the battle and the worry of your accident, I am glad we decided to yield to Lady Blatchett's persuasion and take a house in Brussels as she did."

"Indeed," Caroline replied warmly. "It was such a refreshing change to travel out of the country. And we had all the benefits of a change of scene, but with the company of so many of our old friends."

"Oh, yes!" Flora agreed. "The picnics, the expeditions, the balls—why, even the Duchess of Richmond's ball, agitating though it was with all the officers leaving for the battlefield..." She sighed and returned to her needlework. "We seem to live very quietly now."

"I assure you, Flora, that the tranquility of this household is still most welcome to me," Caroline assured her.

Brother and sister had moved in with their youthful aunt two years ago after the death of Sir Thomas Franklin, their father. The calm and order of Flora's home was still a source of wonder and comfort to Caroline after the turbulance and alarums of life with the baronet.

"We may not burn the candle at both ends, but we contrive to entertain ourselves most satisfactorily, do we not?"

"Unfortunately, my dear, your experience of one who did burn the candle at both ends was not a happy one." They both knew to what Flora alluded. "To have had the burden since the age of fifteen of your unfortunate father's habits—of having to assist him to his chamber bed night after night when he was in his cups and to lie awake listening to noisy card parties in the salon below was quite insupportable."

Caroline's lips twisted with wry recollection. "Frankly, aunt, that was the least of it. The mortification of having tradesmen dun one on one's own doorstep was a far greater burden."

And even, on one occasion, a discarded and disgruntled mistress had forced her way in, although she had no intention of telling her aunt of that, even several years after the event.

Caroline had been more intrigued than shocked by her scandalous visitor, and had offered the woman tea after explaining that her father had gone to New-market for the races.

The woman's painted face and brassy manner belied her age and Caroline had felt a strange liking for her. They had talked long into the evening and she could remember asking about her protectors. "Do you not love them?" The girl had laughed shortly and explained her very practical philosophy of life. When she had finally departed with some of Caroline's guineas in her reticule, she had left a thoughtful young woman behind her.

No wonder she had understood so many of the allusions Jervais had made to the "muslin company"! Life with Sir Thomas and the revelations of one of that sisterhood had only served to confirm Caroline in her observation that marriage was a state to be entered into with extreme caution. This reserve had led her to refuse an earl's son for his propensity to gamble, a baronet for his short temper towards servants and one wealthy young man for his lack of intelligence.

As though reading her thoughts, Flora remarked, "I cannot help but feel I have failed in my duty since you have been in my care. If only I could see you suitably bestowed..."

"Why, Flora, if I cannot catch myself a husband in three Seasons, I am at my last prayers and destined to be an old maid!"

"It is not a subject for levity," Flora scolded. She was despairing of seeing Caroline married, especially after her rejection of the future earl. But she recognised the impossibility of persuading her niece against her will: Caroline could be very obdurate.

"Why not ring?" Caroline suggested, turning back to her idle scrutiny of the street. "They will not be much longer on such a cold day."

She sat on the window-seat and continued to watch the street below. Although four months had passed since Waterloo and her mysterious disappearance, Caroline still felt very strange. Occasionally she felt dizzy. Her head had long since stopped aching, although the loss of the time after she had left the

Brussels house persisted, as did the dreams which came every night.

Emotionally, she felt drained and deeply unsettled. The dreams were always of Jervais, although the scene changed: sometimes they were on his horse together, sometimes they were in his chamber. One feature was constant: when she woke she could still feel the touch of his lips on hers and an aching sense of loss that he was gone.

''Here they come!'' The two uniformed figures were strolling from the direction of Grosvenor Square, cloaks swirling in the rising wind, collars turned up against the cold. Flora tugged the bell pull, then hurried to the glass to tease out her curls more becomingly. Caroline was just turning from the window when she saw the pair stop and hail someone.

Curious, she turned and looked. A big, raw-boned grey horse was pacing up Brook Street from the direction of New Bond Street, a scruffy hound trotting at its heels. From above the rider was unrecognisable.

But the animals were instantly familiar. The world tilted and swayed and Caroline clutched the muslin drapes for support, straining to see. Astride Caesar was a man in riding clothes, his hand raised in greeting as the horse and men converged to meet under the window. The rider reined in the grey, holding it with a strong hand as it fidgeted in the wind.

Looking down, Caro saw the chestnut brown hair, ruffled as he raised his hat; the long, capable hands on the reins; the broad shoulders under the dark cloth.

''Jervais.'' The name was almost soundless as the man from her dreams dismounted and shook the hand of Major Gresham.

"What is keeping them?" Flora enquired, still primping.

"They have... I think they have met someone they know." Caroline hardly knew how she got the words out, or how her aunt had failed to notice her extreme agitation. Her heard was thudding so hard she felt sick and the curtain was knotted hard in her fist.

"Another military man?" Flora walked over to join her.

"Yes."

"But, my dear, how can you tell? He is not in uniform. What a hideous horse!"

"Oh, I just assumed...by his bearing, I mean." Fortunately her aunt had eyes only for Major Gresham and still did not notice her strained demeanour.

The two young women watched the tableau below in silence, Flora smiling happily at the handsome picture her tall Major made, Caroline with her heart in her mouth. Vivian was obviously urging Jervais to enter the house, and Major Gresham was adding his entreaties. Jervais, after a moment's polite hesitation, allowed himself to be persuaded and handed the reins to the waiting footman.

"Oh, my heavens!" Caro whispered under her breath, turning in agitation from the window. Her first reaction had been of incredulous pleasure and recognition, soon engulfed in apprehension as the reality of the situation came over her. How could she possibly receive this man? Her last encounter with him had been in his bedroom—virtually in his bed, certainly in his arms! She had to escape before he came in: surely, even if he were enough of a gentleman to say nothing, nothing could disguise his amazement at finding one he believed to be of the "muslin company" in a fashionable house in Mayfair!

"Flora...one of my dizzy spells... I must have got up too suddenly. Please make my excuses to Major Gresham..." She was already halfway to the door, panic lending her speed.

Flora asked anxiously, "Should I ask Peters to send for Dr Shepherd?"

"No, please... I will lie down for a while, it will pass...but I am not fit for company." Caro was out of the door and fleeing up the stairs even as booted feet sounded in the hall below.

Safe on the landing she peeped down through the curling acanthus leaves of the banisters as the three men came upstairs. She wanted to see Jervais so much, discover if he was well again: she pressed her face up against the metalwork the better to observe him.

The men paused outside the salon door and Jervais suddenly glanced up, as though he could feel her eyes upon him. Caro recoiled into the shadows of the unlit landing, but even so his gaze seemed to follow her. Then Vivian opened the door and the three disappeared from view.

In the safety of her own room Caroline paced up and down, wringing her hands in perturbation. Her mind was so full of remembered images she could scarcely order them, never mind comprehend the enormity of Jervais's presence.

"I cannot think!" she said out loud, sitting down, then springing to her feet again. The memories were filling her brain, clamouring. With Jervais downstairs, rational thought was impossible. The sensible thing would be to stay where she was until he had gone: that was what a prudent, well-brought-up young woman would do. There was no reason why she should ever see him again after all. The meeting had been a chance one; he was not one of Vivian's friends.

Calmer, she went and sat at the dressing-table, smoothing her hair and dabbing a little lavender water on her temples. Yet, perhaps she was not as safe as she thought. He was obviously a friend, or at least an acquaintance, of Major Gresham, and the Major was surely on the point of making Flora a declaration. Captain Barnard could well become a regular visitor to the house and she could not plead a dizzy spell every time he called.

She should go to Longford: that would be sensible. Vivian rarely used the country seat he had inherited, preferring London life to the rambling manor in Hertfordshire with its unhappy memories of their father. She could use that as an excuse to leave London, say she felt the house might be neglected and the servants needing supervision.

Then the flaws in the plan struck her. She could hardly stay at Longford for ever, and besides, Flora would soon become suspicious and would descend to find out what was amiss.

No, she must beard this lion now, while she was prepared. At least she had the advantage of being forewarned and the shock of seeing him had spent its force. Caroline looked steadily at her reflection in the mirror: perhaps he would not recognise her. She certainly looked different from either the painted, bedraggled demirep of the barn or the drably dressed young woman of the Brussels house.

Her afternoon frock was a simple affair of figured muslin, but the elegant lines imparted by a fashionable modiste were quite unmistakable in the tiny pleats at the waist and the pretty puffed sleeves. Her hair was glossy and freshly cut in the latest mode, with demure curls escaping provocatively from a gauze ribbon to frame a complexion owing everything to nature and nothing to art.

No, there was every chance he would not recognise her. He would never expect to see her in the setting of a tonnish town house, furnished with every appurtenance of elegance. And besides, although their encounter was memorable for her because it had been so shocking and intimate, for him she was probably just another young woman amongst a host.

No—it was worth hazarding: before she could lose her nerve Caro ran downstairs and opened the salon door. Flora was bent over the tea-tray, the Major attentively at her side. Vivian had his back half-turned to the door as he made conversation with the Captain. Jervais Barnard occupied the sofa, nodding in agreement with something his host had just said.

They all turned at the sound of her entrance so that only Caroline saw the look of stunned recognition on Jervais's face. Vivian jumped to his feet and came to take her hand, saying in low tones, "Are you feeling quite yourself again?"

Caroline nodded, not trusting herself to speak, maintaining a polite social smile learned during the course of several Seasons. There could be no doubt that Captain Barnard had recognised her, but by the time she brought herself to look at him he had his face well schooled.

"Caroline, this is Lord Barnard who has lately returned from Belgium. Lord Barnard, my sister Miss Franklin.''

Jervais was on his feet, bowing over her proffered hand. Caroline forced herself to look at him. His face was politely composed as it should be, meeting a young lady for the first time. But his eyes reflected his thoughts and she read there a message of reassurance that she met with a look of blank incomprehension.

As she met his gaze without a sign of recognition, his brows drew together, then his expression cleared and became politely bland. Yet aware of him as she was, Caroline recognised a flash of something else in those brown eyes. Puzzlement perhaps, which she could understand, but also a hint of anger which confused her.

Caroline was determined to press her advantage while she was so composed. If she could only establish beyond a doubt that she remembered nothing of their previous encounter, then as a gentleman he would have to accept that. To say anything of their Belgian adventure would be to humiliate and embarrass her in front of her friends and he would have to assume she would deny everything angrily if her loss of memory was genuine.

I do so hope he will keep silent, she prayed inwardly, and that he is sufficient of an actor not to betray that he knows me. If Flora or Vivian were to discover what had really happened during those missing days in Belgium, she and Jervais would find themselves married out of hand. She might try and refuse, but no honourable gentleman would hesitate to do the decent thing, having compromised her so thoroughly. It was a bitter twist of fate to find a man to whom she was attracted and found so intriguing, only for him to prove to be the last one she could honourably consider marrying.

She sat down beside him on the sofa, accepting a cup of tea from Major Gresham with a word of thanks. If she could only maintain the pretence, Jervais would find it impossible to broach the subject of their adventure and they would both be safe.

"Were you in the army in Belgium, sir?"

"Yes, Miss Franklin, but I sold out last month. I am now a man of leisure." He was speaking lightly, but Caroline could almost hear his mind working on the problem she was presenting him.

"Take no notice, Miss Franklin," the Major said jokingly. "One would scarcely call the management of an estate the size of Dunharrow a sinecure, Barnard. It's no secret that your late cousin let the place fall into wrack and ruin."

Caroline pulled herself together. She had been in such a state of turmoil she had missed the significance of Jervais being introduced as Lord Barnard. "You have recently come into the title, then? I do not believe I knew your late cousin: were you close?"

"He died two months ago, and no, we were not close. In fact, Cousin Humphrey was best described as a curmudgeonly old recluse." His mouth twitched at a sudden memory. "I used to pay him duty visits; I was the heir, after all, but he did not welcome my opinions on the state of the land. Last time he threatened to set the dogs on me."

"How sad that you were estranged," Caro commented coolly. She was rather taken aback that he should seem so unmoved by his near relative's lack of affection. "So, inheriting the title caused you to sell out?"

Jervais regarded the polished toe-cap of his riding boot. "I had been in the army for many years, it was time to settle down. And with Napoleon defeated, the army will be a very different place now."

"Did you fight at Waterloo, my lord?" Caroline was astounded at her own coolness, yet it would seem unnatural to avoid the subject.

"Yes," he replied shortly.

"And was honourably wounded," the Major supplied.

"Oh, not badly, I hope?" Caroline said without thinking, then bit her lip. This was too near the knuckle for comfort, she could feel the blush staining her cheeks.

"It was not pleasant at the time," Jervais said evenly, his eyes on her face. "In fact, the entire aftermath of the battle was a strangely confusing experience."

Caroline put her cup down with a rattle. What devil had prompted her to turn the conversation in this dangerous direction? And how was she to get out of it? "Another cup of tea, Captain Barnard?" She picked up his cup and her own and took refuge beside Flora.

Waiting while the tea was poured, she watched him from under her lashes as he talked easily with her brother. This was the man she had dreamed of so feverishly night after night. She could feel his skin under her fingers as she lay in his arms, the touch of his lips on hers...

He was watching her like a hawk across the room, his face inscrutable. Caroline writhed inwardly with embarrassment. He must never, ever, know she remembered what had been between them. She must guard her tongue and hope this was the last she ever saw of Lord Barnard.

He got to his feet as she returned with the cups and she noticed with a pang of relief that there was no sign of any stiffness in his leg.

"And where is your estate?" she enquired politely.

"Hampshire…" he was beginning when they were interrupted by a commotion outside the door. After a moment it opened and the flushed face of the underfootman appeared.

"I'm sorry, I'm sure, Ma'am, but I can't do a thing with this dog…"

As if to prove the point, he was almost sent flying by the hound in its eagerness to find its master. It bounded over, tail thrashing perilously near a pie-crust table covered in enamelled boxes, and prostrated itself at Jervais's feet.

"Sit!" Jervais glowered at the beast which immediately obeyed. "I do apologise, Lady Grey, I left him tied up in the hall."

The big hairy head turned to look reproachfully at his master and then saw Caroline. With a soft "wuff" of recognition the dog flattened his ears and sank his muzzle on her knee.

"Hello, Per…boy," she caught herself just in time, but no one seemed to have noticed the near slip.

"Anyone would think he knew you," commented Jervais in a low tone to Caroline, dragging the big dog off by its collar. "He is usually very wary of strangers."

"I like dogs. I think they can tell, do you not agree?" She was determined not to show him how flustered she was feeling. Percy's greeting had told him nothing he did not already know: she must not allow herself to be panicked into betraying herself.

The party broke up shortly afterwards, Major Gresham announcing he was almost late for a meeting at the House Guards and Jervais rising to accompany him.

"I hope you will call again, Lord Barnard," Flora invited warmly. "Any friend of Major Gresham's is welcome in this house. We are usually At Home on Wednesday and Friday afternoons."

"I would be honoured," Jervais bowed over her hand. "Perhaps I can persuade you and Miss Franklin to drive with me in the Park one day?"

"But surely you will be returning to Dunharrow?" Caroline asked, too abruptly for politeness. "You must have so much to overlook if the estate has been so neglected."

Flora shot her a quelling old-fashioned look, then turned, beaming, to the Captain. "We would enjoy it immensely, would we not, my dear?"

"Yes, of course." Caroline tried to sound enthusiastic. "How kind."

As soon as the door had closed on the gentlemen, Flora turned on her niece in a swirl of skirts. "Really, Caroline, that was almost rude! I could despair of you sometimes! Here is the most eligible man to enter our acquaintance for months—so good-looking, too—and you treat him as though he were a boring young subaltern."

Caroline recognised one of the rare occasions when her aunt was annoyed with her. "He might not be eligible," she protested. "He could have a wife and ten children for all we know."

In reply her aunt pulled a thick, red bound book off the shelf and ran her finger swiftly down a page. "Baldock, no, Ballard...here we are. Barnard. Well, he was not married last year, and as he has been in the army he will have had scant chance!"

Caroline recognised when she was beaten. "I am not seeking for a husband," she insisted stubbornly.

Flora sprang to her feet and began to pace upon the hearth-rug. "Really, Caroline, I do not know what to do for the best!" She took a deep breath the better to remonstrate with her niece about her obdurate behaviour but was arrested by the sudden change of expression on Caroline's face. "What is it?" she asked, alarmed.

"Those words...you used the self-same words in Brussels, that day I left the house. Why, I remember now what happened!"

"But we had already settled upon what must have happened, my love—" Flora began.

"Yes, I know...but now I remember." It was true. Whether it was the shock of seeing Jervais or whether the echo of Flora's despairing words as panic had seized the city, she knew not, but it had been enough to recall that frightening morning when neither of them knew what to do for the best.

"Caroline!" Flora pressed her down onto the sofa. "Sit down and tell me all about it."

Caroline took a deep breath and tried to organise her thoughts. She could have kept her counsel, she supposed, but she did not like to deceive Flora and watching her tongue endlessly would be very wearing. Yet she could not tell her aunt everything—no mention of Jervais must cross her lips.

"You know I went to enquire about the wisdom of our leaving Brussels?" she began.

"Yes, of course, and you took Gypsy from the stables because you said it would be quicker to ride rather than to walk with such crowds on the streets."

"It was a foolish decision. I should have remembered he had not been out of his stable all week, and he has always been nervous of loud noises.

"I got lost." She frowned at the remembered frustration. "So many streets were blocked with carts and refugees and I tried to avoid the main roads because of the troop columns. I must have taken a wrong turn, for I found myself near the outskirts of the city in an area I did not recognise. And by then it was already mid-afternoon and I was so tired and frightened."

"But why did you not turn back?"

"I was going to. I realised I must be heading towards the battlefield because no one was going in that direction, but then a horse came bolting down the road and panicked Gypsy. I managed to hold on, but it was all I could do to stay in the saddle."

"I knew that gelding was too much for you," observed Vivian who, unheard, had re-entered the room.

"He was not!" Caro protested indignantly. "I would have liked to see you fare any better."

Her brother grinned wickedly, but stopped teasing. "Go on, Caro, what happened then?"

"We went for miles, I thought he would never stop. At last he began to tire: I was so relieved for I thought we were going to find ourselves in the middle of the battle!''

Flora exclaimed in horror. "Thank heaven you managed to control him at last!''

"It was due to no skill of mine," Caroline admitted ruefully. "He stumbled in a pot-hole and threw me right over his shoulder into a deep muddy puddle."

"And you let go of the reins?" Vivian demanded from where he stood at the fireside.

"I must have done." She shook her head. "Poor beast, I wonder what became of him."

"If he was not killed, he was no doubt appropriated by a grateful soldier. The carnage among the horses was appalling, several people had more than one horse shot away from under them." Vivian's face darkened as it always did when he spoke of the battle.

Flora took her niece's hand. "My dear, it must have been a nightmare! What did you do next?"

"I..." Caroline's voice died away. The door into her memory had swung to once again. "I suppose I picked myself up and started to walk back the way we had come."

"You can recall no more?" demanded Flora, shocked.

"No, there is still a void. I think I can remember it getting dark and being very tired, but being afraid to stop. It must have been as we supposed and some kind and respectable people found me and helped me back to Brussels."

"But what I do not understand is why you did not come straight back to the house when you reached Brussels," Flora said.

"Why, because Caro had lost her memory of who she was," Vivian interjected. "It is no wonder she cannot remember," he added. "A fall like that is enough to rob a strong man of his senses, let alone a young woman."

"Of course, I am becoming so muddled trying to piece it all together." Caroline could only be grateful for her aunt's vagueness, it prevented her from asking more awkward questions.

"I do wish we knew who had helped you," Flora continued anxiously. "I would like to write and thank them. Still, we must be thankful that the conundrum is gradually resolving itself. No doubt it will all come back to you in due course."

Indeed, Caroline hoped most fervently that it would be so. Comforting though it might be to have more of her memory restored, these recollections did nothing to explain how she had come to be found by Jervais wearing a most immodest gown and with paint on her face, nor where she had been for two nights.

There was a silence while they sat and mused, each lost in their own thoughts, then Vivian asked, "But how did you come to be in the Grand Place?"

"I must have left my rescuers' house thinking a walk might prompt some recollection, or that someone I knew might see me."

"Thank heavens it was I," exclaimed Flora. "Can you imagine the scandal if anyone else had found you! As we said before, you must be careful, dear, to speak of this to no one. What would people think if they knew you had spent all that time in circumstances we cannot account for? How tongues would wag!"

Caroline nodded meekly and sat back against the cushions, relieved that some, if not all, of the truth was out and that her family accepted her explanation of what had happened. But her precarious peace of mind was short lived.

"Caroline, we must go out tomorrow morning and buy that handsome bonnet we saw in Miss Millington's shop yesterday," Flora announced: her train of thought appeared to have moved on from Caroline's adventure.

"But we agreed it was far too dear!"

"Nonsense, it would be just the thing to set off your new walking outfit. You want to look your best, after all."

"Why?" Caroline enquired mutinously, knowing only too well.

"For your drive with Lord Barnard, of course," Flora said unanswerably.

Chapter Four

"They are all most handsome: do you have a preference, Caroline? For myself, I cannot choose between them." Flora turned from the shop window to smile at her niece.

"I care for none of them," Caroline declared flatly.

"But you admired that one in green so much the other day," protested Flora with a sinking heart. Persuading Caroline to visit Miss Millington's exclusive establishment in Conduit Street had proved suprisingly easy: she should have known better, with Caroline's strange new mood, than to believe the rest of the expedition would go as well.

"I cannot imagine what I was thinking of, it is positively dowdy."

"Dowdy? Surely not? Well…perhaps we could ask Miss Millington to exchange the grosgrain ribbon for some curled plumes in a darker green. That would give it a touch quite out of the ordinary and it would look very becoming with your new walking dress and pelisse."

"Very well," conceded Caroline, nodding to the

young woman who opened the door for them. If the truth be told, she was not averse to buying a stylish new hat, but being dressed up to be paraded in front of the one man in London she wanted to avoid was galling. Although not as galling as the knowledge that in other circumstances she would have needed no persuasion at all!

Miss Millington darted out from behind the tasselled velvet curtains which concealed her inner sanctum and a workroom full of apprentices. "Lady Grey, Miss Franklin...what an honour. Drusilla!"

Miss Millington fluttered like the small bird she resembled while her assistant, a willowly young woman, arrayed gilt chairs and a small table for the comfort of the two ladies. "A glass of ratafia, Lady Grey?"

"Are you seeking a hat for a particular occasion or would you care to see our latest creations?" the milliner enquired once the ladies were settled.

"Oh, all the latest ones, please," Caroline asked firmly.

"But, Caro dear," Flora hissed out of the corner of her mouth, "you know why we are here! A hat for your drive in the park!"

"But we may as well see the new ones," Caro wheedled. "Oh, now do look at this one—it will suit you admirably." And indeed the rose pink villager-style bonnet with its deeper pink ribbons would set off Flora's brunette prettiness to perfection.

"I am not in need of any new bonnets," Flora said, with a hint of wistfulness.

"Major Gresham would admire it so much..." Predictably, Flora blushed and dropped her long lashes over her dark eyes in confusion. People often thought that aunt and niece were sisters, although those who knew them well could see Flora's resemblance to her brother, Caro's father, in his younger days, while Caro had inherited her mother's dark blue eyes and much of her slender grace.

"We will see," was all Flora would say as Drusilla brought in more stands displaying the dashing new modes.

At the end of an hour's agonising debate, the ladies had settled on two bonnets apiece—including the pink villager for Flora. Miss Millington bowed them out with promises of speedy delivery of three of the hats, whilst a page boy carried the green bonnet safe in its ribboned box out to the waiting barouche.

Flora and Caro settled back under the snug carriage rug, warmed by the glow of a successful shopping expedition. "Shall we call at Hatchard's?" Caro suggested, as they turned into Regent Street.

"More books, dearest? You will be thought bookish if you do not take care!" And will never catch a husband, was Flora's unspoken warning.

"Why, I found you sighing over the most frivolous novel only the other day!" Caroline riposted. "And I want to see if Miss Austen's lastest book is available yet."

Flora raised no more protests and climbed down with willingness when their coachman drew up outside the busy bookshop. Despite the relatively early hour of their visit, the bench outside the bow-fronted shop was already occupied by a number of liveried footmen awaiting their employers who browsed and gossiped within.

Flora and Caroline arrived back at Brook Street

eventually with not only a book apiece and the hat box, but a myriad of parcels containing silk stockings, ribbon, some embroidery floss for Flora's latest project and two pairs of kid gloves found at a bargain price.

"Take those directly to my chamber, William," Flora was directing when her eye fell upon a number of calling cards on the salver on the hall table. "We have had several visitors whilst we were out, Caro," she commented, flicking over the rectangles with a gloved finger. "Mrs Rivington and that sulky son of hers... Aunt Lloyd—oh dear, we will have to pay a duty visit, there is no avoiding it now she is back in Town. It is most reprehensible of me to say so, but I had so hoped she would find herself suited in Bath with Mrs Chatto as companion. Who else... Caro! Look, Lord Barnard has left his card with a note. He begs the honour of taking us for a drive in the park this afternoon."

She turned to Caroline, her eyes shining. "I knew I was correct in my view of him! And so considerate to ask me, too—so many young men would fix upon the object of their interest and quite ignore any other ladies. Not that I shall go, of course." She was already hurrying upstairs, stripping off her gloves as she went. "How providential that we brought the green bonnet back with us. I shall get Jackson to press your new walking dress and pelisse at once."

"But I have not yet decided to go," Caro protested. "I am certain it is going to rain and I want to read this new book..."

"Caroline, will you please join me in the small sitting-room?" Flora said, directing a quelling look at her niece and closing the door firmly behind them.

"Now what reason can you have for acting in this contrary manner? There is not a cloud in the sky, no sign of rain and you can read your book at any time."

Caroline was fidgeting with some small boxes on a side table, not meeting her aunt's eyes. Flora took her by the hand and forced her to look into her face. "I can understand you wishing to be careful in your choice of husband. After all, we both know that your poor mother had much to bear…"

"And you yourself," Caroline said gently.

"Lord Grey may have been a little older than I…" Flora began hesitantly.

"Nearly thirty years older," Caroline said indignantly. "And I know he was very indulgent, but you cannot deny he was a difficult man when he had the gout."

"We are not speaking of Lord Grey," Flora replied with some dignity. "And you cannot compare a man in his fifties to Lord Barnard. Why, he is handsome, intelligent, well-bred and obviously much taken with you. What more can you ask for? I warn you, Caroline, if you persist in this attitude to your suitors you will get a name for yourself and no one will want you. No man enjoys being humiliated."

"And I find the whole Marriage Mart humiliating!" Caroline countered with spirit. "It is all anyone talks of—who is engaged to whom and how much the settlements are. Who has refused whose proposal, which men have not come up to scratch. I tell you, aunt, I am heartily sick of it!"

Flora was taken aback by Caroline's vehemence, then rallied. "Well, the sensible thing is to find a man you can respect and admire and accept his proposal—and I fail to see what there is not to respect and admire in Lord Barnard.'' She subsided into an armchair, flushed and ruffled.

"Oh, I am sorry, Flora." Caroline came and sat at her feet, resting her head on her aunt's knee. "I do not wish to provoke you or seem to be ungrateful for your concern. But I know him not at all; we have scarcely exchanged half a dozen words and you have us married off already." It was not the truth, of course; she knew far more than was either wise or comfortable about Jervais Barnard!

There was a long pause then Flora patted Caro's head absently. "It is most curious. It had not come to me before, but the reason I think you would be so well suited is the feeling I had that the two of you knew each other already. A rapport like that must surely mean something."

Caroline caught her breath. It was serious if Flora, not given to introspection, had sensed a familiarity between herself and Jervais. She forced herself to sit still and conceal her agitation. Of all the ill fortune to be rescued by this man when it seemed, because of his friendship with Major Gresham, she was fated anyway to meet him in London. Thousands of men could have found her on the battlefield and would have treated her as well—if not better—than Jervais Barnard.

If she had met him for the first time yesterday there was every chance something might have come of it. Now she was totally confused: was he asking to see her because of what had occurred in Belgium or because he was genuinely a suitor? But whatever his motives, as a gentlewoman it was her duty to see matters went no further. He was her rescuer and it was her duty not to compromise him by revealing what had passed between them.

Duty had never seemed quite so bleak, but without a display of quite shocking bad manners she could not refuse his invitation. With a resolution she was far from feeling, she scrambled to her feet and smoothed down her dress.

"Very well, I will go. You are right. It would be ill-mannered to refuse. Now, we are both in need of a little luncheon and then you shall help me change and ensure my new hat looks its best." The two linked arms and went through to the dining-room in perfect amity.

Caroline was sitting, pretending to read a volume of poetry, one of her new purchases, when the knocker sounded at half past two. Her heart leapt with an unpleasant lurch, but she forced herself to carry on scanning the lines until the footman announced, "Lord Barnard, my lady."

She put the book down with studied calm and waited while Flora greeted Jervais.

"Lord Barnard, what a pleasure to see you. Will you take a glass of sherry?"

"Thank you, no." Without appearing to stare, Jervais noted with interest Flora's attire: she did not appear to be dressed to leave the house in Brook Street that afternoon. Caroline, on the other hand, was becomingly attired in a dark green walking dress and a neat pair of buttoned kid walking shoes peeped from under the hem.

He walked over to shake her hand, noting how the richness of the gown brought out lustrous tints in her dark hair. The demure elegance could hardly be a greater contrast to how he had first seen her. Her eyes dropped before the frank admiration in his.

Caroline could feel Flora willing her to make polite conversation and break the silence that had fallen. "Will you not sit down, Lord Barnard?"

He sat, picking up the discarded volume of poetry as he did so. "Do you admire Byron?" He flicked the uncut pages with his thumb. "Perhaps not, as you do not seem to feel it worthwhile to go past the first page!"

"I bought it only this morning," Caroline said, angry to find herself sounding so defensive. "And perhaps it was a foolish choice: on the whole I find his work overrated. Quite impossibly Romantic."

"And you do not believe in Romantic adventures?" he asked with a dangerous twinkle that caused the corners of his eyes to crease.

"Certainly not." Caroline was brisk. "The sort of adventures heroines in novels have always sound dirty, dangerous and thoroughly disagreeable, and I cannot conceive how they ever get themselves into such a plight in the first place!" She caught Flora's eye and subsided. Her aunt's expression said clearly that if anyone had had an adventure recently, it was Caroline and the less said on the subject the better.

"Well, if I cannot interest you ladies in adventuring, perhaps I can offer a gentle drive in the park in my phaeton." He turned politely to Flora. "Lady Grey?"

"I am afraid not: I must visit my aunt who is unexpectedly come up to Town from Bath. Please forgive me, Lord Barnard."

"May I drive you both to your relative's house?" Caroline liked the way he accepted the refusal so graciously and was about to agree with relief when Flora intervened.

"I would not dream of spoiling your afternoon by taking you so far out of your way as Cavendish Square. No, do not alter your plans—I have already ordered the carriage to be sent round for me later. Caroline, dear, go and get your pelisse and bonnet."

That was neatly done, Caroline mused, as she went to her room: she had not realised Flora possessed such tactical skill!

When she joined him in the hall Jervais congratulated her on her promptitude.

"It is chilly," Caroline replied calmly. "I would not wish you to keep your horses standing."

The phaeton was waiting, the groom at the head of a neat pair of match bays.

"You do not drive a high-perch carriage?" Caroline enquired as he handed her up and adjusted the rug over her knees.

"I did not think it suitable for two ladies, but I will bring it next time if you wish."

So there was going to be a next time, was there? Caroline thought grimly. Part of her thrilled to be sitting there beside him, so close their elbows almost brushed, but every time she saw him the pain of knowing she must rebuff him grew stronger.

She realised he was talking to her. "I do beg your pardon, my lord, I quite missed what you just said." Her attention was wandering into the most dangerous paths; it was time to direct it firmly back or she would be in danger of betraying herself.

"I was asking if you drove yourself—you seemed knowledgeable about carriages. And I wish you would call me Jervais."

"But, my lord, that would be most improper on such short acquaintance!" Caro knew she was blushing hotly: she only hoped he would interpret it as maidenly modesty and not a recollection of what had occurred in the short time they had spent together. Hastily she tried to turn the subject. "I have driven a small carriage down at Longford, but only with my old pony between the shafts and he is so slow that 'slug' is too active a description for him! I should like to learn," she added wistfully.

"Then I will teach you with pleasure, if Lady Grey permits it."

The traffic was heavy and Caroline did not answer at once, sitting silently watching his handling of the team as he threaded expertly through the crowded streets between Brook Street and Tyburn Lane while she tried to think what to say. The bright, cool afternoon had brought out many driving parties to take advantage of the parks before the true onset of autumn and she could have had no better demonstration of Jervais's skill in driving.

"Green Park or Hyde Park, Miss Franklin?" he enquired as they reached Hyde Park Corner.

"I have no particular preference," Caroline replied, then realised she had still not responded to his offer. Much as she yearned to accept, it was too dangerous. "And thank you, I would very much like to learn to drive, but I do not think my aunt will permit it. She is very nervous of open carriages."

Jervais negotiated the turn into Hyde Park without replying. Caroline hoped she had struck the right note: she would hate to be thought ungracious in refusing—and indeed she earnestly desired to learn—

but the thought of the intimacy it would thrust upon them made her shiver.

Stealing a sideways glance at his gloved hands as he steadied the team she could almost feel them closing over hers, the strong fingers guiding and tutoring. That thought was too disturbing to be pursued...

"Indeed, Lord Barnard," she stated firmly before she could weaken, "I would be reluctant even to raise the subject with my aunt, she is so nervous about it."

"She must have had a most alarming experience in the past," he said sympathetically.

Well, that was one danger avoided, Caro thought, stifling her regret at the missed lessons. "How quickly the leaves are turning now," she observed brightly. "And how beautiful they look with the sunlight upon them."

"Yes, it is a pleasure to see an English autumn again. I have spent so much time abroad these past six years, it almost feels like a foreign country to me."

"Surely autumn on the Continent is not so very different to our own? The countryside of Belgium struck me as very similar whilst I was there." As soon as the words were out she was regretting them. She had given Jervais a perfect conversational entrée, yet how could she ignore the dramatic events of the past year? To studiously avoid all mention of Belgium and the battle would be highly suspicious and it would seem rude to ignore what must have been a momentous time for her companion.

"You were in Belgium long?" he enquired casually, raising his whip to acknowledge a passing rider.

"We went out in April. Vivian, my brother, had

just been posted there and Lady Grey thought it would be an ideal opportunity to travel on the Continent. So many of her friends were planning to go: after all, who could have foreseen Napoleon's escape?''

"Indeed! None of the Allied governments, that seems certain!''

"We found Society in Brussels very pleasant, and we made several delightful short outings.'' Caro found herself babbling like one of the featherheaded debutantes she despised, yet she could not stop herself. "Bruges is so picturesque and quaint—have you been there?''

"I did not have much time for pleasure trips once the regiment reached Belgium,'' Jervais remarked drily.

Caroline racked her brains for a safer conversational topic than the Belgian countryside. "I had heard that the British officers contrived many impromptu parties despite the rigours of camp life.''

"I would not have expected a young lady to know anything of the rigours of camp life.'' Jervais flashed her a quizzical glance which, with her secret knowledge, filled her with consternation.

"Why, only what Vivian has told me, of course,'' she returned lightly. "Oh, look over there—is that someone waving at us?''

"At you, I believe,'' he observed, reining in the horses, allowing the other phaeton to approach. "I am not acquainted with any matrons of quite such a formidable aspect, I am happy to say.''

"Caroline!''

"Oh, no! It's Aunt Lloyd—and Cousin Frederick driving.''

"And Lady Grey, overcoming her terror of open carriages in the most courageous manner, I observe. Although I must say," he added *sotto voce,* as the two carriages drew up alongside each other, "she would have felt safer with us than with that cow-handed youth."

"Caroline, my dear! What an unsuitable bonnet! And who is this, pray? Introduce us, girl!" Caroline's great-aunt had never felt under any obligation to say anything other than precisely what she thought on any subject and swept on, ignoring Caroline's obvious embarrassment. "Well, young man? Cat got your tongue?"

"Jervais Barnard, ma'am." Knowing him as she did, Caroline realised he was amused—and not in the least discomforted by the rude old lady.

Flora hastened to intervene. "Aunt, let me introduce Lord Barnard. My lord, Lady Lloyd, my aunt. And may I make her grandson, Mr Frederick Lloyd, known to you?"

The Honourable Frederick bowed stiffly in acknowledgement. His grandmother had made her intention that he marry his cousin Caroline very clear and he had no desire to lose the old lady's good graces—and handsome allowance—by being cut out by a rival.

The fact that Caroline had never given him the slightest encouragement had not deterred him: he was too thick-skinned to fear that any lady might rebuff him. But equally he was not stupid enough to fail to recognise at a glance the threat that Jervais Barnard posed.

Somehow Caroline got through the next five minutes before her great-aunt announced it was far too cold to sit around gossiping—and she was much too busy to do so.

"I do apologise," Caroline said, red-cheeked, as soon as they were out of earshot. "But I assure you she made no exception in your case—she is always that rude, even to her closest friends."

"Think nothing of it, we all have relatives we blush for—only consider my late, unlamented, cousin. He wore a ginger wig and was a virtual stranger to soap and water." Caroline giggled at the picture he painted.

"Is that the cousin from whom you inherited your estate?"

"The very same. Fortunately, he was buried in the wig and I was not compelled by the terms of the will to wear it myself."

Caroline was so preoccupied with stifling her laughter that she was caught completely off-guard when he said, "I'm filled with admiration for your Aunt Flora. Such poise in concealing her fear of open carriages in order to do her duty…"

There was a long silence, punctuated by the hoof beats on the tan surface. Caroline swallowed hard, reviewed several implausible excuses and decided frankness was the only answer.

"Lord Barnard, I have dissembled…been less than honest with you…"

"Well, I did suspect as much." He was smiling down at her in a most disconcerting manner.

"Oh dear, how can I put this…you must believe I am not normally given to falsehoods…"

Jervais pulled up the team and sat watching her as she pleated the skirt of her gown with nervous fingers.

"I wondered when you were going to tell me," he said gently putting one hand over hers to still the fidgeting.

"Oh dear, was I so obvious?" Caroline made herself meet his eyes, but let her hand remain under his. His expression was curiously tender, certainly his demeanour was more intimate than seemed warranted by the occasion of the confession of her small fault.

"Not at all. In fact, I was wondering whether I was imagining things," he said quietly.

"What I said about Flora being too nervous to allow me to learn to drive... I am afraid that is not the truth. She does not enjoy driving, but she does not mind me doing so, and she would never prevent me learning if she believed me in safe hands..."

"Ah." Jervais's expression was now unreadable, but she had the strangest feeling she had disappointed him. He released her hand. "So why do you not want me to teach you to drive?"

"Well, I was afraid I had sounded as though I were angling for you to offer to teach me," Caroline improvised feebly.

"Not at all," he assured her firmly, moving the team into a walk again. "You gave me no such impression and I am delighted to have found something I can do that would give you pleasure."

There was no response to that other than to accept gracefully, but the seemingly innocuous words evoked that heady moment in his arms in his room in Brussels. Her cheeks were flaming and Caroline turned her betraying face away from him as she fought to regain her composure, a task made more difficult by the knowledge that she was blushing, not out of maidenly shame, but because she wanted to relive that moment when he had invited her to his bed.

"Is your new home in good hunting country?" she finally managed to ask before the silence became oppressive.

"Moderately good, although the coverts have been neglected—my cousin was not remotely interested in the chase. If I hunt this autumn, I intend to join some friends in a rented hunting box in Leicestershire."

If! Why could he not be more definite about his plans? Then at least she would have the comfort of knowing he would soon be safely away. Her memories of Belgium seemed dreamlike and unreal, despite having the flesh and blood man sitting beside her: knowing what was the right thing to do, the safe way to behave, was far more difficult than she had imagined.

"No doubt you are like my brother and not overfond of balls and parties," she said lightly, trying to keep the conversation going along a safe path yet test how likely he was to stay in London. "Will we be seeing you at Almack's, perhaps?" The thought of Jervais in satin knee breeches, submitting meekly to the scrutiny of the starchy patronesses, was an unlikely one. Nor could she imagine him performing a quadrille or country dance!

"It is a distinct possibility. I enjoy dancing and have had little opportunity of recent months." The amusement was back in his eyes as he sensed her surprise. "The Duchess of Richmond's ball was the last occasion."

"You were there, too?" Caroline asked in amazement. There was no good reason for her surprise:

every officer in the vicinity who could be spared had been at that glittering dance on the eve of Waterloo.

"Indeed, I was." He looked at her, speculation in his eyes. "How strange that we should not have met then and been introduced."

"Surely not, it was such a crush! And no doubt, like the other officers, you had to leave early." Was it coincidence or was he leading the conversation at every turn back to Belgium, back to their first encounter? "But it is a coincidence that you should know Major Gresham and we should meet in London."

"And it is always so important to be properly introduced," he added smoothly. "Are you cold? You are shivering?"

He was too acute, too aware of her for comfort. "The air is a little chilly, perhaps we should return."

Jervais turned the team out of the park and into the busy traffic of Oxford Street. Caroline felt an enormous relief now his attention was off her and concentrated upon negotiating the throng of carriages and pedestrians making their way home as the day drew in.

"I have kept you out too long, Miss Franklin," he remarked, his eyes still on the road.

So, he was as aware of her as she was of him. "Not at all," she protested. "Why should you think that?"

"You sighed just then. If you are not tired, is anything wrong? Perhaps I can help." Jervais sounded warm and concerned and the temptation to admit that she remembered everything that had passed between them in June and end this tense charade was almost overwhelming. She wanted to be friends with him, perhaps when they knew each other better, more than that...

No, she pulled herself together sharply, he was a gentleman. If he knew she remembered, then he would have no choice but to marry her and she would never know whether it was his free choice or not.

"No, nothing is wrong," Caroline replied stiffly. "And I hope I would never presume to trouble a mere acquaintance with my concerns."

They had reached the house in Brook Street as she spoke. Jervais reined in the bays and sat looking down at her. "But I hope I may become more than a mere acquaintance before much longer."

He was not to be rebuffed. Caroline was used to suppressing pretension with a few cool words, but Lord Barnard was too self-assured to be fobbed off like a callow youth.

The footman was running down the steps to help her down, but neither Jervais nor Caroline noticed him. Jervais picked up her gloved hand and held it for such a long moment that she raised her eyes to his in confusion. As she did so he lifted her fingers to his lips and brushed them lightly.

Caroline felt her own fingers tighten in his and recalled herself hastily. Compared with what had passed between them in Belgium this was insignificant, yet her heart was beating and she could hardly formulate a few polite words of thanks for the drive.

"When may I call again?" he enquired as she reached the flagstones safely and glanced up at him.

"I... I do not know. I cannot say what our plans are now my great-aunt is in Town. But if we are not at home when you call, we may, after all, meet at Almack's."

"Miss Franklin? It's a cold wind, Miss..." The footman was patiently waiting with the front door open. Caroline realised she was standing gazing down the street after Jervais as he skilfully took the corner into David Street.

Really! She must be losing her senses! Caroline gave herself a brisk mental shake and passed through the front door with a word of thanks to the footman. What if someone were to see her standing like a moonstruck girl in a public street?

"Is Lady Grey at home, William?" she enquired, handing him her hat and gloves and drifting towards the sitting room.

"Not yet, Miss Franklin. She sent to say she would probably be late at Lady Lloyd's and not to wait dinner for her."

That was a relief. She would not have to face Flora's enquiries until she had reduced the drive to a commonplace incident she could speak of comfortably. None the less she felt a pang of guilt at the thought of her young aunt having to endure single-handed the interrogations of Aunt Lloyd.

Caroline sat down on the sofa with the book of poems and a paperknife to cut the pages. Half an hour later, when the tea tray was brought up, she realised with a start that they still remained uncut and her thoughts were quite elsewhere.

Chapter Five

Lord Barnard called at Brook Street on three occasions over the next fortnight, finding the ladies not at home on two and engaged with an animated tea-party on the third.

Caroline, who had looked for him in vain on the several occasions she had danced at Almack's, could not help but feel piqued that he had not called more frequently, although for a recent acquaintance his behaviour was most correct.

She no longer suffered from the fevered dreams which had come every night in the months following her return from Brussels. Now the real man was close he was filling her waking thoughts and disturbing her equilibrium in a way she found difficult to counter. The nagging mystery of how she had come to wake up beside him in that barn remained but Caroline was learning, for her own peace of mind, not to dwell on it.

When Jervais finally found them at home, ten days after the drive in the park, she was in the act of passing a cup of tea to Miss Babbage, a serious-minded debutante with somewhat of a reputation as a bluestocking.

"Lord Barnard, my lady," Dorking the butler announced, causing Caroline to spill tea into the saucer as Flora shot her a meaningful look.

"Lord Barnard, what a pleasure," Flora beamed, rising to shake hands. "May I hope you will join us for tea? Whom may I make known to you?"

As her aunt performed the introductions, Caroline noticed that beside her Miss Babbage, bluestocking or no, was not immune to the arrival of a good-looking man. There was a slight pink tinge to her complexion as she patted her curls and her face fell a little as, the introductions complete, Lord Barnard took himself and his tea-cup to join Major Gresham at the window.

Caroline watched Jervais discreetly under cover of handing round a dish of almond macaroons. She rather regretted that as he was no longer a serving officer he could not wear the uniform of the Eleventh Light Dragoons that suited him so well. But there was no doubting that the coat of dark blue superfine cloth showed off his broad shoulders to admiration and his long, well-muscled legs could stand the fashion for tight trousers better than many gentlemen.

Caroline turned in her chair to place the empty plate on a side table and was startled to find Jervais at her side. "You have given them all away," he said, low-voiced. "And almond macaroons are quite my favourite."

"How did you know," she said without thinking, her eyes flying to his face, "when you were not even looking?"

He seemed not to notice the implication that she

had been covertly watching him. "But how could I be unaware of the presence in the room of my favourite…delicacy?" he asked gravely.

"You are teasing me, Lord Barnard," Caroline riposted. "I do not believe you gentlemen really care for such sweetmeats, but to test you I shall ring for more—and I shall expect you to eat several!"

The chair beside Caroline was free, Miss Babbage having joined Flora to admire some new prints. "May I?" He scarcely waited for her murmur of agreement before dropping into it. A long silence ensued, long enough to goad Caroline into speech.

"You are very silent, my lord!"

"I do beg your pardon, Miss Franklin, I was not aware you were desirous of conversation and I was preoccupied in anticipation of the macaroons. You notice I dare give you a hint that you have not called for more as you promised."

"Why come and sit by me if you do not wish to converse?" she demanded, tugging the bellpull, too rattled to be polite. "And do not say it is because of biscuits!"

"For the pleasure of your company, Miss Franklin, why else?" He smiled, white teeth mocking her.

"Yet you do not wish to talk to me?"

"Being near you is enough," Jervais replied blandly.

What game was he playing with her? Perhaps he was just determined to tease her. Taking a firm hold on her temper which was rising dangerously, Caroline managed a sweet smile and enquired, "Are you by any chance flirting with me, my lord?"

"I never flirt, Miss Franklin. I would scarce know how. You behold in me just a bluff soldier, unused to feminine company.'' He managed such a look of pained innocence that Caroline nearly choked on her tea. Unused to feminine company, indeed! She had never come across anyone who seemed more familiar with it! She suppressed a snort of indignation.

"Miss Franklin, I fear you are laughing at me," Jervais reproached her.

"Indeed I am," she responded, smiling despite herself. "I have never heard such a tarradiddle: I am certain you have laid siege to the hearts of young ladies across the length and breadth of Europe."

"But never one like you...Caroline." He had dropped his voice so that they could not be heard and the ring of sincerity sent a shiver down her spine. She could not even reproach him for using her Christian name.

"Lord Barnard..."

"Jervais, please."

"Really, my lord, I could never address you so..."

"Never? Very well, as you wish, but I shall call you Caroline when we are driving. I cannot shout at you if I have to address you as Miss Franklin in every sentence."

"Shout at me!" Caroline was indignant. "And why, pray, should you shout at me?"

"I shall have no compunction if you jab my horses' mouths or take my hat off with the whip!"

"Then I shall not come out with you! I shall ask Cousin Frederick to be my tutor."

"Without wishing in any way to be disrespectful of a relative of yours, I have to tell you that he is cow-handed to a degree." Try as she could, Caroline could not school her mouth to the expression of severity his levity deserved. "And there is also the consideration that I do not believe you would willingly be alone with your cousin."

"And I would have no such compunction with you, sir?" Caroline's chin came up challengingly.

"You have shown none in our acquaintanceship thus far." He reached for a macaroon whilst keeping his eyes on her face.

The colour flooding her cheeks, she said, "How could...?" before she checked herself, realising she had nearly betrayed herself fatally. He could not, surely, have intended such a blatant reference to what had passed between them in Belgium? "I cannot feel that one drive alone in the park can be taken as an indication of my willingness to be alone with you, Lord Barnard."

"As you would have it. These macaroons really are excellent. Would you consider me totally without self-control if I asked for another?"

He was laughing at her, she was sure, although his face betrayed nothing beyond polite enquiry.

"I am certain your self-control is beyond reproach, my lord." Caro said waspishly. "Now, if you will forgive me, I must see to my other guests."

The party began to disperse soon afterwards, the young ladies casting demure glances at Lord Barnard as they went. Caroline, watching them with well-concealed irritation, remarked quietly to Flora, "All off to tell their mamas to add a new name to their invitation lists, no doubt!"

Flora arched her brows. "My dear Caroline, I do declare you are jealous."

Before Caroline could riposte, Major Gresham and Lord Barnard came to take their leave.

"I have a favour to ask you, Lady Grey," Jervais said, bowing over her hand.

"Indeed, sir?" Flora, warmed and flattered by the affectionate attentiveness of her beau at her side, was inclined to be gracious.

"I was hoping for your permission to teach Miss Franklin to drive. I believe she is desirous of learning and I imagine her brother has little leisure at present."

"What an excellent scheme! If you are certain it would not be an imposition…?"

Jervais bowed slightly. "It would be a pleasure, ma'am."

"I see no objection. What is your opinion, Major?"

"I am entirely of your view. There is no man in London at present with a better pair of hands."

"You flatter me, sir."

The Major noticed with amusement Miss Franklin's delicate blush and downcast eyes. So, his beloved Flora was quite correct in her belief these two would make a match of it. So much the better! He was having the devil's own job to persuade Flora to agree to marry him while her niece was unattached.

"You will use only a quiet horse—and not a high-perch phaeton?" Flora asked anxiously.

"You may rest assured. Miss Franklin has told me how nervous you are of open carriages. I would do nothing to alarm you, or to put Miss Franklin in danger."

Caroline shot him a darkling glance which he blandly ignored. Flora, unaware she was supposed to be nervous in carriages, merely looked somewhat puzzled at this solicitude for her nerves.

"Shall we say tomorrow at ten, Miss Franklin? If the weather is fine we can go to Richmond Park where it will be quieter for you."

"That will be delightful, my lord." Caroline recognised when she was beaten.

The next morning dawned bright and sunny, dashing Caroline's craven hope that poor weather would postpone her first lesson. Yet despite her qualms at being once more alone with Jervais, she could not suppress a frisson of excitement at the memory of his hands on hers last time they drove together.

She again wore the dark green costume, this time with a pert curl-brimmed hat newly delivered from Miss Millington's emporium. It was a fetching deep gold in colour with no feather to tangle in her whip and a coarse veil to shield her complexion from the wind.

Flora, pausing on the landing on her way to inspect the linen cupboard, walked round her niece tweaking invisible creases from the soft fabric. "There!" she announced, just as Caroline was reaching the limits of her patience. "You look charming. Now, do you have those new tan gloves? Will you be warm enough? It would be a shame to spoil this outfit by having to wear a mantle."

"Flora, please! I am simply going for a drive, not being presented at Court!" Caroline reined in her fraying temper and managed a conciliatory smile, recognising it was not her aunt who was responsible for this irritation of her nerves. "I shall be quite warm enough: the wind has dropped since yesterday."

Any further conversation was curtailed by the

sound of the knocker. Caroline, anxious that Lord
Barnard should not come in and be engaged by Flora
in a conversation which might prove embarrassing,
caught up her skirt and was almost out of the door
before she called back, "Goodbye, Flora!"

She paused on the step to catch her breath and saw
Jervais half rising from his seat. "Please do not get
down, my lord," she said, nodding her thanks to the
groom who was now handing her into the carriage.

"Thank you, Cooper, there are no errands this
morning," Jervais said, dismissing the groom who
touched his hat with one finger before walking off
down Brook Street. "Once more you are most
prompt, Miss Franklin, and, if I may say so, in great
beauty."

Behind the veil, which did nothing to conceal the
slight flush which mounted to her cheeks, he saw her
flash him a quick glance, half-flattered, half-
suspicious.

"If I am prompt, sir, it is because I am looking
forward to my lesson and do not wish to keep your
horses standing." She could think of no suitable re-
joinder to his blatant flattery, so ignored it. "That is
a very fine pair of bays: have you had them long?"

"They were one of the few possessions of my late
cousin which showed any sign of taste or discrimination!" Jervais's eyes narrowed as he concentrated
on a corner partly obstructed by an approaching coal
wagon. "They are rather more docile than I would
have chosen for myself, but that makes them ideal
for our purpose today."

As if to belie his words the nearside horse shied
violently as the coal heaver tipped his sack down a

coalhole in the pavement with a rush and a cloud of dust.

"Steady!" Jervais skilfully reined in the nervous animal. "Perhaps they are fresher than I realised. But the drive down to Richmond will shake the fidgets out of them, there is no need to be nervous."

Caroline, who had neither shifted in her seat, nor grasped the side of the carriage, replied composedly, "I am not at all nervous, my lord."

She was conscious of his narrowed, sideways glance which seemed to convey more than mere approval. "I think it would take a good deal to rattle you, Caro."

He had used the one word above all he could have chosen to rattle her. "No one but my family ever calls me Caro, sir," she said coldly. Her heart was beating uncomfortably hard at the memory of the hay bed in the barn and Jervais spelling out her name from the jewels in her ring.

Involuntarily she glanced down at her had, but she had left the ring off that morning before pulling on her tight-fitting gloves so as not to stretch the leather.

"And was it your brother who gave you your ring?" he asked casually, his eyes fixed on the road ahead as they neared the river crossing.

"My ring?" Caroline said feebly.

"The one you usually wear on your middle finger with the stones which spell CARO," he said patiently.

"How observant you are, sir." Caroline swallowed hard, half fearing the moment had come when he would drop the pretence that they had never met in Belgium.

"I notice everything about you, Caroline." That

statement was unanswerable. There was a long silence while she contemplated telling him once again to stop addressing her by her first name, then she gave up: he would take no notice. And besides, she liked the sound of it on his lips: it was a dangerous, indulgent pleasure.

By the time they reached the entrance to the park and Jervais reined in to show his ticket of admission to the keeper at the gate the bays were trotting calmly without a sign of skittishness.

Caroline looked round admiringly at the rolling grass, still verdant under the autumnal trees. ''Richmond Park always puts me in mind of the countryside around our home at Longford; I never tire of coming here.''

A group of strollers admiring a small herd of fallow deer was visible under the nearest stand of trees. Further off another phaeton bowled along one of the numerous carriageways which crisscrossed the parkland, but otherwise they seemed to be alone.

When they were well into the park and away from the entrance, Jervais reined in the horses.

''Now, have you ever driven a pair before?'' He shifted on the seat to look at her, his manner serious now he had begun to teach.

''No, only a pony in a dog cart about the estate— I told you about that.''

''It will take a little time to become accustomed to the feel of two sets of reins. Here, hold them thus.'' He handed her the reins, adjusting them until she could feel the gentle tension from the horses' mouths to her hands.

Caroline had expected to be very conscious of the touch of his fingers on her own, but in the event was concentrating so hard on his instructions and the horses, it was no more disturbing than if her brother were her tutor.

Following his directions, she allowed the pair to move forward in a gentle walk whilst she concentrated on the signals she was receiving from the animals: it felt very strange to be controlling two animals after dear old Rollo who plodded obediently along the lanes of Longford which he knew better than she did.

For half an hour Caroline walked the team around the park, totally absorbed in what she was doing, scarcely aware of the man by her side except as a reassuring presence. She was quite oblivious that he watched her face as much as her hands, smiling as she caught her lower lip between white teeth in concentration or muttered instructions to herself under her breath.

So intent was she that when he spoke she jumped slightly and the nearside horse jibbed.

"You look quite fierce, Caroline," Jervais said, sounding amused.

"I know," she admitted ruefully. "It is a very bad habit. Vivian tells me I scowl horribly when I am concentrating and Flora warns me I shall have dreadful lines by the time I am five and twenty."

"An unlikely prospect," Jervais murmured, looking unashamedly at the smooth skin of her brow. "Here, give me the reins for a while. You will find you are more tired than you imagine."

"Indeed, I am quite stiff," Caroline exclaimed, easing her shoulders with relief and flexing her fingers as he took back control of the horses. "I had no notion it would prove so taxing."

"You must learn to relax both your hands—indeed, your whole body—or you will become very tired."

This reference to her form was quite unseemly and Caroline reacted sharply. "That is a most improper remark to address to me, my lord!"

"Either I will teach you to drive as I would teach a man, Caroline, or I will not teach you at all!" His voice was curt. "I had believed you an intelligent woman…"

"I am!" she said indignantly.

"Then you must understand that it would be unsafe to modify my tuition to compensate for your sex. Unless, of course, you were not serious in wishing to drive a pair."

Caroline flushed at the open rebuke. His good opinion was important to her. "My lord…"

"Can I not persuade you to call me Jervais, at least whilst we are alone?" He still sounded irritated with her, which perversely made his request seem innocuous: he certainly was not flirting now!

"Very well, Jervais," she capitulated, "but only whilst I am having my lessons."

"But of course," he said smoothly, bowing slightly. "Now, are you fatigued, or would you like to try trotting?"

The increased pace was invigorating and seemed quite safe on the smooth, straight track with Jervais at her side, only occasionally now intervening to correct her handling of the reins.

Looking back on it afterwards, Caroline realised she had become over-confident, that her concentration had become blunted by the novelty of the experience.

"There is a bend approaching," Jervais cautioned, "steady them now as I showed you."

But Caroline hardly heard him. The team seemed steady under her hands and the bend looked innocuous enough to take with scarcely a check. Perhaps it would have been if it were not for the sudden eruption of a stag from a thicket of thorn on the apex of the curve just as Jervais said sharply, "I said steady!"

The horses shied violently, breaking into a canter, sending the phaeton swaying dangerously around the bend. Jervais grabbed for the reins, but in trying to release them, Caroline let them go and they fell to the floor of the carriage in a tangled heap.

Without any control the pair bolted in earnest, throwing both Caroline and Jervais violently to the left. Caroline seized hold of the side with both hands as Jervais flung one arm across her to keep her in her seat. With his free hand he scooped up the reins, struggling to order them and control the frightened bays.

The entire episode could only have occupied the space of thirty seconds before he had the carriage at a standstill, the horses still restless and sweating between the shafts.

Caroline found both her hands were clenched on the carriage side and she could not seem to let go.

Jervais jumped down, looping the reins over the branch of a nearby tree before coming to stand and look up at her. "You can let go now." His voice was half-teasing, but Caroline could see the concern in his eyes.

"That is simpler to say than to do," she said unsteadily, summoning up a smile. Jervais gently prised her fingers free and held out his arms to lift her down.

"Come down and walk a little, it will steady your nerves. Come, Caro, I know you well enough to believe you will not let this overset you." He took her firmly by the waist and Caroline let herself be lifted down.

As her feet touched the ground, her knees gave way and she sagged slightly in his arms. "It is not my nerves that need steadying, but my legs," she jested, not entirely successfully, irritated with herself for behaving so weakly.

Jervais tightened his embrace, holding her close. He was no longer simply supporting her. She became very conscious of the warmth of his closeness and her hands, already resting on his shoulders, tightened of their own accord as her eyes travelled up slowly to meet his. Being in his arms felt natural, right, as did his kiss when it came.

His lips on hers were gentle, almost tentative, as though he expected her to draw back. Instead her mouth softened, yielded to the familiarity of his lips, welcoming the kiss she had been dreaming of for months.

Jervais broke away and looked questioningly at her upturned face. Caroline smiled back, warmed by the tenderness she saw in his expression. She knew she should draw back, rebuke him for taking advantage of her weakness, but instead she caught his hand and raised it to her cheek.

He needed no further invitation, catching her hard against him, crushing her lips under his in an uncompromising kiss which sapped the remaining resistance from her body.

All thoughts of propriety, prudent behaviour or the probable consequences of their actions fled. Caroline kissed him back with an ardour born of all those restless nights when she had thought she would never see him again, yet his face and the memory of his lips had haunted her sleep.

How long they would have stood there locked in each other's arms she did not know—perhaps forever—if a loud voice had not caused them to spring apart.

"You will observe, gentlemen, this fine example of the puff-ball, *Lycoperdon giganteum*, as Lineus would have it."

Caroline, frantically straightening her veil, caught sight of the expression on Jervais's face and, despite the mortification of her situation, could scarcely suppress a bubble of hysterical laughter.

"This is quite a small specimen: I see your surprise, gentlemen, but the giant puff-ball may reach the size of a man's head." The speaker emerged from the far side of the thicket, revealing himself to be an elderly clergyman, carrying a wicker basket and leading a small group of soberly dressed young men, obviously undergraduates.

"Sir, madam! Good morning to you! And what a fine morning it is, too!" Undeterred by the frigid politeness of Jervais's bow he turned to his party. "No doubt we are in the presence of fellow enthusiasts: see, they are admiring a most handsome specimen of the bracket fungus which, gentlemen, as you know, is most commonly to be found on the beech tree."

"Indeed, yes," Caroline responded warmly. "I

have rarely seen a finer at this time of year, although I am only a simple amateur.''

The clergyman, encouraged to find a fellow enthusiast, was intent on showing Caroline the contents of his basket containing the spoils of the expedition when Jervais took her firmly by the arm. ''My apologies, sir, but we have a most pressing luncheon engagement. Good day to you.''

As soon as they were out of sight of the fungus foray, Jervais reined in the horses and let out a great shout of laughter. Caroline was laughing, too, the tears running down her face and it was a few moments before they both sobered.

The silence which followed was uneasy. Jervais let the bays walk on before commenting lightly, ''Rarely can a young lady have had a more effective chaperon than a clergyman and three scholars!''

''They should not have been necessary! I cannot believe I permitted…that we could…'' Caroline was deeply shaken by what had happened, by the intensity of the feeling his touch had evoked. She could not voice the true fear that shook her: that he would suppose her to remember everything that had passed between them before. Yet if she did not remember then her response to him was even more outrageously forward. She was caught on the horns of a dilemma: all she could do was to express what any well-bred young woman would under the circumstances.

Her colour high, she said stiffly, ''I cannot account for my recent behaviour, sir, other than to say I must have been more shaken by the incident with the horses than I had supposed, but I must tell you that such conduct is very foreign to my nature.'' And why should I alone feel so guilty? she thought indignantly, after all, he kissed me first. "And as to your actions, sir..."

There was a short pause, then Jervais said coldly, "Entirely inexcusable, Miss Franklin. I can only attribute it to my relief at discovering that you were unharmed." Caroline could sense that only his good breeding was restraining him from challenging her with the knowledge of what had passed between them in Belgium. More than ever she was convinced that he knew she could remember, but the more intimate their relationship became, perversely the more difficult it was to admit it.

"We will say no more about it," Caroline declared firmly, turning the conversation to the scenery they were driving through. To her relief Jervais followed her lead but the conversation was still constrained and impersonal when they arrived back at Brook Street. Caroline, despite the calming effects of social conversation, was still overwhelmingly preoccupied with what had passed. Her heart fluttered uncomfortably and she could not bring herself to look at Jervais.

As the alert footman opened the front door, Flora descended the steps. "My dear, have you had a successful lesson? Thank you, Lord Barnard, for taking such good care of Caroline. I cannot permit you to leave us without refreshment—will you not join us? A light collation awaits in the dining room."

To Caroline's amazement, Jervais accepted with alacrity. "Thank you, ma'am, that would be delightful. If your footman would direct me to the stables, I will join you as soon as maybe."

As he handed her down from the carriage Caroline gave him a reproachful, speaking look, scarcely able to credit that he would wish to join them after what had occurred. To her embarrassment Jervais not only did not take the hint, but challenged her directly.

"Come now, Caroline: if you do not wish to see me again after what has just passed between us, you must say so and that will be an end to it. However, such an action is bound to cause much unwelcome speculation…"

Furiously, she whispered, "If you were a gentleman…"

"If I were not a gentleman, Caroline, I would take what was offered to me—as well you know." His voice was harsh, his eyes angry, although his words were too low to reach the ears of Lady Grey waiting at the front door.

"I have no idea what you mean, my lord—and I have no wish to find out!" Caroline turned on her heel and marched angrily into the house, hot colour staining her cheeks.

Flora observed the signs of fury with concern. "Caroline, have you quarrelled with Lord Barnard? Tell me quickly before he returns from the mews."

"Yes, I have quarrelled with him! The man is insufferable!" Caroline stripped off her gloves and flung them on the hall table. Knowing she was as much in the wrong as Jervais did nothing to temper her anger, and the thought of taking luncheon with him was almost insupportable.

"What occurred?" Flora was concerned. "Please tell me, dear; you were so happy when you left here this morning."

"He…" She could hardly say he had kissed her, and she had liked it, had responded. "He shouted at me!'' She knew she sounded petulant, almost child-like.

"Oh dear, what did you do wrong? Gentlemen do worry so about their horses! I remember Lord Grey became apoplectic if anyone jabbed the mouths of his favourite pair..."

"But, Flora!" Caroline was shocked that her aunt would readily accept such behaviour.

Flora took her by the arm and smoothed her sleeve. "All men are difficult about something, dear. You are very young. You will discover that there is something about even the most perfect of men to be tolerated. If you and Lord Barnard were to be-come...that is to say..." She became hopelessly en-tangled in her own explanation and broke off, slightly flushed.

"I should have known you would be on his side, Flora! I am going to my room to wash my hands and brush my hair."

When Caroline entered the dining room, Jervais was sitting chatting to Flora with every appearance of ease. "I was just telling Lady Grey of our dis-turbing incident this morning," he said smoothly as he stood up.

Caroline was speechless: surely he had not told Flora of the kiss!

"Do sit down, Caroline," Flora chided, "do not keep Lord Barnard standing."

"What has Lord Barnard been telling you?" she finally managed to ask between stiff lips.

"Why, naturally I told Lady Grey about the stag and the horses bolting. I would not wish to conceal anything from her as she has entrusted your safety to me. After all, she may not wish me to take you out again.''

Caroline was mercifully saved from replying by Flora's interjection. ''My dear Lord Barnard, such a thought had not crossed my mind. Such an incident could have happened to anyone. The fact that Caroline is safely home proves you are just the person to take care of her and to teach her to drive.'' She looked reprovingly at her niece. ''Caroline, do pass Lord Barnard the cold chicken.''

The meal passed pleasantly enough. Caroline called on all her reserves of social training and courtesy to make tolerable conversation. After a while she relaxed, finding Jervais a warm and witty guest. With Flora as chaperon, Caroline felt safe from the undercurrents that made conversation so dangerous when they were alone.

Jervais was scrupulous in his attention to both ladies, but Caroline felt he was speaking only to her, that he admired her conversation and opinions as much as her looks. When finally he rose to leave she was warmed and flattered and quite off guard.

Flora insisted Caroline see him to the door while she remained in the drawing-room.

Reaching the hall, Caroline found the normally ubiquitous footman was quite absent. Below stairs had quite as good an idea of what was taking place as their masters upstairs and the servants knew when to make themselves scarce.

Caroline clicked her tongue in annoyance and turned to the bell pull, but Jervais caught her hand. ''No, wait. I must talk to you.''

She looked up at him questioningly. ''Indeed, we have not set another time for a lesson: if you are

willing to risk your horses once again, that is!'' She
was still lulled by the mood of the meal, quite unprepared for what he said next.

His fingers tightened on hers, compelling her attention. ''Never mind the lessons, Caroline, there are
more important things we have to discuss.''

''I do not understand you, sir.'' She was perplexed, but made no attempt to free her hand from
his.

''Why do you not trust me, Caroline?'' he urged.

''But I do, Jervais,'' she replied, puzzled by his
intensity. ''If you mean what occurred this morning,
why I am at least as much to blame as you and I
intend to put it quite from my mind—have I not just
said I wish to drive with you again?''

''Caroline, stop! That is not what I mean and you
know it! There is that between us that must be spoken of openly.''

Caroline freed her hand abruptly and stepped back
from him, suddenly aware of the pit yawning at her
feet. He was referring to Belgium; he must be going
to make her a declaration because—and only because—of what had happened there.

She did not want him to propose because of that,
simply because he had compromised her and now
must do his duty. No, it was his love she wanted
because she realised, with a clarity that shocked her,
she was in love with Jervais Barnard.

Somehow she must convince him that she had no
recollection of their ever having met before Major
Gresham had brought him to the house in Brook
Street. If he believed that, then she might be sure
that he was courting her out of love, not duty.

''I have no idea to what you are referring, Jervais," she forced herself to meet his eyes and speak lightly. "I declare you are being quite Gothick with your hints of mystery."

Jervais watched her between narrowed lids. Then his face relaxed and he shook his head slightly. "As you will." When he spoke again, it was almost as if to himself. "Perhaps I was imagining things..."

"You are very mysterious, sir," Caroline said lightly, almost flirtatiously, prepared to use feminine wiles to her own ends. Inside she felt an enormous tide of relief, so sure was she that she had finally convinced him that she remembered nothing.

He took her hand and kissed her fingertips lightly. "Until tomorrow at the same time? Shall we say Green Park for your next lesson? We will be safe from both stags and clergymen there."

Chapter Six

It might have been supposed that for a young woman to discover herself to be in love with an eminently eligible man, who in his turn was paying her the most marked attentions, would have been the pinnacle of her happiness.

But it was not so for Caroline, left alone with her thoughts. Major Gresham called to escort Flora to an exhibition at the Royal Academy, but even the promise of a new work by Mr Constable was not enough to tempt her to accompany them. Pleading tiredness after her lesson she took the new volume of Lord Byron's poetry into the small sitting room intending to peruse it.

"This will not do!" she admonished herself out loud, after several minutes had passed without a poem read or a page turned. "What good will it achieve to sit here moping? It is no use to wish Jervais and I had never met in Belgium: we did and there's an end to it!"

However, such rallying thoughts were of no practical help to Caroline in her dilemma. Surely Jervais had some tender feelings towards her for him to look at her with such warmth in his eyes, to hold her hands in his, to kiss her with a passion which even now made her head spin? But then she remembered the other embraces, the kisses he had pressed on her, and the circumstances in which they had taken place.

There was no question of love and tender feelings then! Why, he had thought her a lightskirt and had been quite prepared to take advantage of the fact. Jervais was a man of the world, of strong passions, who had hazarded his life across Europe. Of a certainty, he had not lived like a monk and was unlikely to behave like one now.

Perhaps in her innocence she was refining too much on the passion of his kiss in Richmond Park. She could hardly ask Flora how a gentleman behaved when alone with his inamorata—her aunt would be deeply shocked to discover that the slightest intimacy had taken place, even though she made no secret of her approval of Jervais as a suitor.

This is getting me no further forward, Caroline scolded herself, forcing herself to consider all the possibilities. At worst Jervais could be nothing but a heartless rake bent on completing the seduction he had begun in Belgium, at best he was in love with her and what had passed between them after Waterloo had no influence on his actions now.

But it was the middle course that seemed most likely: that Jervais found her attractive enough, no more, and it was only his sense of duty that was prompting him to pay court to her. And given that she was in love with Jervais Barnard, this was a most melancholy thought.

By the time Flora and her major had returned, bickering amicably about the differing merits of the paintings they had been to Somerset House to see, Caroline had argued herself into a mood of cheerful determination. Drooping about at home would not solve the riddle of Jervais's true feelings; she was resolved to put all her doubts behind her and enjoy his company. Surely, as she came to know him better, she would learn to read his heart?

"Shall we go to Almack's this evening, Flora?" she asked, as her aunt rang for the butler and they sat to await the tea tray.

"Why yes, although I should prefer to have a gentleman to escort us and you know Vivian finds it such a bore."

"May I offer my services?" Major Gresham enquired hopefully.

"Why, Anthony, I thought you were on duty tonight." Flora was almost coy.

"No. Did I not tell you? After today's parade, I am released from duty for an entire week. Seven days which I intend to devote solely to the entertainment of both you ladies."

But despite his words, it was obvious that Flora's enjoyment was his prime concern. Nor was her aunt unhappy at the prospect: her cheeks were flushed and her downcast eyes were shining. Caroline was suddenly impatient with this staid courtship: why did he not make Flora a declaration and be done with it? It was obvious they were deeply in love and neither had reason to delay the marriage.

Flora's party arrived early at Almack's. The rooms were somewhat thin of company and only one of the patronesses, the formidable Mrs Drummond Burrell, was to be seen.

They had extracted a reluctant promise from Vivian to join them later. "Now do not forget the doors shut at eleven," Caroline had reminded him. "And those pantaloons will not do! Dress uniform or knee breeches or you will be denied admittance."

"Very well," he sighed. "But you know I find the entertainment insipid: the stakes at the tables are so paltry."

"Chicken stakes, I agree," his sister commiserated. "But think of all the delightful young ladies you will meet, Vivian."

Her teasing was met with a dark glance. "And all their delightful mamas as well, no doubt."

As the major had handed the ladies into the carriage to take them the short distance to King Street, Caroline remarked, "I do wish Vivian would find himself a nice girl—he shows not the slightest inclination to settle down."

"There's time yet," the major said tolerantly. "He is enjoying himself in the army, time enough to settle down."

Caroline watched the young ladies chatting and deploying their fans as the rooms gradually filled, reflecting that she could think of no one who was ideal for her brother. Now in her third season, she was no longer a debutante, and she was permitted more latitude than the wide-eyed girls, overawed to find themselves in the heart of the *ton,* but with all the tolerance she could muster, they still seemed an insipid group.

So deep was she in thought that when a man spoke low-voiced behind her, she took it to be Major Gresham. "Why so pensive, Miss Franklin?"

"I suppose I should not worry about Vivian, but

none of those girls would make him a suitable wife,
you know.''

''Why does your mind run so on nuptials?'' It was
Lord Barnard at her side, not the Major. Caroline
caught her breath at the unexpectedness of it.

''Oh, all sisters matchmake for their brothers, sir!''
she responded in rallying tones. ''Do your sisters not
do so for you?''

''Unhappily I have none.'' He sounded not in the
least regretful.

''Nor brothers either?'' Caroline turned, giving
him her full attention, blue eyes wide on his face.

''No, no brothers.''

''Then you are quite alone? How sad.'' She could
not imagine being without the warmth of Flora and
Vivian around her.

Jervais regarded her solemn face with some
amusement at the intensity which brought a slight
crease between her dark brows. ''Do not frown so
on my account, Miss Franklin, I entreat you! Remember your aunt's warnings about wrinkles.'' But
even as he teased her he found it hard to imagine
anything ever marring the beauty of her creamy skin.

''Why, my lord, you are not at all polite to speak
of wrinkles! You remind me I am in my third season
and at my last prayers.'' A smile tugged at her
mouth: they were both quite well aware that she was
looking her best that evening, her slender figure set
off by a gown of cream net over an under-dress of
jonquil yellow silk.

''Indeed, I had no idea you were so decayed! I am
surprised you do not take your place on the chaper-
ons' bench. And why do you not wear a cap? Surely
such an elderly lady...''

"Sir! You are ungallant!"

Jervais smiled back at her mock outrage. "I protest, I was only deferring to your age, as you make much of it."

Caroline was caught by his eyes and the warmth of admiration in them. He was still tanned, his face fined by the pain of his wound, and his bearing was military: she was aware of the quickening of her pulse and an unworthy feeling of satisfaction that all the other young ladies in the room were green with envy because she had his attention.

The orchestra struck up a waltz and Jervais held out his hands. "Will you dance, Caroline?"

His arm was strong around her waist and she was very conscious of the closeness of him. The waltz was so familiar to her that normally she thought nothing of it, but suddenly it was as though this was the first time she had performed the daring dance with a man.

She forced herself to relax and let him guide her confidently through the other couples crowding the floor, but she found it impossible to raise her eyes above the level of his shirt front.

"Have I offended you in some way?" he enquired as her silence stretched on.

"Why, no!" Caroline looked up startled, then found herself unable to look away. If only this dance would go on forever, the circle of his arm isolating her from everyone else, the flame in his eyes warming her. "No...of course not."

"I could not attribute your silence to concern for your steps: you waltz very well. May I hope you will dance with me again this evening?"

"Yes, of course," Caroline said, amazed to find herself slightly breathless.

"Are you not going to make even a pretence of consulting your card?" he asked her gravely.

"No." This was ridiculous! She must find something to say—she was behaving like a gauche schoolroom miss.

Jervais continued to sweep her around the floor, apparently content to leave her to her silence. When the music drew to a conclusion and he handed her to one of the gilt chairs lining the wall, Caroline looked at her card and declared, with a fair assumption of calm, "There, I was correct—a country dance is free after supper."

"Ah, but a country dance will not do," he said, low-voiced. A frisson ran down her back and she forced herself to meet his eyes. "I will settle for nothing less than another waltz."

"Then you must be disappointed, my lord!" Caroline rallied slightly. "I can hardly break engagements I have already made." Further conversation was thankfully curtailed by the arrival of her partner for the cotillion which was just forming.

When the dance was over the young man escorted her over to where Flora and the major were seated. As they approached, Anthony Gresham sprang to his feet to give Caroline his chair. Caroline curtsied to her partner as he made his apologies and left to collect the next young lady on his card, then sank down beside Flora with a little sigh.

"I declare I have not danced so much for a month."

Flora regarded her niece's glowing face and sparkling eyes and patted her hand. "You looked so right dancing with Lord Barnard."

"Indeed, he is a very good dancer," Caroline said hastily.

"That is not entirely what I meant," her aunt replied drily. "Has he not said anything to you?"

"Why, any amount—and most of it nonsensical this evening!" Caroline said gaily, choosing to misunderstand.

"Lady Brancaster was remarking upon his attentiveness," Flora pursued relentlessly. "She is not the only one who expects him to make a declaration before many more days are past."

"Well, I am sure I have given no one any cause to think I was expecting—or encouraging—such a thing," Caroline said hotly. The thought that she and Jervais were the object of gossip was deeply distasteful. "Why, he pays me no attention out of the ordinary—I should be most surprised if he says another word to me all evening!"

"Then I fear you are about to be surprised," Flora said archly. "For here comes Lord Barnard now."

"May I take you in to supper, Miss Franklin?" he enquired smoothly, bowing over her hand. "I see Major Gresham intends to escort Lady Grey."

Past his shoulder Caroline could see the Dowager Lady Brancaster regarding them beadily through her lorgnette. The polite refusal died on her lips: the old tabbies could say what they liked, she would go with him.

"It would be a pleasure, sir," she said demurely, putting her hand in his.

"Which is more than can be said for the repast on offer in this establishment," Jervais remarked acidly, surveying the simple fare of cakes and bread and butter laid out before them.

"I always make the point of dining well before coming to Almack's," Caroline agreed, accepting a glass of lemonade and a slice of sponge cake. "I am sorry there are no almond macaroons," she added with a mocking glint in her eyes.

"Are you not going to allow me to forget my greed? I suspect, Miss Franklin, that you are a very unforgiving person."

Caroline put her cup down with a rattle. There was something pointed in the seemingly light-hearted comment that jarred, spoiling the mood of the evening. Could he be referring obliquely to Belgium, suggesting that she remembered and harboured a resentment about his treatment of her?

She gave herself a little shake, trying to convince herself he was only teasing, unaware that a shadow had taken the sparkle from her eyes.

"Miss Franklin?" Jervais took her hand in his, raising it to his lips for a fleeting moment, ignoring the shocked stares of several dowagers. "Forgive me, I have put you out of countenance."

"Well, sir, you succeed in putting me out of countenance every time we meet," Caroline said with some asperity, freeing her hand. "I should be used to it by now!"

"I have hopes you will become even more used to me," he began, soft-voiced, then broke off as Vivian appeared by their side.

"Vivian!" Caroline cried. "I had quite given you up—surely the clock has already struck eleven?"

"Indeed it has—and I arrived at one minute to the hour! Although why I troubled myself I do not know.

Good evening, Barnard.'' Vivian bowed to the older man, then swept a disparaging glance over the refreshments. He winced as his eye was caught by a notorious husband-hunting mama. "Caro, I rely on you to protect me: if Lady Hilton tries once more to entrap me into dancing with that bran-faced daughter of hers, I swear I will return to Belgium forthwith!''

"Have a soothing cup of tea, Franklin," Jervais suggested drily. "I think you will be safe from abduction while drinking it.''

Vivian shuddered, then, surveying the other choices, decided that tea was the lesser of the evils on offer. "I did not look to see you here, my lord," he observed to Jervais.

"Surely your sister has told you of my addiction to dancing?" Jervais said blandly.

Vivian glanced from Caroline to Lord Barnard. "That's all a hum if you ask me," he remarked sceptically. "Shan't believe that until I see you standing up for a country dance!''

"Do you doubt my word, sir?" Jervais countered lightly.

Vivian grinned. "Yes, I do! I suspect you are like me, dragooned here by the ladies…oh lord! Here comes Lady Hilton. Excuse me, I am certain I just saw George Tomlinson—got to talk to him about a horse…" He made his escape with the agility of an eel, leaving his unfortunate sister to greet Lady Hilton.

"Oh, dear, I seem to have missed your brother, Miss Franklin." Her ladyship was a wispy, innocuous-looking woman with a pale complexion and slight frame which belied her implacable will. It was well known she would stop at nothing to secure eligible husbands for her three daughters.

"I am so sorry, Lady Hilton, he cannot have seen you. May I introduce Lord Barnard?"

She observed with hidden amusement the calculating look which entered her ladyship's eyes as she shook hands with Jervais. As she observed later to Flora when they had returned to Brook Street, "It was almost as if she was measuring him for his wedding clothes!"

"We have not had the pleasure of your company here at Almack's before I think, my lord," Lady Hilton simpered, making play with her fan.

"This is the first time I have come here for several years."

"Lord Barnard has been with Wellington's army," Caroline supplied demurely, enjoying Jervais's efforts to deflect the lady. "And was most seriously wounded. His friends are glad to see him out and about again, but I was just telling him, he must not overstrain himself by too much dancing. One can never tell..." she added darkly.

"Oh, dear," Lady Hilton's sympathy was very perfunctory and she soon took her leave.

Jervais observed her fluttering retreat with some puzzlement. "Did I say something to upset her?"

"No, it was my reference to your wounds, I believe. She intends, I understand, to secure only the most robust husbands for her daughters."

"Good heavens!" Jervais raised his brows. "Perhaps I should hurry after her and assure her that, despite your improper hints, my wounds are healed and will in no way impede my duties as a husband."

Caroline was thrown into total confusion by this

daring remark. "Sir!" was all she managed to get out.

"Miss Franklin, you misunderstand me: I merely refer to the probability of my living to a good age. What can I have said to discommode you so?"

Caroline shut her mouth hard, aware she was blushing like a peony. Her mind was full of the memory of being in his still, shuttered bedroom, of his husky voice entreating her to come into his bed, to allow him to pleasure her...

"Caroline, you are quite flushed. You have been dancing too hard." It was Flora on the arm of Major Gresham, Vivian at her side. "Here, take my fan and cool your face."

"I have been trying to persuade Miss Franklin to take another glass of lemonade," Jervais remarked, taking the fan from Flora and deploying it to cool Caroline's burning cheeks.

"So kind, Lord Barnard," Flora smiled benevolently on them, well satisfied with the way things seemed to be progressing.

"Shall we all sit down?" Jervais gestured towards an alcove near by.

When the party had settled themselves around the circular table and drinks and cake had been fetched, Jervais continued, "I am glad to have the chance to speak to you all together, for I have a proposition which I hope may be acceptable to you. By mid-December I expect the west wing of Dunharrow, at least, to be habitable and I would be honoured if you would all consent to spend the Christmas season with me there. I intend inviting two of my brother officers who should be returned to England by then, and my cousin Serena to act as my hostess."

"For myself and Caroline," Flora said immediately, "I accept with pleasure. To be in the country at that season sounds delightful and I have never been into Hampshire." She turned to her nephew. "Will you be able to be spared, Vivian?"

"I have already spoken to the Colonel," he replied. "I had intended that we go to Longford, but this sounds a capital scheme!"

"Gresham?"

"I would be delighted, Barnard; beside the pleasure of such a congenial party, I would be most interested to see the improvements you are making." He turned to Flora. "You remember, I was telling you that Barnard had schemes for the improvement of his agricultural land?"

"Excellent!" Jervais seemed delighted by their enthusiasm and seemed not to have noticed Caroline's silence. "But I give you fair warning, I shall expect you all to work for your suppers: Gresham, I would value your opinion on the better management of the estate. Ladies, the interior of the house has been sadly neglected by my late cousin, your natural taste will be of assistance in suggesting improvements."

"And what will my task be?" Vivian asked with amusement.

"I am sure you and my gamekeeper will have many interesting conversations! You must see if there is at least one pheasant to be found within my neglected preserves."

"And your cousin Serena—I do not think I have met her," Flora said enquiringly, while Caroline sat mute, still somewhat flushed and quite unable to decide whether she was happy or not at the thought of spending so much time in close proximity to Jervais Barnard.

"I very much doubt if you have made her acquaintance. She is Lady Shannon, her husband has estates in Ireland and they rarely come to London. However, Serena has hopes of launching their eldest daughter Julia next year: she intends to come direct to Dunharrow with Julia for Christmas so the girl can experience a few private parties before entering Society."

"And her husband?"

"The Earl is no lover of Society. He will remain at home very happily with his racehorses!"

The orchestra struck up for a cotillion and Vivian asked his aunt to dance.

"A very dutiful nephew, indeed," Jervais remarked, as they turned to watch Vivian gracefully handing Flora in the moves of the dance.

"No such thing!" Caroline laughed. "If he is dancing with Flora, then he is not standing up with a debutante, which suits him very well: I quite despair of him!"

Major Gresham laughed. "This fear of entrapment is merely a phase young men go through. He was much in the company of young ladies while we were in Belgium: it is all these matchmaking mamas who have alarmed him. Never fear, he will be settling down and establishing his nursery before you know where you are." He shot a swift glance at Barnard and Caroline. "Now, if you will excuse me, I promised Bellamy a hand of whist."

"That was neatly done," Jervais remarked.

"What do you mean?" Caroline, feeling abandoned by her supporters, was inclined to be sharp.

"Gresham shows more tact than one would have expected: with his departure we are alone..."

"Hardly, my lord. There are at least two dozen people in this room."

"Indeed, and we are monopolizing this table: let us remove from here and allow that party over there to sit." He rose and held his chair for a grateful lady.

Caroline permitted herself to be guided from the room, but instead of re-entering the ballroom, Jervais turned left and entered the conservatory. The room was quite deserted, the groups of tall ferns and potted palms creating a sense of intimacy amongst their shadows.

"My lord..." Caroline began.

"I thought I had made it plain I do not wish you to address me so when we are alone," he admonished, his voice huskily intimate.

Alarmed, Caroline moved away across the tiled floor and began to examine a handsome Chinese pot which formed the centre-piece of the room. "Do you not admire the Chinese style?"

"I do not, and pray do not change the subject."

"Was there a subject?" She turned to face him, chin raised, suddenly determined to stand her ground.

"I was asking you to use my name." Jervais took two quick strides towards her across the tiles and Caroline whisked neatly round the Chinese pot away from him.

"But we are not driving now, my lord." Her heart was fluttering, and she felt light-headed in the heated, earth-scented atmosphere. There was a gleam in Jervais's dark eyes she had seen before and it both alarmed and excited her.

"You are driving me insane," he said, so softly

she thought perhaps she had imagined the words. He almost reached her side before she darted away again to an array of orchids displayed on a tier of shelves to one side.

"I do not believe these are plants at all: look at them, they are like strange small creatures." As an attempt to distract him it was a singular failure. Jervais ignored the exotic blooms, stretching out a hand to take hers.

Once more Caroline evaded capture, running behind a bank of palms. There was silence, broken only by the tinkle of a wall-fountain and the distant sound of the orchestra. Where was he? Her pulse drummed loudly in her ears as she twisted and turned, trying to descry him in the scented gloom.

Still, there was no sound from Jervais. Perhaps she had annoyed him by her evasions enough to drive him back to the ballroom. "Oh," she whispered, deflated, as she tiptoed out from behind the screen of plants.

Yes, the room was deserted, the only sign of movement that of the palm leaves in the Chinese pot, swaying where he had brushed against it.

"Jervais?"

"Yes?" His voice was right in her ear and as he spoke his arms encircled her waist from behind, drawing her back against him.

She stiffened and began to wriggle in his hold, but Jervais drew her hard against his body until she could feel the warmth of him down the length of her back, his breath stirring the hairs on her nape.

Still holding her tightly, he began to nuzzle her neck along the hairline, trailing kisses up behind her ear until she was shuddering with delight at the sensation. All thought of evading him had quite gone, all reality was centred in the circle of his arms, his heart beating against her shoulder, the sudden catch of his breath as she stirred against him.

After what seemed an age his lips left her skin and he stood holding her, quite still except for the rise and fall of his breathing, saying nothing.

"Jervais?" Her voice sounded very small in the gloom as she twisted in his arms to face him. She looked up, trying to read his face. She was more than ever certain that she loved him, still as uncertain whether he loved her in return or merely desired her.

"You are a very serious temptation, Caro; I have to keep reminding myself that you are a respectable young lady."

"And this is treating me as a respectable young lady, Jervais?" She intended it lightly, but her voice shook. She was standing so close she could see a nerve jump in his cheek.

"No, it is not, as well you know." He opened his arms, freeing her, and stepped back deliberately putting a distance between them. "Caro, there is something I must ask you…"

"Yes, Jervais?" Caroline was unconsciously twisting her hands in the fragile fabric of her skirt, hardly able to breathe.

For the first time since she had met him she saw doubt cross his face. "I…no. No, not yet. I do wish, Caro, you would bring yourself to trust me."

"But I do trust you," she urged, puzzled by his reticence.

"Do you? I wonder, Caro. I wonder sometimes whether I know you at all." He turned away and walked across to the orchids, standing looking down at them for a long moment. When he turned back to her he was his usual assured self again. "I go into Leicestershire tomorrow to join my friends for the hunting. I will be away six weeks."

"That long?" Try as she might Caroline could not keep the dismay out of her voice.

"I shall go direct to Dunharrow from Leicestershire. I shall return to London in mid-December and we can all travel down together."

"Oh, that will be nice," Caroline said inanely. It seemed hard to believe that a moment ago she had been standing in this man's arms, that he had been kissing her neck, holding her tight against him. Surely he could not behave now as though nothing had just occurred? It seemed he could—and there was nothing she could say!

When he said, "Shall we go into the ballroom, Miss Franklin?" she could only nod.

As she rejoined Flora, her aunt exclaimed in horror, "Caroline, what have you done to your gown, the front is quite crushed!"

Caroline looked down at the creases she had inflicted on the delicate fabric with her twisting hands. "Oh...I do not know. Flora, may we go home? I have such a headache."

Chapter Seven

"He is on the point of making you a declaration! I know it, I feel it in my bones!" Flora waved the sheets of hot-pressed notepaper at Caroline across the breakfast table.

"Who can you mean?" Caroline asked casually, pushing the crumbs on her plate about and not meeting her aunt's eye.

"Caroline!" Flora clicked her tongue chidingly. "You know I refer to Lord Barnard. He writes to say he is now home at Dunharrow and to suggest travelling arrangements for our Christmas visit." She scanned the sheets covered in Jervais's bold black script once more. "He apologises for the fact we will all be cheek by jowl in one wing: but I scarcely feel we could complain of that, for the rooms we will occupy with be newly refurbished…"

Caroline hardly heard as Flora chattered on, fluttering the pages as she read them. All she could think of was Jervais's face, the tone of his voice, his arms as he held her close in the dark conservatory. A frisson passed down her spine and she shivered visibly.

Flora looked up in alarm. "My dear, you are not

sickening for a chill, are you? I knew I should never have allowed you to go out driving with Vivian in that cold wind yesterday. And you get such a red nose when you have a cold..."

"I do not!" Caroline was indignant. "And thank you for being concerned more for my appearance than my health!"

"We must be practical about these things." Flora was unabashed. "A chill is easily got over, the lasting effects on your marriage prospects of being seen at less than your best, however, are more serious."

"Flora, if he truly loves me—which he does not— he will offer for me, red nose or no. And what woman of spirit would accept a man who would be so easily deflected? Not that he is going to make me a declaration."

"Really, Caroline, I declare you protest too much." Flora folded up the letter and passed it across the table. "Why should he go to so much trouble to furbish up Dunharrow for Christmas when he could easily have a congenial party of his army friends who would not care in the slightest what condition the house was in?"

"He has to undertake the repairs at some time, you heard him tell how badly the estate had been neglected." Caroline buttered a piece of bread and considered the range of preserves, finally settling on honey.

"But hardly at this time of year: the spring would have been far more sensible," Flora observed unanswerably.

"I really could not say, I know nothing about these matters." Caroline was secretly convinced that Flora was indeed correct and that Jervais was about to make a declaration. The more she considered it, the more she was certain he had been on the point of doing so that evening in the conservatory.

His reluctance to come to the point must be because he was only considering it out of a sense of duty. Yet, inexperienced as she was, there was no denying that Jervais desired her; when he held her in his arms and kissed her, the look in his eyes was not that of a man doing his duty! Caroline had had more than a month to resolve the conundrum of whether he loved her—and if he did not, whether she was prepared to accept him if he still proposed to her.

All her thinking had made no difference. The same wearisome doubts circled like the kitchen dog in his treadmill turning the spit, and to rather less effect.

"...do you not think so?"

"Oh, I am sorry; Flora, I was not attending. What did you say?"

Flora sighed patiently and repeated herself. "I think we should take only my dresser, and Vivian and the major will share Anthony's batman in lieu of a valet—I feel we should not inflict too many servants on the household while they are in disarray with building work. Vivian is proposing to drive down in his curricle with Anthony and we can take the travelling carriage. Plumb can travel with us and the batman and the luggage will go in the other carriage."

Caroline nodded her agreement, glancing at Jervais's letter as she did so. "I see he proposes to come to London simply to return at once with us to Dunharrow. Surely that is not necessary, for we will have Vivian and the major as escort."

"I think it shows a degree of sensibility that is

most pleasing,'' Flora rejoined smugly, pleased to be able to point out yet another virtue. ''And you know full well that your brother will not want to dawdle along at our pace.''

''And I am certain Lord Barnard will not want to be cooped up in a travelling carriage with us for a whole day either,'' Caroline riposted.

''No doubt he will ride, the gentlemen usually prefer to do so,'' Flora said. ''Now, that is settled. He writes that he hopes we will reach Dunharrow on the twentieth of December, that only leaves us nine days to prepare. Have you any further shopping you need, Caroline dear?''

Caroline needed very little persuasion to embark on yet another shopping expedition. Since Jervais had departed for Leicestershire, Flora had been amazed at her niece's willingness to be fitted for new gowns, to try on new bonnets and to spend hours shopping for fashionable trifles. This behaviour was so uncharacteristic she could only attribute it to Caroline desiring to look her best for Lord Barnard. Caroline, for her part, was simply aware of a need to fill every waking moment with activity.

''Grafton House, Forster,'' Caroline directed the coachman as they took their places in the closed carriage. The ladies pulled the fur-lined carriage rug over their knees and watched the damp and foggy streets unroll as they traversed the short distance.

Once under cover they discovered that many other ladies had decided to while away a raw December morning in like fashion.

The ladies purchased a few necessities: toothpowder, Hungary Water and eau de Cologne, then settled down to some serious frivolity. Over cups of chocolate at Gunter's two hours later they compared their acquisitions.

"See this fan, Flora—such a novel decoration." Caroline unfurled it, fluttering the fragile arc experimentally. "I like those stockings, how much were they? Perhaps I should purchase some for myself…"

At last they rose to leave. "Could you bear it if we went to Bond Street now, Flora?" Caroline enquired, slipping her hands into her muff. "I still have to find a gift for Lord Barnard. I have made all the rest of my Christmas purchases, or else I am making gifts, but I am quite at a loss to know what to give him."

"It is difficult," Flora commiserated, giving directions to Forster. "There are so few things one can, with propriety, give to a gentleman to whom one is not connected, and yet it would be most discourteous to take nothing for your host. I have left it to Anthony to select something on my behalf, but have you no notion of what to give him?"

"I had thought of a book. After all, Lord Barnard can have had little opportunity to buy many volumes whilst on military duty and I believe he said his cousin's library was much decayed, fit only for the bonfire. But other than the fact he despises Lord Byron, I have no notion of his tastes."

Browsing through the shelves of Caroline's favourite bookshop in Bond Street, the ladies found three volumes for themselves, but nothing for the elusive Christmas gift. Caroline had almost despaired when her eye fell upon Gilbert White's *Natural History and Antiquities of Selborne* lying open on a table.

"Why, this is the very thing! Selborne is in Hampshire and I am sure he would find it of some interest, it is so very well written and observed."

The next eight days seemed to crawl by, despite all there was to do. Presents had to be completed and wrapped, a final choice made from wardrobes and trunks packed. The ladies' bedrooms were soon a drift of silver paper and ribbons and Vivian began to complain he could find none of his linen because it was either being laundered or had already been packed.

Miss Plumb, Lady Grey's highly superior dresser, was in her element, directing footmen to bring down heavy fitted dressing-cases from the attics and irritating the butler by sending his staff on seemingly endless errands to the jewellers with items to be cleaned.

"I am not one to complain, Miss Plumb, as you know, but how am I supposed to run this household—what with the door to be answered and the trunks moved and all her ladyship's errands to be run—when if I call for William or Peter I find you have sent them round to Gieves and Hawkes?"

"Well, I am glad to hear you do not wish to complain, Mr Dorking," Miss Plumb responded with asperity, "for what could be more important than her ladyship presenting her best appearance at such a house-party?"

"Under the circumstances," Dorking dropped his voice, "I should say it's more important that a certain other party looks her best—if you follow my drift, Miss Plumb."

The appearance of a passing parlourmaid prevented the dresser from immediate reply; the speaking glance she gave him, however, conveyed volumes.

Mr Dorking was therefore not surprised, when opening the door at seven o'clock in the evening of the nineteenth, to find Lord Barnard upon the doorstep.

"Good evening; my lord." Dorking bowed Jervais into the hall, closing the door on the swirls of mist which eddied around their feet. "A pleasure to see your lordship again, if I may make so bold. I regret to say her ladyship has just left for a supper at the opera: I believe she did not look to see you until tomorrow morning, my lord."

"Indeed? I am sorry to have missed Lady Grey. Is Miss Franklin at home?"

Dorking hesitated, then appeared to reach a decision. "Miss Franklin is at home, my lord, I believe she is reading in the small salon. Shall I announce you?"

"No, thank you, Dorking." Jervais was already shedding his multi-caped driving coat into the waiting arms of a footman. "I will see myself up."

Behind Jervais the footman's eyebrows shot up as Mr Dorking permitted this latitude. As his lordship disappeared around the bend in the stairs, the butler turned to his underling. "Don't you stand there gawping, lad! Take the port and the brandy up to the small salon—in about ten minutes. There is no hurry." He permitted himself a small smile and made his way magisterially down to the housekeeper's sitting-room to convey this gratifying development to the senior staff.

Caroline had just laid aside her book and was

walking across the room to ring for Dorking when she heard the door open behind her.

"Ah, there you are, Dorking," she said, without turning round. "I was just about to ring for supper. It is a little early, I know…"

"Caro."

She whirled round, her hand dropping from the bellpull, her cheeks turning quite pale at the surprise of seeing him after so many weeks' absence.

"Jervais…Lord Barnard!" She collected herself rapidly and advanced, her hand outstretched to shake his. "We had not expected to see you until tomorrow morning: did you not believe we would take your instructions to the letter? I assure you we are quite packed and ready to set off at eight o'clock tomorrow morning."

Jervais took her proffered hand, but instead of shaking it, stood holding it, staring down intently into her face. Caroline, further unnerved, found herself prattling on. "And you have just missed Flora: she was quite unexpectedly invited out to the opera by the major…"

"I know." Jervais was still holding her hand, all his attention focused on her.

"You know? How could you?" Then she saw the betraying twinkle in his eye and gasped indignantly. "Why, you put him up to it! Whatever made you do such a thing?"

"Well," he said reasonably, "I could hardly do this with Lady Grey present." And with no more ado he took Caroline firmly in his arms and kissed her with a thoroughness which robbed her of her breath.

When he finally let her go she put her hands to

her burning cheeks and exclaimed, "Jervais! What are you about?"

"If you do not know, Caroline, I had better do it again."

This time she was too quick for him, dodging behind a tambour table, panting slightly.

"Let us sit down—look, I will sit here, at a safe distance." Jervais dropped easily into a bergère armchair, crossing his long legs at the ankle and regarding her benevolently as she sat cautiously, as far away as she could. "I have missed you, Caro. Have you not missed me? I had rather hoped you had."

"Well, naturally, from time to time…but we have had much to do." This was ridiculous! Here she was making conversation with a man who had just had the effrontery to kiss her—in her own home. "This is most improper. I do not know what Dorking was about, letting you up like this; he knew my aunt was out."

"I suspect he guesses why I have come." Jervais got to his feet and strolled across to sit beside her. Caro slid along the sofa away from him, her heart thudding uncomfortably. "Do you know why I have come?"

"I…my lord…"

The door opened to reveal Peter bearing a tray with decanters. "Mr Dorking thought you might be desirous of refreshment, my lord." He set the heavy tray down and bowed himself out, managing with an effort to keep from staring at the startling sight of the young mistress, quite unchaperoned, sitting on a sofa with a man.

"A glass of sherry, Caroline?" Jervais seemed quite unperturbed by the intrusion. He crossed to the tray, poured himself a brandy and brought it and the sherry across to Caroline.

The interruption had given her a moment to gather her wits and to discover she was not a little irritated by Jervais's air of assurance.

"You take a great deal for granted, my lord," she said frostily when he presented her with the glass.

"Oh, I am sorry. Would you have preferred madeira?"

"That is not what I am referring to, as you know full well."

He watched her, admiring the fair complexion, heightened by the flush of annoyance in her cheeks. Although she had planned an evening alone, her slim figure was dressed, with the easy elegance he had come to associate with her, in a simple silk gown of a deep cornflower which echoed the blue of her eyes. As she looked up to meet his scrutiny one of the dark curls framing her face tangled in her pearl earring and she gave a little exclamation of annoyance.

Jervais reached out one finger and gently unhooked the fine hair. Caroline froze as the tip of his finger brushed fleetingly against her skin: looking into his eyes she could see them soften.

"Caro, you must know why I am here..."

Caroline, quite unable to speak, shook her head slowly, hardly able to believe he was, in truth, about to make her the long awaited declaration.

"Dammit! I had no idea this would be so difficult." He got to his feet and paced across to the fireplace, uncharacteristically at a loss. He squared his shoulders and turned and she had a sudden glimpse of how he must have looked going into battle. Abruptly formal he knelt beside her and took her hand. "Miss Franklin... Caroline... I have the honour to ask if you will be my wife."

All the weeks of worry and indecision vanished in a rush of love for him that brought tears to her eyes. The fact he had not said he loved her was lost on her in that moment, all that mattered was that he was there beside her, asking her to be his wife.

"Yes...oh yes, Jervais."

He needed no further encouragement to take her in his arms and this time his kiss was a long, sensuous, gentle declaration of mastery. Caroline sensed she was being claimed, owned, yet she did not care, so swept up was she in joy at the thought she was to be Jervais's wife, married to the man she loved.

At length he gathered her up, lifting her onto his knee and holding her tightly against his chest. Caroline, very conscious of his lean body against hers, snuggled her head under his chin and listened to his heart beating rhythmically under her ear.

"This is very improper you know," she murmured after a while. "Have you asked Vivian's permission to pay your addresses?"

"Under the circumstances I thought it best to speak to you first," Jervais muttered, his lips nuzzling gently in her hair.

"Circumstances?" Caroline twisted out of his embrace and sat upright on his knee to stare at him in perplexity. "What circumstances? Oh, do you mean that Vivian is so much younger than you? I can see it might seem ridiculous, to find yourself, a more senior officer, asking his permission!"

"No," he said slowly, and apparently with some reluctance. "I mean the circumstances of our first encounter."

Caroline felt the blood drain from her face. So, it was true: he had only offered for her because he had compromised her in Belgium. "Whatever was there in your first visit to Brook Street..."

Jervais took her by the shoulders and gave her a little shake. "Caroline, stop this play-acting! It is no longer necessary—indeed, it never was necessary. You know as well as I that I picked you off the road on the battlefield, that we spent the night together before our return to Brussels, that you ran away from me."

"You knew I had regained my memory?" she said very slowly. "You knew right from the beginning that I remembered all about it?"

"When I walked into this house and saw you, I was too taken aback to consider it rationally. I recognised you at once, but it was obvious you had no wish to acknowledge the fact we had already met. Then you seemed so unconscious of any awkwardness that I concluded that the brain fever, or shock, or whatever had caused your first loss of memory, had also robbed you of your memories of me: that you had, in confusion, wandered from the house and been found by your friends."

Caroline got to her feet and moved away from him to the fireplace. There was such restraint in the way he was speaking, such reserve that she knew he was controlling some emotion only with difficulty. Jervais stood, too, but made no attempt to approach her. Suddenly she was very cold and she shivered as she held out her hands to the blaze. "Then what betrayed me? When did you become suspicious?"

"You knew my rank, although I had been introduced as Lord Barnard, and you knew Percy. After that you betrayed yourself to me in so many little ways—although no one else would have guessed.''

''Thank goodness for that,'' she said shakily. ''I was in a terror that Vivian or Flora might realise something was amiss: they had accepted my explanation of a fall from my horse and having been taken in by a respectable Belgian family. I could have scarcely told them the truth!''

''Caroline,'' Jervais asked patiently, ''why could you not have trusted me, told me that you remembered? I asked you to trust me, do you not recall?''

''How could I trust you on such short acquaintance? When you think of the circumstances under which we were together!'' She shuddered and averted her face.

The look of patience vanished from his face to be replaced by anger. ''So you did not trust my discretion? When I saw you here I never doubted you were exactly who you purported to be: a lady. Do you think so little of me that you fear I would damage your reputation in Society by carelessness or spite?''

''Your delicacy does you credit, my lord!'' Caroline flung back at him, goaded by the reproach in his voice. ''What a shame it was not much in evidence when you were trying to inveigle me into your bed!''

''I thought you were one of the muslin company,'' he began indignantly. ''You knew that.''

''I did not know who I was! You leapt to the conclusion that I was a loose woman on the flimsiest of evidence—why, it was the merest chance I was not ruined, in fact! And then you ask me to trust you after you took advantage of me in that outrageous manner? Oh, no, my lord, I am not quite so gullible.''

"Leapt to conclusions!" Jervais raked his fingers through his hair in angry exasperation. "What the hell am I to conclude when I find you in a dress only a courtesan would wear and with paint on your face?"

"You might have given me the benefit of the doubt!" Even as she said it, it sounded weak and improbable: all the evidence had been against her respectability, not least her own ready comprehension of what he had been suggesting.

"What doubt? And to cap it all, you showed a knowledge of things no innocent young lady should have had an inkling about."

Caroline drew herself up and said icily, "From your conduct, sir, I should imagine your acquaintanceship with innocent young ladies is somewhat limited!" She had no intention of telling Jervais about her father and his string of mistresses.

"You still have not explained to me what you were doing in that dress," he persisted.

"Not that I owe you any explanation, Lord Barnard, but the truth of the matter is that I have no recollection."

"Truth? I am beginning to doubt you have any conception of the meaning of the word. Your loss of memory is strangely convenient, it seems to me."

Caroline, goaded beyond prudence, took two jerky steps towards Jervais and slapped him hard across his cheek. He caught her raised hand painfully in his and pulled her against him. "I ought to turn you across my knee for that!"

"And when Vivian heard of it he would call you out!" she gasped, still too angry to think what she was saying.

"So you have confided all the details of your little adventure to your brother, have you? I had not thought him so complaisant."

"I tell you I cannot remember..."

"Oh, yes, you can, but you dare not admit it. What was it, a dare between you and one of your feather-headed friends that went disastrously wrong? Consider yourself lucky, madam, that it was I who picked you up and not a common foot-soldier: there would be no talk of respectability then."

Caroline stared aghast as his harsh face. "You think...you believe I would dress up in such an improper garment for a game...risk my reputation...and at such a time? In the midst of all our worry about Vivian and the battle?"

"What else would you have me believe if you persist in lying to me?" His expression was grim. "How long were you away from home?"

"From Saturday midday, which was when I rode out to seek advice on whether we should leave Brussels..."

"And I found you at midnight on Sunday: thirty-six hours to be accounted for. Can you not think of a convincing explanation?"

"My horse bolted and took me out of the city. I fell off and hit my head!"

"You went riding in the dress I found you in?" He was making no attempt to hide his scorn at her story.

"Why, no, of course I did not—I was wearing a riding habit."

"Then with whom did you spent those thirty-six hours?" he demanded.

"No one! Or, at least, I cannot remember..." Her

voice trailed off at the look of disbelief on Jervais's face, then she recovered herself. "I do not lie! Why did you ask me to marry you if you think such terrible things of me?" Caroline freed her wrist, shaking Jervais off. "I would not marry you, sir, if you were the last man on earth!"

"I am delighted to hear it, because believe it or not, Caroline, having asked you I would have felt it my duty to honour my offer regardless. Now I can see I have had a fortunate escape."

"You are no gentleman, my lord!" Caroline could hardly choke the words out past the tears that threatened to overwhelm her.

"If I am no gentleman, then ask yourself what lady would be prepared to ally herself with a man she mistrusted as much as you mistrust me." He ignored the tears which were running down her cheeks. "Perhaps you had other reasons: had you made some enquiries into the size of my inheritance? As you are no doubt aware, it is substantial. Or after your little escapade did you think you had better take the first man who offered for fear of scandal?"

"Go!" was all she could manage to say, burying her face in her hands.

"With pleasure, madam," Jervais replied softly. "With pleasure."

It was three hours after the front door had shut behind Jervais that Caroline heard the unmistakable sounds of Flora and the Major returning from their visit to the opera.

During those interminable hours she had passed from sobbing despair to dumb misery. At first she had wanted nothing more than for Flora to return so she could pour out the whole story. Then she realised she could not. Once she learned the truth of what had really happened in Belgium, Flora would insist on telling all to Vivian and he, regardless of how violent the quarrel had been between the couple, would demand that Lord Barnard marry his sister.

And she would never agree to that. Jervais had made it as clear as though he had told her so that he had offered only because he had compromised her. Nor could he love her if he was not prepared to accept her word that her memory had only partially returned, that she still had no recollection of how she had come to be on the battlefield. As to what he believed she had been doing... Caroline could hardly bring herself to think about it.

By the time Flora returned, Caroline had decided that all she could do was to tell her aunt that Jervais had proposed, that she had refused him and that it was too embarrassing to expect her to spend Christmas at Dunharrow as his guest.

Flora would be extremely displeased with her, and it would mean the break-up of the party at the last moment, but rack her brain as she might, no other solution offered itself.

Where was her aunt? It must be quite fifteen minutes since Caroline had heard the buzz of arrival in the hall. Perhaps she had gone direct to her chamber, but there had been no sound on the stairs.

Caroline looked at her reflection in the glass and hesitated, then decided that her swollen eyes and pale cheeks could be attributed to maidenly distress at rejecting a suitor. She walked slowly downstairs, finding the hall empty and the house quiet.

Then she saw the study door was ajar, light spilling out across the marble checkerboard floor. Flora must have decided to take a book up to bed with her, or perhaps she was penning a note.

Caroline pushed open the door, then froze. In a cruel parody of what had passed upstairs only hours before she saw the back of the Major's head as he sat on the chaise longue, Flora in his arms.

"Anthony, my dear, I cannot say when we can be married," her aunt was saying. "I must see Caroline settled first. I promised her dear mama I would not leave her until she was married…"

Tiptoeing silently out of the study and back upstairs to her room Caroline felt sick at heart. It was a double blow: both to lose the man she loved and, in doing so, deprive Flora of her chance of happiness. She knew her aunt too well to believe she would yield easily to any persuasion either she or the Major might employ. Caroline had turned down the only man she would ever love, condemning both herself and her aunt to unhappiness.

Nor could she tell her aunt she was not going to Dunharrow. To spoil her happiness now would be a cruel blow; somehow she would have to break the news, but not yet, not just before Christmas.

When Jervais arrived tomorrow to collect them— if, indeed, he did—she would have to speak to him and plead with him to betray nothing of what had passed between them that evening.

Then all they had to do was to play act for two interminable weeks; she as though her heart was not broken, he as though he did not hold her in the deepest suspicion and contempt.

Chapter Eight

The appointed hour of eight o'clock came and went without sign of Lord Barnard. The entire household was in that state of restlessness consequent upon being fully prepared and having nothing to do but wait. The travelling carriage was packed with all the necessities for a long journey on a cold winter's day and the coach with the trunks had left at dawn.

The dank mists of the past fortnight had been banished overnight and replaced by a sparkling hard frost. Dorking had hot bricks waiting in the bread oven until the last minute before the ladies, well wrapped in fur travelling rugs, stepped into the carriage and he could pack them around their feet.

Vivian and the Major had already left as agreed, Vivian driving the curricle gingerly across the icy cobbles.

Flora, still in a secret, happy daze from last night's agreement with her Major, was doing her best to soothe her agitated niece. Her instincts blunted by her own happiness, she misinterpreted Caroline's unhappy restlessness.

"It is but twenty minutes past the hour," she said

placidly from her seat by the fire. "There is bound to be some small delay, especially with the weather so icy."

Jervais was not coming. She must have been mad to think he would after what had passed between them last night. Such bitter words could not easily be unsaid, and they had both uttered accusations which in the cold light of day appalled her.

As the minute hand of the clock crept round and Flora continued to sit placidly waiting, Caroline steeled herself to tell her aunt the truth—all of it. She could not live with this feeling of guilt for deceiving her: now Jervais was not coming she could pretend no longer. She must persuade Flora that Caroline's mother would never have intended her sister-in-law to sacrifice her own happiness by interpreting her promise so literally, not after Caroline had ruined her own chances of marriage so disastrously.

"Flora…"

The sound of the knocker reached them faintly from the floor below. Caroline spun round and craned to see down through the frosted window. But the horse standing by the kerb, its breath making white plumes in the bitter air, was an ordinary hack, not Caesar.

As she watched, a groom emerged and mounted the horse, walking it slowly away down the treacherous road. Shortly afterwards Dorking entered the salon, carrying a silver salver with a note on it. "Lord Barnard's compliments, my lady."

Caroline sank down onto the window-seat. She should have said something sooner to Flora; now the shock of discovering Caroline's behaviour and the consequences for her own alliance with the Major, would be all the greater.

As Caroline watched her aunt scanning the note, she saw her brow furrow and she made a soft sound of distress. What could he have said? Caroline's heart contracted as she imagined the contents.

"Oh dear, how distressing for Lord Barnard," said Flora in a worried tone.

"Distressing! Is that what you call it? I suppose he has told you all..."

Caroline broke off at the sight of the perplexed expression on Flora's face. "What are you talking about, Caroline? Of course Lord Barnard has told me all!"

"All! On one sheet of paper?" Caroline cried.

"My dear, you are not well, you speak so strangely!" She looked at Caroline's strained, pinched face. "Are you feverish? Oh dear, oh dear, I must send to Lord Barnard immediately—we cannot travel if you are unwell."

"Travel?" Caroline croaked. "We are still going to Dunharrow?"

"But, of course, this is only a short delay." Flora put a cool hand on Caroline's brow. "You do not seem to have a fever. I know what it must be—you are over-excited, and you did not sleep well last night. I heard you moving about in your chamber." She looked closely into Caroline's face. "I do not know how I can have failed to notice it before, but your eyes are quite heavy."

"I am quite well, but I did not sleep much—it is the thought of the journey, for some reason I found it unsettling." She could contain herself no longer.

"May I see his lordship's note? How does he account for the delay?"

Flora handed her the missive and she scanned it with anxious eyes. Caesar, it seemed, had slipped on the icy cobbles in the mews and had strained a tendon and there would be some delay whilst another horse was saddled. Jervais would be with them directly.

Relief threatened to overwhelm her and she turned away to hide her face from Flora. He had said nothing of her secret, nor had he withdrawn the invitation to Dunharrow. Caroline knew she should be relieved on her aunt's account, but all that she was conscious of was thankfulness that he had not severed all contact, that she would see him again, however difficult it would be. It seemed you did not stop loving someone just because you discovered they held you in distrust and considered you a liar.

She had scarcely laid the note aside when Jervais strode into the room, his heavy caped riding coat brushing the furniture. Without a glance towards Caroline, he bowed over Flora's hand, his gaze intent upon her face.

"Why so solemn, my lord?" Flora teased. "Did you think you were in for a scold for keeping us waiting? I can assure you that in this house we are so inured to Vivian's unpunctuality as to almost expect it of everyone! But I should not joke—how is your poor horse? Not badly hurt, I trust?"

"You are most forgiving." Flora saw his face relax and thought with satisfaction that he must care very much for Caroline's good opinion if he was so concerned at being late. "And thank you, but Caesar will be well enough in a few days."

Caroline swallowed hard and forced her unwilling legs to cross the room to him. "Good morning, my lord." She held out her hand, and he took it briefly. "You will not be hunting him for a while, I imagine."

She had schooled her face into an expression of cool politeness and was wounded to see no hint of emotion of any sort in his.

"If you ladies are ready, shall we set out? We have a long journey and the weather is against us: the only consolation is that it is too cold to snow."

As Plumb helped her into her warm pelisse and handed her a fur muff, Caroline reflected grimly that if this cold correctness were to characterise their relations over the next few weeks, then so be it. She could be as chillingly punctilious as he.

Once clear of the treacherously slippery streets of London, the horses were able to increase their speed more safely on the metalled road. Jervais, mounted on a black gelding Caroline had not seen before, cantered beside the carriage, his expression as frozen as the weather.

Flora talked animatedly as they drove, apparently unaffected by the bounding of the well-sprung carriage on the frozen surface. Caroline sat abstracted, answering her aunt in monosyllables. Plumb, as was her place, sat jealously guarding her mistress's dressing-case, regarding the frozen countryside with the deep disapproval of the town-bred.

Caroline watched Jervais, telling herself she should be grateful that his correct demeanour would do nothing to raise suspicion that anything untoward had passed between them. But her irrational longing was for him to storm at her, or take her in his arms—

anything to show he felt something, that he cared for her.

"Lord Barnard must be frozen," Flora remarked. "When we change horses at Guildford, see if you cannot persuade him to ride inside with us, Caroline."

"He should be warm enough," said Caroline indifferently, watching the rider as she spoke. He was wearing a heavy caped greatcoat which hung down over the flanks of the gelding and quite covered his riding coat and buckskins. The coat was of military cut and brought back the memory of him in uniform, of sitting up behind him as they rode back to Brussels.

For a fleeting moment she was back in the heat of that June day, remembering again how he had looked after her, protected her despite his wounds, his gentleness and understanding of her fears.

Angry tears pricked at the back of her eyes and she blinked them away. She was angry with herself for still loving him, despite everything; at him for failing to trust her, at the unfairness of life.

It was well after dark when they reached Dunharrow and the clock over the stable block was striking six as the carriage drew up at the front door. Despite Flora's best efforts at persuasion, Jervais had continued to ride and the ladies had long since run out of conversation so it was a cold and weary party, grateful to have reached its destination, which finally shed its coats in the hallway.

"Are the rest of our guests here, Chawton?" Jervais enquired as the butler took his coat.

"The Major and the Lieutenant arrived an hour since and are in the drawing room with Sir Richard and Major Routh, my lord. The heavy luggage is also here and has been taken up.'' He turned as a homely woman came in and curtsied to the ladies. ''Mrs Chawton will show the ladies to their chambers.''

Miss Plumb nodded stiffly to the housekeeper, obviously considering such bucolic servants beneath her touch. Caroline and Flora followed her gratefully, wanting nothing more than to change out of their travel-stained clothes, wash and warm themselves by a good fire.

''What a handsome staircase,'' Flora remarked as they ascended. ''This part of the house seems of recent construction.''

''Indeed, ma'am, I believe it was built by his late lordship's father some fifty years ago,'' the housekeeper replied as they reached the first landing. ''This is your room, my lady, I trust you will be comfortable.''

The chamber she showed them into was spacious and Caroline guessed that in daylight it would afford a fine view down the driveway towards the gatehouse.

''And this room is for you, Miss Franklin.'' The woman opened the door into the adjoining chamber which must, from the arrangement of its windows on two walls, be on the corner of the new wing. ''There's a handsome prospect of the park from this side,'' the housekeeper commented. She ran a critical eye over the arrangements in the room. ''There is hot water coming and the maid will unpack for you if your dresser will direct her. Is there anything else you require, Miss Franklin?''

Before Caroline could reply Flora entered, untying her bonnet strings as she did so. ''Why, what a beautiful room! His lordship has had it decorated in the most exquisite taste.'' Her discerning eye travelled over the delicate cream panelling set off by rich jonquil yellow draperies at the windows and above the four-poster bed. The bed curtains themselves were a froth of fine muslin, swagged and tied with matching yellow ribbons. ''Do you know, this colour scheme puts me in mind of that gown of yours, the one you wore to Almack's the evening Lord Barnard invited us here.''

The housekeeper turned from stirring a bowl of pot-pourri on the tallboy. ''It was originally going to be a green room, my lady, but his lordship sent orders for it to be changed at almost the last minute—why, I declare the paint is hardly dry!''

Flora shot Caroline a knowing look, amused by the colour which was staining her niece's cheeks. ''Indeed, Mrs Chawton. And are all the refurbished rooms as fine as this one?''

''Well, my lady, they are all very fine and a great improvement on what there was before—his old lordship did neglect things something awful, as everyone does agree—but I think this room is the finest.

''I do wonder whether his lordship intends to make this into the room for the lady of the house. At present, that is the chamber at the back overlooking the Fountain Court, and to be sure Lady Shannon has that as hostess, but he hasn't had it decorated as lovely as this. And this would be as convenient as that is,'' she added with a twinkle, ''there being a door through to his dressing room from this one. It is locked, of course, just now.''

''So I should hope,'' said Flora firmly, but her tone

belied the triumphant light in her eyes. To her, there could not have been a more blatant indication of Jervais's intentions towards Caroline than to install her in the bedroom of the mistress of the house.

Caroline turned away to unbutton her pelisse, almost unable to bear the thought that he had intended all this for her, not just for a short visit, but for the rest of her life as his wife.

The thought was still uppermost in her mind as, changed out of their travel-stained garments, they entered the salon an hour later to join the rest of the party before dinner.

The room seemed full of people and Caroline felt relief that she was not going to be thrown together with Jervais without the company of others.

Tonight he was dressed with severe formality in evening dress, his dark blue tail coat in sharp contrast to the dress uniforms of the male guests, all still serving officers. His expression as he approached the ladies seemed blandly welcoming, but Caroline caught one, brief betraying glance in her direction that hinted at hidden depths to his thoughts.

"Lady Grey, may I introduce you to my cousin, Lady Shannon, who has kindly agreed to act as my hostess. Serena: Lady Grey and her niece, Miss Franklin."

"How do you do." Lady Shannon shook hands with them both with a frank, welcoming smile. "What a terrible journey down you must have had! I do hope you are quite warm and rested now and that you have everything you require. Let me introduce my daughter, Julia, to you."

As Lady Julia made a rather shy curtsy Caroline saw how like her mother she was. Both were blonde,

fine-boned and full-figured. Lady Shannon had a ma-
tronly dignity that in time Julia would acquire, but
for the moment she was still very obviously just out
of the schoolroom with a wide-eyed innocence of
expression that was very endearing.

Lady Shannon turned to include the two officers
standing by the fireside. "And may I make known
to you Captain Sir Richard Holden—" the tall young
man in question bowed politely, the light glinting off
red hair which clashed unfortunately with his scarlet
jacket "—and Major Simon Routh."

The Major was older than Sir Richard, a stocky,
dark man with a roguish twinkle in his eye as it
rested on Caroline. "Enchanted," he said.

Flora, observing his ready admiration of her niece,
promptly engaged him in conversation, drawing Anthony Gresham into their discussion of the latest
news from Europe.

Caroline smiled at Julia who was standing to one
side, her eyes cast shyly down. "I understand you
live in Ireland: have you been to England before?"

As Caroline skilfully drew out the debutante, Lady
Shannon turned to her cousin. "So, Jervais," she remarked in an undertone, "this is the cause of your
sudden desire to entertain! I must congratulate you
on your discernment, Miss Franklin appears to be a
charming young woman—everything I could have
hoped for."

"I have no notion what you mean, Serena," he
replied lightly. "You know full well you inveigled
me into holding a house-party to help you launch
Julia."

"Nonsense, Jervais. We would have been quite
content to spend a few weeks quietly in London at-

tending to Julia's wardrobe! And do not attempt to gull me into believing you have had this wing lavishly redecorated in the depths of the winter merely for the sake of your brother officers. So long as the food and the shooting are good, they would not notice if they were billeted in the barn!''

"You will excuse me, Serena," Jervais said abruptly. "I must speak with Chawton about the wine for dinner."

Lady Shannon watched him move across the room, noticing he did not so much as glance in Miss Franklin's direction. She might be married to a bluff country-loving peer with more regard for his horses than for intellectual pursuits, but she herself was a shrewd observer of people. There was something deeply amiss with her cousin, however well he hid it from his other friends: she knew him too well to be deceived.

Serena looked consideringly at Miss Franklin who had succeeded in drawing out Julia into a laughing conversation. So, she was as kind as she was beautiful, Julia's mother mused, knowing not many young women would have relished the competition afforded by her daughter's burgeoning looks. And they were so different that they made a charming pair, the one so blonde and rounded, the other slender and darkly elegant.

Caroline was dressed with deceptive simplicity in a deep rose gown with a hem quilted in a darker shade and a spider's-web gauze scarf. Lady Shannon commended her taste and resolved to enquire the direction of her dressmaker.

So what was Jervais about? Serena would have expected him to confide his intentions to her, yet he had almost snubbed her just now. He made no attempt to single out Miss Franklin: that might simply have been discretion...and yet, it was more than that, she could sense a deep unhappiness in him. And that was most perplexing.

Dinner was a most convivial occasion: even Caroline, miserable as she was, found herself relaxing. The food and wine were excellent, the gentlemen were lively and amusing conversationalists and Lady Shannon had skilfully disposed her guests around the table to overcome the problem of the extra gentleman.

Jervais, at the head of the board, was out of Caroline's line of sight, for she found herself placed near her hostess at the other end of the table between Sir Richard and Major Gresham.

Opposite her, she was amazed to see, Vivian had struck up an animated conversation with Julia. He seemed to have found just the right note to take with her, for she showed none of her previous shyness and was chatting happily.

Caroline was concentrating on drawing out Sir Richard who, although pleasant, was rather hard going as a dinner companion, being rather serious and high-minded for her taste. She glanced up at one point and met the admiring eye of Major Routh, diagonally opposite. Her immediate impression on meeting him that he was something of a ladies' man was underscored by the warmth in his face as he raised his glass in a toast to her.

Caroline smiled back, somewhat repressively. He was obviously a rogue, but, in her judgement, a likeable and harmless one.

At the end of the meal Lady Shannon gathered the

ladies with a glance and rose, saying with a laugh, "Well, I suppose we must leave these men to their port and what they will tell us afterwards is a serious discussion of affairs!"

The drawing-room, lit by branches of candles, was cosy, the firelight flickering on its pale oak panelled walls. Flora immediately engaged Lady Julia in conversation, drawing her out about her plans and hopes for the coming Season.

Lady Shannon gestured in a friendly manner to the sofa beside her, "Do sit by me, Miss Franklin, and tell me your opinion of Jervais. I own I have been a little concerned for his health since he returned from Belgium; his wounds gave us such cause for anxiety when we heard of them. I wrote at once to beg him to join us in Ireland, but he would have none of it. I could not, at the time, imagine why." The sideways look she gave Caroline was full of meaning.

"Lord Barnard is in the habit of visiting your estates often, I collect?" Caroline tried to ignore the suggestion implicit in that last remark.

"Well, we are the only family he possesses. Even when his late cousin was still alive, Jervais came more to us than to Dunharrow."

"I would not want to speak disrespectfully of the late Lord Barnard, but he does seem to have been somewhat...eccentric."

"Eccentric! The man had maggots in his head— did Jervais tell you about his fearful ginger wig?" She lowered her voice and added, "And there was not a family in the village who would permit one of their daughters to work here. No doubt Jervais and I have several relatives down in Dunharrow Parva!" Seeing the look on Caroline's face, she said immediately, "Forgive me for putting it so frankly, my dear! I am used to plain talking, and you seem such a poised young woman, I quite forgot you are still single."

"I have been out for several Seasons," Caroline replied absently, still meditating on the appalling habits of his late lordship.

"Indeed? And you are not, I believe, engaged to be married?"

"My aunt tells me I am far to nice in my requirements of a husband," Caroline replied evenly, uncomfortable with the direction the conversation was taking.

So, Lady Shannon mused inwardly, he has done something to upset her, has he! How unexpectedly clumsy of Jervais. "Julia, my dear," she called across, much to Caroline's relief, "did you bring down your pianoforte music? You know Jervais likes to hear you play." She lowered her voice again. "He has no more fondness for amateur playing than the next man, but she needs to overcome her nervousness at performing in company."

As Julia opened the instrument somewhat reluctantly, the men joined them. Major Routh was saying as they entered "...sounds capital! I'm ready for a game; Holden, Gresham, Franklin—will any of you join us to try Barnard's new billiard table? If the ladies will excuse us?"

"Yes, of course," said Lady Shannon gracefully.

"For myself, I would remain, if the ladies have no objection to my company," said Vivian, to Caroline's complete amazement. When she saw Julia's flushed cheeks and downcast eyes, she understood what had made him lose interest in masculine company.

"Lady Julia is about to play for us, Vivian," Caroline informed him slyly, only to be confounded when he leapt to his feet and asked:

"May I turn the music for you, Lady Julia?"

"I do hope you do not object to my brother showing such a marked partiality to Lady Julia," Caroline murmured as the first chords were struck. "I am amazed, he normally flees from debutantes!"

Lady Shannon was regarding the young couple indulgently. "It is early days yet, they have only just met and she is not yet out. I would not want her fixing her interest whilst she is still so young, but it will do her no harm at all to enjoy a light flirtation with a young man such as your brother."

Caroline rather doubted if a light flirtation was what Vivian had in mind. He was usually so impervious to the charms of young debutantes that she suspected he was falling in love. But there was no need to raise that possibility yet.

"Will you excuse me a moment, ma'am?" she asked, getting to her feet. "I seem to have left my reticule in the dining-room."

Having retrieved the little bag which had fallen under her chair, Caroline paused to order her hair in the glass over the mantelpiece. The door behind her closed with a sharp click and in the mirror she saw Jervais reflected. He crossed the room to her side, showing no surprise at finding her there.

Caroline turned, her heart thumping at the shock of being alone with him, but she believed she had succeeded in keeping her thoughts from her face. "My lord..."

"Miss Franklin. Is anything amiss?" He was closer than was quite comfortable—or quite proper, but with the fire at her back she could not retreat.

"I forgot my reticule."

"That is not what I meant." He was looking almost sinisterly saturnine in his dark clothes and the subdued light. His face was expressionless apart from his eyes which showed some emotion she could not interpret.

Caroline opened her mouth to make a light riposte, then found herself unable to maintain the pretence that nothing had happened any longer. "What could be amiss, my lord? Other, of course, than the fact that you and I are closeted here together for the next two weeks when, after last night, you heartily wish me elsewhere!"

"You seem very certain of my feelings," he replied evenly.

"How can you pretend it could be otherwise after what passed between us last evening! What do you imagine must be my feelings at having to pretend nothing is amiss? I realise that you could not withdraw the invitation to Dunharrow without reason, without having to explain all to my aunt..."

Caroline knew her colour was high, and she could feel her fists clenching at her side. She had known this conversation was bound to occur, but what she had not anticipated was how she would feel. Anger was uppermost, but underneath the anger she wanted to be in his arms and the need made her tremble.

"Perhaps I was afraid your brother would call me out if he knew what had..." a fractional pause "...passed between us," he said calmly.

"Sir, you are insufferable!" she cried, goaded.

"And you, Caroline, are a very irritating young woman."

"Oh!" The attack was so unexpected it took her several seconds to formulate her reply. "Irritating! No one has ever described me so—how dare you!"

"There are many things I dare do, Caroline," he said, suddenly husky and before she realised what he was about, she was in his arms being thoroughly kissed.

For perhaps five seconds she stiffened angrily, struggling, then the warm strength of him overcame her and her struggles were only to free her arms to twine them round his neck, to draw him closer.

Drugged by the intensity of her feelings, she clung to him, hope welling up that the harsh and bitter words they had exchanged last night were behind them, that he had come to believe her and was prepared to trust her after all.

It was Jervais who broke the embrace. "This must stop. I was a fool to let myself be alone with you— I should have learned by now you are a temptation I find it impossible to resist."

So that was all she was to him: a temptation. No doubt his late, unlamented cousin had found the serving girls an equal temptation!

"I had not observed much attempt at restraint in you, sir," she began angrily, ashamed that she had gone into his arms so easily.

"Caroline, you wrong me." There was colour in his face now. "I assure you I am exercising considerable restraint to prevent myself making what would probably be the biggest mistake of my life."

"If by that," she stormed, "you are inferring that you are restraining yourself from making me another offer, I can assure you that nothing would suit me better! And if you think I would permit you to lay one finger on me again…''

There was no question of Jervais hiding his feelings now. He was at least as angry as she as he said icily, ''That, madam, I have no trouble in assuring you! Gratifying as your ready response to my caresses has always been from the moment I picked you up on the battlefield…''

Angry tears stung her eyes so that she could not see him clearly. ''Let me past! I hate you…''

Jervais stepped aside without a word, making no attempt to restrain her as she ran from the room.

Chapter Nine

Caroline dashed the angry tears from her eyes and realised she was in a deserted, dimly lit passage in part of the house she had not seen before.

In her flight from Jervais she must have taken a wrong turning, although how many minutes she had spent angrily pacing she could not guess. Not long, she realised after a little thought, for she was still quite warm and the stone-flagged passage was chilly.

Resolutely Caroline turned her thoughts from Jervais and diverted herself to looking about. This had to be one of the older wings of the house, she deduced, wandering further. It did not seem to be the servants' wing for there were some fine, although dirty, portraits on the walls and when she turned a corner her heart leapt in her mouth until she realised the lurking shadow was only a suit of armour.

The sound of voices ahead of her drew her on, although cautiously, for she had no wish to encounter anyone with her cheeks still tear-streaked.

A door was ajar, spilling light onto the flagstones. Caroline tiptoed forward, drawing her skirts tight in her hand to stop them rustling. A sharp click and an exclamation of "Damn good shot!" made her realise she had inadvertently found the billiard room.

Unable to resist a peek into this male domain, Caroline looked through the crack at the hinge side of the door and found she had a good view of the room and its inhabitants.

Anthony Gresham, jacket discarded, was leaning across the table, lining up a tricky shot. Sir Richard, also in shirt sleeves, was moving the pointer on the score-board whilst Major Routh lounged against the wall, drawing on a cigarillo and squinting through the smoke at the lie of the billiard balls on the baize cloth.

"Come on, Gresham! Hazard the shot, man—I'm growing old while you work out your angles."

"Typical artillery approach," Sir Richard drawled. "Thank goodness he doesn't have to calculate elevation as well, we'd be here all night."

Ignoring the attempts to distract him, Gresham potted a perfect shot and straightened up, chalking the end of his cue. "And we all know why you do not want to be here all night, eh, Routh?"

"Why not?" Sir Richard enquired absently, circling the table to set up his own shot.

"Because he's got a little ladybird stashed away down in the village, that's why."

He had all Holden's attention and Caroline, who had been on the point of tiptoeing away, also stopped to listen. "I say, old chap, that's a bit much, isn't it—I mean, guest of Barnard's and all that…"

"I'm not asking him to feed or house her," Routh replied breezily. "And if I left Fanny alone in London, she wouldn't be alone when I got back, if I know her."

"Even so..." Amongst his friends Sir Richard was known as something of a stuffed shirt: one or two had even suggested he was in the wrong profession and was a natural-born bishop.

"Damn it, man," Routh riposted, grinding out his cigarillo butt. "If he hadn't got the ladies staying, Barnard would not turn a hair if I had Fanny here. In fact, knowing him, he'd want to know why I hadn't brought her friends."

"Indeed?" Gresham enquired. "You do surprise me; I had no idea our host was a womaniser."

It was no surprise to Caroline, remembering all too vividly his reaction to her in Belgium, the easy way he seemed prepared to take her under his protection. She suppressed an indignant snort and reapplied her eye to the crack. It was totally improper to be eavesdropping at all—her aunt would have the vapours if she knew—and to be listening to such scandalous revelations was quite beyond the pale. But if they were talking about Jervais, she wanted to hear every detail, however shocking.

"Well, to be fair," Routh remarked, raising an eyebrow as Sir Richard missed his shot by several inches, "womaniser is not the word I'd use to describe him. One woman at a time, that's his style—and looks after them well at that. Do you remember that little Spanish piece who followed him all over the Peninsula, Holden?"

"Portuguese, I think," Holden corrected him coldly, the conversation obviously not to his liking.

"Well, whatever." Routh waved his hand dismissively. "The point is, he stuck to her right through the campaign and made sure she was well provided for when we crossed the frontier into France."

A stab of jealousy struck Caroline, much as she tried to tell herself that she could expect nothing more or less from an unmarried fighting man, hundreds of miles from home, never knowing from day to day whether he'd survive to nightfall.

"And just how do you propose visiting your paramour?" Sir Richard enquired. "Climbing down the wisteria?"

"No need for anything so crude, old chap. I've slipped the butler a few sovereigns and got the back-door key. Can come and go as I please."

The clock in the billiard room struck the quarter and Caroline realised with a shock that she had been away a full half hour. What would Lady Shannon be thinking of her? Hastily she tiptoed away, breaking into a run once she was around the corner. In only a short time she found herself opening a door which led into the hall.

She patted her hair into order, brushed a lingering trace of dust from her hem, and wracking her brain for a plausible excuse for her absence, once more entered the drawing-room.

"Oh, there you are, my dear," said Lady Shannon placidly. "Jervais explained how you had torn your flounce. I would have sent my maid up to you, but Jervais insisted you had said it would only take a few stitches to catch it up."

Miffed that his lordship was, as usual, quite in control of the situation, Caroline shot him a far from grateful glance. He was sitting next to Flora, helping her sort coloured silks for her embroidery and managing to look entirely domesticated. Caroline tried to imagine him, battlestained in the Spanish dust, returning to a dark-eyed girl who would soothe away all the horrors of the day and found the resulting vision so disturbing that she turned abruptly to Lady Shannon.

"Are you to take a house in Town for the Season?" she enquired, managing to retain a look of bright interest as her hostess recounted the trials and tribulations of finding suitable rented accommodation.

"Jervais offered us the use of his town house, but to have the house full of chattering debutantes and callow youths would be asking too much of his good nature! After all, if Julia's darling papa cannot face the thought, I really do not think it fair to inflict it upon Jervais."

Caroline laughed and offered some suggestions as to suitable house agents until Flora began to pack her silks away in their box. "Thank you, my lord, I find those pale colours so difficult to match in anything but daylight—your eyesight must be excellent! Caroline, my dear, I think we should retire, for it has been a long day."

"Indeed, yes," Lady Shannon concurred. "You must have risen at the crack of dawn." She looked across to where her daughter was sitting near the piano, turning over sheet music with Vivian, her cheeks pink with animation. "And you, too, Julia!"

Caroline was woken the next morning by the rattle of curtain rings as the maid pulled back the heavy drapes, letting in the sunlight to fill the room. The light had a cold clarity as it reflected off the hard hoar frost, but the girl had already set a taper to the fire and the room was comfortably warm as Caroline scrambled out of bed, pulling a wrapper around her shoulders.

The windows in the side of her room faced southeast, catching the rising winter sun. Caroline took a cup of steaming chocolate and went to perch on the window-seat to admire the view over the park. The frost-whitened lawns swept down to a ha-ha beyond which the park stretched out with fine stands of trees on the slopes and, in the distance, a herd of fallow deer.

She rested her head against the shutter and drank in the cold tranquility, sipping occasionally at the chocolate. The stillness was broken by two spaniels, ears flopping as they raced across the grass, chasing each other in their exuberance. They were followed by a tall figure clad in a caped greatcoat, a low-crowned hat on his head and suddenly Caro's dreaminess was quite gone.

Caroline knelt up on the seat the better to see him as Jervais whistled at the dogs, bending to pull at their ears as they gambolled round his booted ankles.

As she watched he turned to stand with his back to the house, staring out over the winter landscape. She knew instinctively he was savouring the sense of ownership now this place was his. Without ever having discussed it with him, she knew he would want to return Dunharrow to the beauty it used to have before his cousin's neglect had besmirched it.

Lost in a futile dream of how it would be to help him in this task, Caroline was taken by surprise when he turned to stare up at her window. Across the distance their eyes met and locked: a sudden terrible sense of loss swept through her and she had to turn back into the room, away from him. He was the man she loved, the only man she would ever love, and he was irretrievably lost to her unless he could find it in his heart to trust her unreservedly.

He had made it perfectly plain the evening before that much as he might desire her, he would never ally himself to a woman with a mystery in her past she would not confide in him. And Caroline knew that even if she had that missing piece of knowledge about how she had come to be on the battlefield, she would not tell him now. If he could not trust her unreservedly, she must learn to live without him.

Over breakfast Lady Shannon suggested the ladies might like to accompany her on a walk into the village.

"Not that Harrowbridge is truly a village, like Dunharrow Parva which lies to the west, it is more of a small town. There is really quite a good haberdasher's shop—you may be able to match that rose pink silk you have been wanting, Lady Grey."

"That would be very pleasant," Flora agreed. "At this time of year it is such a pleasure to be able to take the air, one can never tell when the weather will turn to rain or snow. Will you accompany us, Caroline dear?" It might put a little colour in her cheeks too, Flora thought privately. Those wan looks would not attract his lordship's eye.

Caroline agreed willingly, and Julia, too, was enthusiastic for the expedition.

Sir Richard also offered to join the party, "...in case you have any small purchases you would wish carried, ma'am. Unless you are taking a footman?"

"Oh, I never trouble in the country, Sir Richard. We should be most glad of your escort."

Vivian also seemed about to make one of the party

when Jervais said, "I've a litter of hound puppies I'd be glad of your opinion on, gentlemen. A little short in the muzzle, I suspect, but I may be wrong."

Sir Richard was, therefore, the only gentleman to accompany the ladies as they set out, well wrapped up, to Harrowbridge.

"It is less than a mile if we take the path across the park," Lady Shannon assured them. "And the ground is so hard, there is no danger of mud."

Harrowbridge was, indeed, a large village with a straggling high street widening into a green with a frozen duck pond overlooked by a church, some houses and a respectable-looking inn, the Barnard Arms.

Caroline excused herself from the visit to the haberdasher's, explaining that she would like to look around the church. Sir Richard immediately offered to escort her. "A most interesting example of early Perpendicular, if I am not mistaken," he said, causing Caroline's heart to sink at the prospect of a prosy lecture.

"Do not get chilled," Lady Shannon cautioned. "We will meet you at the Barnard Arms: ask the landlord to bring coffee to the private parlour if you are there before us."

The party divided. Caroline found to her surprise that, far from being the bore she had expected, Sir Richard was most informative on the subject of church architecture and they spent a pleasant half-hour looking at the church.

As Caroline had expected, the others were not at the inn when they reached it. "Too much to expect three ladies to have done with silks and ribbons in half an hour, I am afraid, Sir Richard," she smiled.

"No matter," he said amiably as the landlord escorted them to a private room with a roaring fire and a commanding view of the green. "This is most congenial, and if you, my good fellow, will bring us coffee and perhaps some macaroons for the lady, we will be comfortable enough."

"Thank you for explaining about the wall-paintings," Caroline said as they took their seats beside the fire. "I had no idea there was so much symbolism in them—I shall look at such things with new eyes from now on."

"I have one or two treatises in my library which you might find informative," Sir Richard was saying when they were interrupted by a soft exclamation from the doorway.

"I beg your pardon, I'm sure," the young woman standing there said, dropping a slight curtsy. "I had no idea the parlour was occupied."

They both turned and looked at her, Sir Richard with a raised brow as he took in the somewhat daring cut of her overtrimmed pink gown that did nothing to disguise the opulent figure it was clothing.

Caroline felt a tremor of familiarity as she looked at the interloper. Like Sir Richard, she recognised a member of the muslin company when she saw one—life with Papa had taught her that much—but unlike him she did not feel a shudder of revulsion. She had always thought such women were as much sinned against as sinning, and her recent experience had taught her just how vulnerable a young woman could be.

"Indeed," Sir Richard was saying frostily, "this parlour is taken for a private party."

Sir Richard's tone appeared to wash over the

young woman, for she twinkled pertly at him and said, "Then I will take myself off, sir, but first I must find my needlework that I left here this morning." There was a swish of skirts as she came into the room to retrieve the calico bag from the window seat. "You know what they say about idle hands, don't you, sir? Must keep busy!"

Sir Richard coloured with embarrassment, but Caroline could not suppress a small giggle. The girl— although now Caroline could see her closely she realised she was nearer seven-and-twenty than seventeen—glanced at her again and a look of surprise, swiftly suppressed, crossed her features.

"Thank you kindly, sir, ma'am." She dropped a slight curtsy again and shut the parlour door behind her.

"Shall I ring for the waiter, Miss Franklin? I cannot imagine what is keeping the fellow." Sir Richard tugged the bellpull irritably. "I suppose one should not expect too much from a village inn—not even the privacy of a parlour, it seems."

Caroline scarcely heard him, although she nodded politely in acknowledgement. Ever since the young woman had come into the room she had been increasingly uneasy, filled with a nagging sense of recognition which was driving everything else from her mind.

Surely she could never have met her before? Even if she were in her late twenties she was still too young to have been one of the late baronet's fancy pieces. And yet...and yet the amiable, pert face was one she had encountered before—and not very long ago. The mass of pale blonde hair was not that unusual, but those green eyes, like a cat's, were.

"Ah! Here you are at last." Sir Richard glared at the waiter who was struggling with a loaded tray and nearly managed to upend the coffee pot and plates in his agitation.

Caroline ignored them, her eyes staring unfocused on the fire. Yes, she had seen those green eyes before, but not in a room. The memory was of them, filled with consternation, staring down at her. And she had been lying down, on something hard and uncomfortable which jolted.

"Miss Franklin!" Sir Richard said, right at her elbow.

"Oh dear! I do apologise, Sir Richard. I have been daydreaming. Yes, that is exactly how I like my coffee. Thank you."

He put the cup down on a small table beside her and moved to the window. "I espy the rest of our party. I think I should go and offer my arm to the ladies, for the street is really very treacherous underfoot. Will you be comfortable here alone for a few moments, Miss Franklin?"

"Indeed, yes, please do not trouble about me," she assured him hastily. "It would be dreadful if Lady Shannon or my aunt fell on this ice."

As he left the room she began racking her brain again in pursuit of that elusive memory. Then her head had been hurting...and she had been wet...and mud was oozing between her fingers as she had tried to sit up...and the reins had broken, her horse halfway to Brussels...

"Of course!" Caroline exclaimed aloud as the last piece of the puzzle clicked into place. That was how she had come to be on the battlefield...

"Has he gone?" She jerked round at the sound of

the whisper. It was the young woman. What was her name? Sarah? No Sally...no...

"Fanny!" Caroline exclaimed, starting to her feet. "I could not remember, but now I see you again, it all comes back."

"It would be surprising if you could remember your own name," Fanny remarked, coming fully into the room. "What with the bump on the head you got falling off that horse." She peeped out of the window. "We can't talk now, that stuck-up cove's coming back, but don't you worry, I won't say nothing about you being with us girls. But what happened to you? I've been that worried..."

"It will take too long," Caroline said urgently. "May we meet somewhere and talk at length? I am staying at Dunharrow."

"That's a laugh! Up at the big house? Along of Simon Routh?"

"Major Routh?" Caroline was surprised. "Do you know him?"

Fanny patted a rather flashy enamelled necklace which curved over her ample bosom. "Oh, I know the gallant major. Who do you think is paying my shot here? Listen, here they come and you can't afford to be seen talking to the likes of me..."

"But I must talk to you," Caroline protested. "Can I come back this evening? Or meet you somewhere?"

"Too cold outside. Look, come back to the inn after dinner. Simon never turns up before two. He likes his cake and eating it, does the major. He won't miss his dinner and billiards to come hurrying down to me—he knows I'll wait up." She began to slip out of the door.

Caroline seized her arm, "Wait! Where will you be?"

"In here. There's no other guests."

Fanny had hardly vanished up the stairs before Flora, Lady Shannon and Julia came in through the door, laughing and shaking the frost off their hems. Sir Richard, handicapped by a bandbox, a parcel tied in brown paper and string and two umbrellas, followed the ladies.

"My dear Captain, I must apologise for burdening you with our purchases," Lady Shannon said. "I really should have brought a footman! Let us leave the box and parcel with the landlord and I will send down for them later."

"Did you have an interesting visit to the church, Caroline?" Flora enquired. "A cup of coffee—the very thing, I do declare my lips are blue with cold." She peeled off her gloves and sat down, accepting a cup from her niece.

Caroline pushed all thoughts of Fanny swiftly to the back of her mind. "Sir Richard made it most interesting, thank you. Did you find the silks you were seeking, Flora?" She passed the macaroons to Lady Shannon and managed to look interested while the other recounted the results of their shopping expedition.

Lady Shannon took them back to Dunharrow by a different route, one which brought them up the drive towards the house. "I often think this is the best view," she remarked to Flora. "I prefer the new wing in the classical style myself, although there are those with a taste for the Gothick who prefer the older wings."

"Parts of the house are very much older, then?"

Caroline enquired as they paused to admire the vista with the house set off on its slight rise by well placed clumps of trees. "I must agree with you that in this light the classical formality of that front is quite magnificent."

"Well, the oldest surviving part is the Elizabethan wing which is in a state of some disrepair. Unfortunately, that is where the kitchens are. It is joined to the modern part by a rather undistinguished section built in 1701 by the then Lord Barnard who had the thought to complete the other three sides of the square. Fortunately, he was killed in a hunting accident before he could do more."

"Mama!" Julia protested. "You cannot be glad the poor man was killed?"

"Nonsense. Anyone with taste would rejoice he met a timely end. Mind you, my dear," she said, turning confidentially to Caroline, "nothing would induce me to visit the old wing after dark."

"Why not?" Caroline was enjoying the rather irreverent Lady Shannon. "Is it haunted?"

"By a headless monk!" Lady Shannon announced dramatically.

Lady Julia was forced to protest again. "Mama! How could it be a monk if the wing is Elizabethan?"

"There! You see the inadvisability of educating girls," announced her fond mama. "I warn you, Julia, take care not to contradict gentlemen in that manner—they do not appreciate it!"

Julia pouted at the reproof, but was unexpectedly championed by Sir Richard. "On this occasion, Lady Shannon, I must support Lady Julia, for it cannot be a headless monk unless, of course, it is a revenant from a monastery slighted at the time of the abolition of the monasteries.''

Further argument was curtailed by the sound of hooves approaching. The party turned to see Jervais cantering up the drive behind them, a pair of hounds following close on his heels. As he drew up to greet his guests, Vivian also appeared from the woods, riding a particularly handsome grey which Caroline did not recognise.

The riders dismounted and walked alongside the others, Caroline dropping back a little to admire her brother's mount. ''It's a very nice goer,'' he confided. ''I offered to buy it, but Jervais won't sell: he's intending to hunt it later in the season.''

As if hearing his name, Jervais stopped and waited for them to catch up to him. ''Serena tells me you are interested in the Elizabethan wing, Miss Franklin. Would you like to see over it?''

''I…I would not want to put you to any trouble, my lord,'' she said uncertainly, not wanting to be alone with him after their encounter the previous evening.

''It is no trouble, I can assure you. I am still exploring the property myself: perhaps you will see possibilities for improvement in the older wing which have escaped my eye.''

Caroline was startled that he should still show any interest in her opinion, and annoyed with Flora for the knowing look she sent her.

''Perhaps you would care to go after luncheon,'' Jervais continued. ''In the safety of daylight,'' he added.

''Is it really haunted, then?'' Caroline asked

lightly, trying to hide her feeling that to be anywhere alone with Jervais was hardly safe.

"Haunted?" He looked startled. "Oh, Serena has been indulging in her taste for the Gothick, has she?"

"Mama says there is a headless monk, but that is not true, is it, Cousin Jervais?" Julia demanded.

"Good heavens, no! I have told you countless times, Serena, it is not a monk but a nun, walled up alive in what are now the cellars. She committed a nameless crime." Mischief danced in his dark eyes as Julia gave a small squeak of alarm. "The monk is only seen on Shrove Tuesday..."

Having reduced Julia to wide-eyed dismay, Jervais swung easily back into the saddle, slipped his booted feet back into the stirrups as the horse fidgeted uneasily. "The horses are getting chilled. I will see you all at luncheon." He touched his hat to the ladies. "And afterwards in the small salon, Miss Franklin?" He did not wait for her answer but cantered off across the frosted grass towards the stable wing, Vivian close behind.

Caroline went directly to the small salon after luncheon and found the room empty. She wandered around uncertainly, picking up some of the small carved ivory pieces which decorated the side tables, then putting them down again with scarcely a glance.

They had eaten early, keeping country hours, and the clock on the mantel was striking half past one when Jervais joined her.

"You are admirably prompt, Miss Franklin," he observed. "I would suggest a warm shawl at the very least, that part of the house is unheated."

"I have one here," Caroline rejoined, wrapping it round the shoulders of her garnet-red wool dress as she spoke. "I thought it sensible to put on stout shoes as well in case the floors were dusty."

As they went out into the hall, Jervais picked up a lantern and tinder box. "It is the shortest day today, we cannot rely on the light lasting for more than an hour in those rooms, the casements are so small."

Caroline followed his broad back down the stone-flagged passage she had paced in her agitation the night before. He paused outside the billiard room and threw open the door. "If you lose any of the gentlemen in the evening, no doubt this is where they will be found." Caroline coloured slightly, feeling guilty about her eavesdropping the night before, but Jervais was already moving on.

The old wing, when they emerged into what have been the Great Hall, was indeed already deep in gloom, but Caroline could see it had once been magnificent.

"Oh, how fine!" she exclaimed, touching the intricate carving on the staircase, then recoiling as her hand came away covered in sticky dust.

"And how dirty," Jervais added drily. "I something think the simplest thing would be to set a taper to the whole thing."

"How could you think of such a thing? I would not have thought you so easily discouraged!" she said indignantly. "All it requires is some resolution, hard work and a good housekeeper. Just think how fine this panelling would look with the application of elbow grease and beeswax." Enthusiasm overwhelming her awkwardness at being alone with him, she walked rapidly into the centre of the room.

"Caroline! Have a care!" But almost as Jervais called out and began to move towards her there was a crack and her right foot went through the floor board as though it were made of kindling.

She gave a sharp cry of pain and stood still, too frightened to move in case more of the floor should give way. Jervais was at her side in an instant, his fingers strong on her ankle as he freed her foot.

As soon as it was disentangled from the splintered wood, he lifted her in his arms and carried her to the foot of the stairs. Unceremoniously he deposited her on the fourth step, ignoring the puffs of dust that eddied round her skirts.

"Jervais! I mean...my lord!" Caroline gasped as he lifted her hem and gently explored her ankle and foot with strong fingers. "Ouch!" she protested, torn between shock at his intimate action, the pain of her wrenched ankle and a guilty pleasure at the closeness of him.

"Be still!" he commanded sharply. "Now is no time for propriety and, after all, I have seen rather more than your ankles before."

Caroline was still simmering at such a tactless remark when he got to his feet and pronounced, "Nothing broken, not even a graze, but it is bruised: I think you will find it a little sore tomorrow. I will ask my housekeeper to bring you some witch hazel."

He put out a hand and pulled her gently to her feet. Caroline found herself standing on the bottom stair which brought her eyes to a level with his mouth.

She stared at the firm, moulded lips, remembering the sensation of his mouth on hers, the pleasure it evoked and the anger with which he had kissed her last night. She shivered.

"Can you walk or shall I carry you?" He was

already reaching for her. Caroline swayed towards him, seduced by his assumption of mastery, her own yearning to be held close against him. At the last moment she realised what she was doing and stiffened.

''No! No... I am quite capable of walking alone, thank you.'' Suddenly she needed to be away from him, away from the danger that she might blurt out her feelings or fall into his arms.

Wincing as her injured foot met the ground, Caroline gathered up her skirts and walked as briskly as she could back to the safe warmth and companionship of the new wing.

Chapter Ten

"Now, my friends," Lady Shannon announced, clapping her hands lightly together to gain the attention of everyone gathered in the drawing room after dinner. "I am not going to permit you to become indolent during these long winter evenings! I have a scheme which I trust will find favour with you all."

Heads turned as she made her announcement, faces showing reactions ranging from the alert interest on Flora's to the apprehension on Vivian's.

"What do you have in mind, Mama?" asked Julia from her seat beside Vivian on the sofa where they had been poring over an album of prints. "Mama has the most amusing schemes," she added enthusiastically as the other gentlemen broke off their discussion of the arrangements for the Boxing Day meet of the local hunt and came across to listen to their hostess.

"Allow me to hazard a guess, Serena," said Jervais with the hint of a laugh in his voice. "You are about to propose a theatrical entertainment?"

"Is there a group of players in the district, then?" enquired Flora.

"I rather fear, if I am correct about Serena's scheme, that we will form the company," said Jervais drily.

"Oh, do not discourage the others before I have explained all," protested his cousin. "We often perform such entertainments at home in Ireland, and it proves a most delightful diversion, does it not, my dear?" she appealed to her daughter.

Julia clapped her hands together in pleasure. "Indeed!" She turned to the others, her eyes sparkling. "But we rarely have such a large party. Why, we can mount a fine production."

Flora looked a little doubtful. "Theatricals, Lady Shannon? Do you consider it quite proper for young ladies to appear on the stage?"

"Not in the ordinary course of things, but this would be quite privately, my dear Lady Grey, merely for our own entertainment, and perhaps that of some friends," Lady Shannon assured her.

"Then we will have no audience for our efforts?" asked Major Routh.

"I had intended asking some of our neighbours to a small party for New Year's Eve," Jervais remarked. "They can form our audience. What is your opinion, Miss Franklin? Will you agree to be one of the company?"

Caroline felt herself flush at being singled out so. Why did he persist in asking her opinion on every topic? It only added fuel to Flora's expectations of an early declaration. And yet, his manner was so cool and correct she felt quite chilled by it. It was as though, having been forced to maintain the invitation to Dunharrow despite everything, he was determined to treat her correctly.

"It sounds most diverting." She addressed herself directly to Lady Shannon. "Did you have any particular play in mind?"

A general discussion immediately ensued, with Lady Shannon proposing scenes from Shakespeare; Julia, supported by Vivian, suggesting they write their own one-act play and Sir Richard offering to scour the library for some suitable works of drama. Flora was still inclined to be dubious and put forward the idea of readings from poetry, a suggestion which met little support.

Conversation was still animated when the footman brought in the tea-tray. As he was leaving, Caroline heard Jervais call him over.

"Richards, will you ask Chawton to make certain the doors are all double locked and the bolts secure. And remind him to ensure the shutters are firmly latched." He was speaking low-voiced, and Caroline realised he did not wish to alarm his guests, but she caught a little of what he added, *sotto voce,* to the Major. "I heard from the head keeper that Pendleton Manor was broken into last night and some plate stolen. I see no cause for concern, but there is no need to take risks."

Caroline thought, with well-concealed amusement, that the improved security would put a spoke in Major Routh's wheel, then realised that she too would be locked in. How was she to reach the inn and talk to Fanny?

The problem exercised her so much that she hardly took any part in the decision that they should perform a work of their own devising. However, her brother volunteering to assist Lady Julia in penning it startled her back into the conversation.

"Are you certain, Vivian?" she asked in amazement, knowing he never willingly set pen to paper and had to be badgered into responding to invitations.

"Come, Caro," he protested, looking hurt at her imputation. "You have no need to make it sound as though I can scarcely write my own name!" He turned to the rest of the group. "Now, we must agree upon a theme."

Later, as the party broke up and Flora and Caroline were ascending the staircase to their chambers, Flora confided, "I do not know what has come over Vivian. I would have thought him as likely to take up *petit point* as play writing!"

"Really, Flora, cannot you see he is besotted with Lady Julia!" Caroline was tart. "You know what will happen: Julia will write some piece of amusing nonsense and Vivian will moon around the library gazing at her and sharpening her quills!"

"You do not sound very pleased at the prospect." Flora halted at the threshold of her room and regarded her niece in perplexity. "I thought you were eager for him to settle down with a suitable wife."

"I would not call a child not yet out a suitable wife for Vivian," Caroline rejoined as she kissed her aunt goodnight.

A few moments later, alone in her chamber, she wondered at herself for being so tart. Why should not Vivian be happy with Julia? She seemed a charming, well-brought up and intelligent girl, just what Vivian needed, in fact. And perhaps having a very young and inexperienced bride to look after would give Vivian an anchor of responsibility. Always at the back of Caroline's mind was the fear that

Vivian, so like her father in looks with his height and blue eyes, would turn to his irresponsible ways.

No, her lack of enthusiasm for her brother's budding tendresse stemmed more from her own unhappiness over Jervais. She felt ashamed of the jealousy which made her feel so grudging. Whatever happened, she and Jervais would never share that first tentative, shy courtship. With a heavy sigh she sat down in the window-seat, turning her mind to the more immediate problem of getting out of the house to meet Fanny.

As the ladies had retired, the men had strolled off towards the billiards room, with Vivian making rather wild wagers on the outcome of a match he proposed with Simon Routh. It seemed certain that the gentlemen would be safely occupied for some time to come.

Caroline remembered the gnarled branches of ivy which covered the wall at the corner of the house. Lady Shannon had remarked upon the shrouding climber as they had walked up the drive, observing that Jervais must have it attended to or it would damage the stonework.

She opened the doors onto her balcony, shivering as the bitter cold cut through her silk gown. By leaning over the balustrade she was able to test the size of the stems, finding them as thick as a man's arm. As she looked down on the branches she could see that many of them grew horizontally, providing what appeared to be a secure stepladder.

If she hurried down now before Chawton made his rounds, she could leave through the front door and return this way and no one would be any the wiser.

Caroline pulled off her evening dress and rapidly

donned her warmest gown and thick stockings. She winced as she laced up her stout walking shoes over the purpling bruise on her foot, but pushed the discomfort out of her mind as she searched for warm gloves.

She drifted downstairs, hugging the shadows as she crossed the hall, pulling the hood of her fur-lined cloak over her face as she did so. The door was on the latch and opened with a well-oiled silence as she slipped into the frosty night.

Everything seemed to conspire with her in her escape—even the moon was full, reflecting off the frosty ground with a light which made walking easy. Caroline set off down the drive at a brisk pace, half expecting a shout from the house as someone saw her, but none came.

She climbed over the gate at the lodge, not daring to risk the wicket squeaking, but there was no light showing at the windows and she passed on unseen.

Getting away undetected had occupied Caroline's mind, but now she was abroad on the highway she began to feel uneasy. The woods on either side of the road were full of dark shadows and furtive noises. Branches cracked, dead leaves rustled and her own footsteps sounded loud on the frost-hardened road.

Caroline had to speak firmly to herself to quell her fears and had succeeded quite well when the night was rent by an unearthly shriek. She broke into a run and did not stop until she arrived at the first cottage on the outskirts of the village, where she stopped, her heart banging against her ribs.

Fool! she rebuked herself. How many times had she heard the cry of a vixen before? To be panicked into headlong flight was thoroughly foolish—and had done her sore foot no good into the bargain.

If her need to speak to Fanny and reassure herself that now she truly did recall everything that had happened to her on the battlefield had not been so great she would have turned tail and gone back to Dunharrow without delay. The prospect of scaling the ivy ladder now seemed foolhardy in the extreme.

The inn looked warm and welcoming and the noise of raised voices and laughter rose from the back of the building. There was light between the drawn curtains in the window of the private parlour. She tapped discreetly on the pane, keeping back in the shadows. The curtain was moved so quickly Fanny must have been waiting for her signal: in response to her gesture Caroline hurried to the front door which was swiftly and silently opened.

"You must be freezing, miss," Fanny declared, urging her into the parlour. "Sit by the fire and have some punch. I ordered it earlier—we don't want to risk anyone seeing you here with me."

Caroline sipped the pungent liquor gratefully, wrinkling her nose in distaste at the unfamiliar smell of rum but welcoming the warmth it spread through her chilled body.

"Take off your cloak and gloves, miss, or you won't feel the benefit when you go out again," Fanny chided, bustling round. When Caroline was settled she sat down opposite her and regarded her with shrewd eyes. "So what's the story, miss? Why are you so hot to find out what happened?"

"Why, anyone would be concerned," Caroline protested. The green eyes assessed her, then Fanny shook her head.

"No, there's more than that. There's a man in this somewhere, I'll be bound."

Caroline found she could not meet the woman's gaze and dropped her own eyes. "Well, yes, there is—the man who found me on the battlefield. But never mind him now—I need to know if what I recollect is what truly happened. For if there is anything, anything else at all, I must know. My memory has been returning, but only in fits and starts." She laughed shakily. "I do not believe I can stand any more surprises!"

"You tell me what you think happened," said Fanny, refilling her own—and Caroline's—glass and settling back in her chair, "and I'll tell you if you go wrong."

"Well, I was riding through Brussels to find someone to advise us on whether we should leave the city. All the rumours were that Napoleon was on his way and his troops would take it by nightfall. I had not ridden for days and my horse was over-fresh." She sipped the warming punch, then continued. "There was such a hubbub in the streets, so many people pushing and clamouring I could hardly hold him…" In her mind she was back in the mêlée, broken carts, screaming children being tugged by their mothers through the crush of bodies…

"I became quite lost. By the time the crowd thinned enough for me to descry my surroundings, I was almost on the outskirts of the city. At least the crowds were less—everyone was going in the opposite direction, of course." She grimaced ruefully. "I should have realised then I was totally out of my way. But I had no time to think—a column of infantry was going past and a musket was discharged accidentally. The wretched animal took off like a bullet himself and the next thing I knew, we were galloping towards the sound of the fighting, across fields.''

"It's a wonder you stuck on so long," Fanny said. "I never could get the knack of this horse-riding lark myself."

"Well, I came off soon enough—right over the top of Gypsy's head and into a puddle."

"And that's where we found you," Fanny chimed in. "Do you remember that?"

"Very well—I was never so glad to see anything in my life as I was to see your wagon," Caroline said with feeling.

"You did look a sight, sitting there in the mud," Fanny chuckled. "Oh, sorry, miss, it's wrong to laugh, but I tell you, we was glad of the diversion. All of us were worried about our boys: we knew Nosey had ordered an all-out attack. And then we'd been bundled into that filthy old wagon, all anyhow—and half our nice things left behind for those filthy Frenchies to steal. Some of the girls were having a good cry, so you were a godsend to take our minds off our troubles."

"You were all very kind," Caroline said warmly.

"And so were you," Fanny responded roundly. "No side to you, treated us just like we was ladies, not working girls at all. A nicely brought-up girl like you should have had the vapours at being picked up by the likes of us."

"A nicely brought-up girl would not recognise your profession," Caroline responded with a flash of humour. "But then life with my late papa gave me an early acquaintanceship with all manner of things I should not know!"

"I do not know when I've been so uncomfortable as on that journey," said Fanny reminiscently. "What with the state that wagon was in, and that old fool of a driver with his endless moaning…"

"And the poor horse," Caroline recalled. "It did hate the thunderstorms so."

"Well, so did I, but you'd have thought it would have been glad to get to its stable in Brussels instead of sticking its hooves in and refusing to move."

"We couldn't have gone on in such a storm," Caroline said reasonably. "That lightning!"

"I suppose you're right," conceded Fanny. "And it did give us a chance to get you out of those mud-soaked clothes and get you washed up a bit."

"I am afraid I have lost your dress, the pretty red silk one you lent me. And the slippers."

"It doesn't matter," said Fanny smugly. "I got a whole new wardrobe from Simon: if we had more time I'd show you." She gave Caro a wink. "Very generous gentleman is the gallant Major."

"I imagine he is." Caroline thought of the frank warmth in Major Routh's eyes when they had been introduced. She shook her head ruefully. "That dress, though, it caused a dreadful misunderstanding."

Fanny grimaced. "No, I 'spose it wasn't the best of choices, not for a lady of quality like you to wear. And the face paint can't have helped." She shook her head. "We only put it on because you looked so white, even after you'd had something to eat."

"It was amusing," Caroline reassured her. "It was something I would never have dared do and I must admit, I enjoyed seeing what a little rouge and eye black could do for my looks." Fanny was still looking doubtful, so she added, "It passed the time until we could set out again, and none of us could have guessed I would not have the chance to wash it off again."

"We all felt so badly about that! Looking back, I suppose one of us should have stayed awake, but we was all too tired by the time we set off again. And in the dark we didn't know the old fool had taken the wrong road!" Fanny threw up her eyes to the ceiling. "Miles out he was come Sunday morning. I know it was dark, but how do you miss a place the size of Brussels, for heaven's sake!"

"So that was why I was so confused," Caroline exclaimed. "I had thought it was the bang on the head, but I could not make any sense of the landscape when daylight came."

"But what happened to you?" demanded Fanny. "One minute we were all there, and the next, when we woke up, there you was gone!"

"I fell asleep as well. I was sitting right by the tailgate—do you remember? I was woken by a terrible lurching of the cart and the next thing I knew, I had tumbled out. For the second time in a day I was sitting on the muddy ground."

"Why didn't you get back in?"

"I was winded and it was dark and raining. By the time I had got to my feet I could see nothing— not even a track. I think the driver must have lost the road completely by then."

"You poor lamb." Fanny was all sympathy. "What did you do?"

"I was cold and wet, but most of all I was frightened of coming across troops—theirs or ours! I found a spinney with a hollow oak in it and spent the rest of the night there. When daylight came I started to walk, but there was no sun to guide me with all that drizzle and for all I knew I was walking away from the city."

She rubbed her forehead, shivering at the unpleasantness of the memory. "I could hear fighting, but it seemed to come from all directions. I was getting hungry and I was more frightened than I had ever been in my life before—or ever want to be again!"

"But you got back to Brussels?"

"No. I found a track at last, but it was getting darker. I can remember feeling faint and dizzy, then nothing... I must have fainted."

"And then?" Fanny's eyes were bright with excitement, she was almost on the edge of her chair.

"I woke up in a barn. With a dog, a horse—and a man."

"Oh, er!" Fanny was wide eyed. "What sort of a man?"

"A gentleman—of sorts," said Caroline bitterly.

"Lawks! Did he...er, I mean...?"

"Very nearly." Caroline made no pretence of misunderstanding the other woman's drift. "He was too badly wounded, however. He assumed I was one of your profession, and because my memory had completely deserted me—so did I, for two days."

Fanny's face showed complete comprehension. "Well, he would, wouldn't he? What other women would be on the battlefield, and with you dressed like that, with a painted face..." She eyed Caroline shrewdly. "This gentleman, he got you home safely, then? And no one any the wiser?"

"He offered me his protection." Caro fell silent, recalling vividly how that protection had felt, how safe, yet how vulnerable Jervais had made her feel. "My friends think I was taken in by a respectable Belgian family. No one other than the man, myself and you know the whole truth."

"Well, you need not worry that I'll let on to anyone," said Fanny roundly. "We girls need to stick together. After all, you can only trust a man as long as your looks last, but your girlfriends stick by you."

"Let me at least give you something for the dress and the shoes," Caroline offered.

"That'd be very civil of you, miss." Fanny, no blackmailer, was obviously used to taking whatever benefits came her way.

"Call me Caroline," Caro urged, pressing a folded banknote into the young woman's hand.

"Thank you kindly, Caroline! Now, you'd better be on your way or you'll be running into Simon Routh."

"Oh, I should have told you," Caroline said as she got to her feet. "He may not be able to come down this evening—the doors are all being double-locked because there are housebreakers at large."

"That's nice," Fanny commented. "The bed to myself for a night. Men are all right, but they do snore... Here, where does that leave you? How are you going to get back in?"

"Up the ivy," said Caroline grimly as she drew on her gloves.

"You're a game one," Fanny said admiringly. She drew back the curtain and peeped out. "Here, look, it's started to snow! Have another noggin before you go, keep the cold out." She pressed the mug into Caroline's hand.

Caroline, her mind on the journey back to Dunharrow, swigged back the punch without thinking, squeezed Fanny's hand with gratitude and hurried out into the snowy night.

The snow was lying light and powdery, already obscuring the road surface. Caroline shivered and pulled her heavy cloak closer round her shoulders. Her bruised foot was throbbing, her head was muzzy from the punch and the cold hurt her throat. The journey back seemed endless and somehow she did not seem entirely in control of her feet.

''I'm tipsy!'' she exclaimed to the dark night in horror. That punch must have been stronger than she had realised: certainly far stronger than the genteel fruit cups she was used to. Fuzzily she recalled Vivian remarking on one occasion that cold made the effects of drink worse. That was all it was…once she was in the warmth of her room, she would feel quite herself again.

The house was in darkness when she finally reached the end of the drive. Unaware of the footprints she was leaving in the snow she trudged across the lawn looking for the root of the ivy. Really, this cold was so extreme it was now affecting her eyesight: there seemed now to be two main streams growing up, one each side of the corner.

It seemed very amusing all of a sudden. Caroline stood swaying slightly. ''Eeny meany… This one, I think.'' The right hand one was the thicker and stronger.

Really, it was surprisingly easy and she was not frightened at all. Her foot slipped and she giggled, but kept on climbing. The edge of the balustrade presented a hurdle, but with a lurch she was over it and safe on the balcony, albeit sitting in the snow.

''Whoops!'' Another giggle escaped her, then remembering she might be overheard by Flora, she whispered ''Sshh!'' and gently pushed the French doors open.

Caroline swayed towards the dark bulk of the bed, shedding clothes as she went. Now where was her nightgown? Lighting a candle seemed far too much trouble and the room was beginning to swim in a most disconcerting manner. By the glow of the embers of the fire she could see something white at the foot of the bed. Ah, there it was!

She reached out a hand towards it, missed and fell headlong onto the bed. Oh well, now she was here...

Everything that followed happened very swiftly. The bed next to her came alive. A large form heaved itself up, throwing bedcovers all over her, smothering her startled scream. As she struggled to free herself from the folds a hand slammed down on her throat, almost choking her. ''One move and I'll break your damned neck!'' Jervais's voice snarled.

Jervais! ''Aargh!'' Caroline managed before the hand relaxed its grip. Seconds later the light of a candle flickered.

''Come out of there and make no false move, my friend, I have a pistol trained on you.'' There was a soft click as a hammer was cocked: this was no bluff, he thought she was a housebreaker.

Caroline peeped gingerly over the blankets and found herself staring down the single black eye of a pistol. Jervais, wearing only a nightshirt, was standing beside the bed, one knee on the edge.

''Caroline! What the hell are you doing?''

She struggled up in the bed with some difficulty. The straps of her shift were sliding dangerously down her shoulders and she hitched them up with great dignity, enunciating carefully.

"Why are you in my bedchamber, Lord Barnard? And kindly do not point that thing at me!"

"Your bedchamber? This is my room, Miss Franklin!" He put the pistol aside, regarding her quizzically, then leant towards her and sniffed delicately. "Rum! I do believe you are drunk, Caroline! How? Where the devil have you been to get spirits?" He seemed amused rather than annoyed.

"Merely a glass of punch...or two. Hic!" Incorrigibly truthful, Caroline corrected herself. "Or perhaps three?"

Jervais, hands on hips, his lips twitching with laughter, enquired, "But where? And, judging by the state of you, I would hazard four glasses at least."

"It is a secret," Caroline responded with dignity. "And it is a well-known fact that cold makes the effect of strong drink worse." Unfortunately another hiccough escaped her. Irritably she pushed at the heavy covers. "Don't just stand there! If this is your bedchamber I must leave—help me!"

Jervais obligingly tossed aside the bedclothes and took her hands in his. "Upsadaisy." He was humouring her, she could tell. "Time you were in your own bed..."

She offered no resistance. His strength pulled her into his embrace with more force than he had perhaps intended. Shift and hair awry, Caroline found herself chest to chest with him, only the thin fabric of two garments separating their bare skin. The tolerant amusement ebbed out of his face. In the flickering candlelight his eyes went very dark.

Jervais bent his head and kissed her hard. Caroline,

all inhibitions gone, returned the embrace with ardour. Her shaky legs lost what little strength they had and she overbalanced, falling back onto the bed, taking Jervais with her.

For a hectic moment their bodies intertwined on the rumpled bedding, then Jervais exclaimed, "My God!" He freed his mouth and stared down at her. "Your feet are frozen! Where have you been?"

"Mmm," Caroline murmured, snaking her arms around his neck to draw him close again.

"Oh, what the hell..." Jervais seemed to have reached a decision. With one hand he pulled her close against him, with the other he dragged the covers over both of them.

Jervais held her tight, wrapping his warmth around her, but making no attempt to kiss or caress her. Caroline wriggled, confused and disappointed by his lack of ardour. The unfamiliar weight of him against her, the strength of his arms, the heat of his body were terrifyingly, wonderfully new.

"Stop squirming, Caro! You are testing my willpower to the utmost. You should not be here, I should not be holding you like this—and as soon as you are warm, and sober enough not to rouse the household, you are going straight back to your own bed."

"Jervais..." she pleaded softly against the satiny smoothness of his neck.

"Caroline...stop it!" The words came out between gritted teeth. "You are going to feel sorry enough for yourself in the morning as it is—do not add to that something you will regret for the rest of your life."

Foggily Caroline knew he was right. She should

not be doing this, should not be there with him. She…they…were behaving scandalously, but the warmth and strength of him were too much for her willpower. There was nowhere else she wanted to be, ever, and she could trust Jervais. Slowly the warmth of his body overcame the chill of hers and the rum was making her drowsy: her eyelids drooped and with a little sigh of content she gave herself up to sleep.

Chapter Eleven

The door crashed open with a sound like artillery firing and the room was suddenly lit by flickering candlelight.

"God! Sorry, old chap...bit unsteady, been drinking with Routh. Here, Barnard—you asleep? If you are I'll go 'way, but had to tell you...lost that bet you made on me! Rolled up, beaten hollow—damned good game you missed." A loud hiccough echoed round the silent room.

Caroline, waking with a start to the sound of her brother's voice, half-rose from the pillow only to be unceremoniously shoved back under the covers by a ruthless hand.

"Hell's teeth, Franklin, I thought you were a gang of housebreakers!" Jervais sat up in bed, achieving, to Caroline's frantic hearing, a credible note of amused tolerance. "What time is it, man? You're as drunk as an owl—get to your bed, we'll talk about it in the morning."

"No, you're a good chap and I'm determined to explain how I came to lose your guineas." Vivian waved a finger in the air, lurching towards the bed.

"Go to your chamber, Vivian," Jervais said evenly.

The younger man gazed at him, looking very like the owl he had compared him to and lurched again.

"Watch those candles, man!"

"Sorry...put them down here." Caroline heard the bump as a candelabra was set down on the night-table beside the bed. "There we are... Think I'm drunk, old man—damn good port, by the by—I'll just sit down here while I explain about the game."

There was a jolt, then the mattress next to Caroline sank as her brother's weight landed on it. With a loud "Whoops!" he lolled back, hitting Caroline's head with one arm. Even through the blankets it was a painful—and unexpected—blow.

Without thinking, before she could stop herself, Caroline protested, "Vivian!"

A dreadful silence followed that none of them seemed capable of breaking. Eventually, unable to bear the stifling darkness, Caroline peered over the top of the blankets at the two men.

Jervais, sitting up against the pillows, had his eyes closed, a look of utter resignation on his features. Vivian, mouth agape, eyes popping, was gazing in stunned horror at the sight of his sister revealed, scarcely clad, in his host's bed.

Vivian leapt from the bed, suddenly sobered by the implications of what he was seeing. "Sir!" he thundered. "How dare you!" His young face dark-ened. "Name your friends, sir—my seconds will wait on them tomorrow. Caroline—" he turned stern fea-tures on his sister "—Caroline, go and pack your bags and wake your aunt. We leave this house im-mediately!"

"Vivian." Caroline also was horribly sober and awake. "It is not what it seems!" It sounded feeble even to her own ears.

Beside her Jervais stirred at last. "Caroline, please be quiet, leave this to me." He swung his legs out of bed, reaching for his brocaded dressing-gown and shrugging it on. "Come and sit down, Franklin—I cannot believe you wish to involve the household in this matter." He guided Vivian's still unsteady feet to the fireside and pushed him into a chair, taking the one opposite.

"Now look here," Vivian persevered. "You need not think to fob me off, my lord! I am not so much in my cups as to forget what I have seen tonight, or my challenge."

Jervais sighed deeply. "I have no intention of avoiding my obligations to your sister, Vivian. It would be quite ineligible of me to fight my future brother-in-law, would it not?"

"You are intending to marry her, then?" Vivian demanded. He was increasingly rational as they spoke, his words sharper and more coherent.

"Of course I am. Why the devil do you think I invited you all down here? Your aunt realised, even if you did not."

"But Flora would not permit this any more than I will," Vivian said icily.

"Well, of course Lady Grey would not!" Jervais snapped, then reverted to a calmer voice. "Listen to me, Franklin. I have every intention of marrying your sister, I have always intended to marry your sister. It is unfortunate that you have discovered us, but you cannot be so naïve as to believe that such an anticipation of the ceremony does not go on in polite society!''

Vivian regarded the older man through narrowed eyes for a moment, then relaxed. ''Well, of course I know such things go on; it is just somewhat of a shock when it is your own sister involved! I will not deny it is a good match and if you intend to do your duty by her—and, of course, I accept your word as a gentleman that you will—I withdraw my challenge. You have my consent to the union.''

Caroline had been listening with increasing embarrassment and anger. How could they discuss her as if she were a piece of livestock to be disposed of at will! Why, it was as though she were not even in the room...

''But not necessarily mine,'' she interrupted icily.

Both men turned to look at her in surprise. ''What did you say?'' demanded her brother.

''I said, you do not have my consent to the match,'' she repeated, struggling out of bed and pulling the coverlet around her chemise for decency.

Vivian was outraged. ''You stand there in your shift, in a man's bedchamber and tell me you will not marry him?''

Caroline's chin came up. To be lectured by her young brother as if he were her grandfather was insupportable, but the anger kept at bay the dreadful embarrassment of being found by him like this. ''It would be nice to be asked.''

Vivian looked enquiringly at Jervais who got to his feet, strode over to her side, went on one knee and took her hand in his. ''Madam, I have the honour to request that you be my wife.''

She looked down at his head, bent as he kissed

her hand. She had no choice but to agree. It was what she wanted above all things... "But not like this," she murmured desperately. Jervais must have heard her for his head came up and he looked her in the eye.

"We have no choice," he murmured back, so low-voiced it could not have reached Vivian. Then he stood and led her over to her brother. "We will speak in the morning. Go back to your room, you will be getting cold."

At her doorway she whispered to Vivian, "Do not tell Flora any of this!"

"Of course I will not—how could I? Really, Caroline, I must tell you I am very disappointed in your behaviour."

"Oh, don't be such a prig, Vivian!" she hissed back, suddenly furious with him and every other man in the world. When she had closed the door on his disapproving face, she leaned back against the heavy panels, sick with reaction and the effects of the rum. Her head throbbed and she felt queasy. And so thirsty.

Caroline poured herself a glass of cordial from the flask on the night table and crossed to the uncurtained window, trailing Jervais's coverlet behind her. The snow was lying thickly now, blanketing the park in silence under the moonlight. It was so beautiful, so tranquil and she was so utterly confused and miserable.

She was going to marry Jervais, the man she loved—but for all the wrong reasons. When they had met again in London she had pretended not to know him so that he would have no compulsion to offer for her. When he had made a declaration she had believed it was because he loved her, only to have that belief dashed when he showed he did not trust her. Even that was better than the prospect that faced her now: the knowledge that unwittingly she had trapped Jervais into marriage.

Getting out of bed the next morning with the worst headache she had ever had in her life was an act of sheer will and determination. Caroline sat on the edge of the bed, attempting to master her rebellious stomach, marvelling that men were prepared to tolerate the after-effects of strong drink on a regular basis.

The maid came in with hot water, full of excited chatter about the thick snow that had fallen during the night. "And they do say the village is quite cut off, miss..."

Caroline flapped a limp hand. "Oh please, Katy, do not prattle so, I have such a headache I can scarcely think!"

"You shouldn't be out of bed, miss." Katy looked concerned as she dragged the heavy drapes back from the window. Caroline winced and shut her eyes against the clear white light that flooded the room. "It's early yet, miss, why not lie down again and I'll ask Cook to make you a soothing tisane." She regarded her mistress, taking in the pale, pinched features and the shadowed eyes.

The temptation was almost overwhelming, but Caroline fought against it. No, she must speak with Jervais before Vivian had the opportunity to tell the entire house-party of his sister's good news.

Seated before the looking glass, she reflected that at least Vivian also must feel somewhat fragile this morning and if luck were with her would keep to his chamber for a while yet. "Something very simple, Katy, if you please!" she exclaimed as the maid approached with hairpins and brush to arrange her black curls. "Leave it loose, simply brush out the tangles."

Food was set out in the breakfast room but as Caroline had hoped, no one of the party was yet at table. She was hesitating, wondering if she dared go to Jervais's bedchamber to talk to him, when she heard the sound of the library door shutting: no one but the master of the house was likely to be about in there at this hour.

Jervais was standing before the cold fireplace, one booted foot resting on the fender. He was dressed for riding, but seemed in no hurry to be out, for he was gazing pensively into the glass above the mantelshelf, drumming his fingers slowly on the marble.

Their eyes met in the reflected image: his dark and unreadable, hers shadowed and anxious.

"Jervais, I looked to find you alone..." she began, moving across the room towards him.

He turned, but made no move to meet her. Instead he looked hard at her face before announcing abruptly, "You look ghastly."

"Thank you, my lord!" Caroline snapped. "You may be assured I feel it."

"That is not to be wondered at, considering the state you were in last night. You need the hair of the dog." As he spoke he was already pouring a small tot of brandy from the decanter. "Here, drink it."

"Oh, no!" she said in revulsion. "I shall be sick!"

"No, you won't," he said grimly. "Knock it straight back."

Caroline did as she was told, closing her eyes with a shudder as the spirit burned the back of her throat. For one frightful moment her stomach rose in revolt, then she opened startled eyes. "Oh! That is better." She set the glass down and smiled shakily at him. "I cannot conceive how you gentlemen drink for pleasure if that is how you feel every morning."

"From that, may I deduce that my affianced bride is not in the habit of imbibing rum toddies nightly?" The words were said humorously, but there was little humour evident in the saturnine face.

"Of course not, do not be so absurd! But never mind that now—we must agree what to do before Vivian starts spreading news of our engagement."

"Do? What is there for us to do?" He put his hands behind his back and rocked slightly on his heels as he watched her. "I had assumed that Lady Grey would be placing a notice in *The Times* and that she and you would be buying your bride clothes once you return to Town. Of course, if you wish to discuss which church we are to be married in, or what arrangements you wish to make for the domestic staff at the town house, I am at your disposal. But after breakfast, surely, is soon enough?"

He offered her his arm as if to take her into breakfast. "Jervais!" Caroline protested. "That is not what I..."

"Expected?" he finished for her. "Forgive me, Caroline. You must think me most undemonstrative, unloverlike. But I hesitated to press my attentions on you, looking as frail as you do. However..."

He took the hand he had tucked under his elbow and raised it to his lips, pulling her close against him as he did so. Caroline gazed up, mesmerised, into his intent face. She felt her lips part involuntarily and drew in a shuddering breath before his mouth came down on hers.

His mouth was hard and demanding, almost cruel in its insistence that she yield to him and Caroline felt her few defences crumble. His tongue touching hers caused a shock that thrilled through her; she moulded herself more closely against his body, all her determination to reject him melting in the heat of his embrace.

Jervais stooped to cradle and lift her in his arms, carrying her languid and unprotesting to the chaise longue. He sank down slowly, taking Caroline with him to nestle on his lap: not once had he freed her mouth and she was scarcely conscious that she was no longer standing, so swept up was she by the feelings he was arousing.

He bent his head to trail kisses across the gentle swell of her breasts where they rose from the confining lace of her bodice. A shudder convulsed her; when he glanced up enquiringly she locked her fingers in his chestnut hair to impel him to continue.

Instead he laughed huskily, sitting up straighter and pulling her back to rest against his shoulder. "Enough of this, my little wanton! I am beginning to think that what I said about anticipating the wedding ceremony has some merit."

The words were enough to recall her to her senses. "But that is what I came to talk to you about, Jervais."

"Anticipating the ceremony?" he queried.

"No! Cancelling it—and as soon as possible, before Vivian tells anyone. Why else do you think I am here so early?"

His face hardened. As swiftly as she had found herself on his knees she found herself seated upon the chaise longue beside him. "Do I understand you aright, Miss Franklin? After what has just passed between us, after having been discovered drunk in my bed by your own brother, you tell me you do not wish to marry me?"

"Yes," she stated baldly, tugging the lace up over her heated bosom.

"And precisely what do you think you were about just now?" His voice was calm, interrogative, but with an underlying danger in it which she chose not to heed.

"Well, you kissed me. You took me by surprise." Caroline got to her feet, smoothing down the tell-tale creases in her muslin gown where it had been crushed against his thighs.

Jervais was on his feet too, very close beside her, but not touching her. "I begin to wonder if you can be as innocent of the effect your actions have upon a man as you would have me believe."

"Sir!" But her outrage did not quite ring true. Caroline was burningly aware that Jervais only had to kiss her to incite her own ready need for him. "Stop it, Jervais—you are distracting me." She ignored the incredulous expression that crossed his face and pressed on. "I mean, we must discuss this before we are joined by the others. I cannot marry you."

"There would appear to be only one explanation for your refusal," he remarked. "If, of course, one discounts the notion that you intend to remain unmarried for the rest of your days. And forgive me,

Miss Franklin, if I find that hard to believe, judging by your responses to me.''

Caroline felt hot colour suffusing her face at his unseemly implication. ''Sir! You are no gentleman!''

''Madam,'' he replied evenly, ''in my arms, I find you no lady.''

Caroline clenched her fists as if to strike the sardonic face, but he easily encircled both wrists with one hand and held her away from him.

''Let us stop beating about the bush, Caroline. Who is he?''

''Who?'' She wriggled ineffectively in his grasp. ''You are hurting me!''

''Only when you struggle. Keep still. I refer to the man you were with last night, the man you had your clandestine meeting with. Is he the same man you were seeking on the battlefield when we first met?''

Caroline was utterly speechless. ''Or is this somebody else who has caught your fancy?'' he added, raising an interrogative eyebrow.

She found her voice, although it emerged as an outraged squawk. ''How many men do you think I am entangled with, for heaven's sake?''

He released her hands and shrugged dismissively. ''I would not like to hazard a guess.''

Caroline controlled herself with difficulty. Eventually she said, with deceptive calm, ''I was on that battlefield for a perfectly innocent reason and if you cannot trust me enough to believe that, then I have no intention of furnishing you with an explanation!''

''So you no longer maintain you have lost your memory?'' He folded his arms across his chest and leaned against the mantelshelf.

''I did lose my memory and now I have regained

it—but not all of it...until last night.'' As soon as the words were uttered she could have bitten her tongue, for his eyes narrowed.

''I had not considered the liberal application of rum to be a memory reviver.''

''Oh, never mind the rum! And what I was doing last night is none of your concern. You are neither my father, my brother nor my husband—and never will be! Jervais, will you please believe I do not wish to marry you!''

She was flushed and panting with emotion and the desperate need to convince him—and herself—that it was so.

Jervais looked down into her eyes and said softly, ''Yes, I believe you.''

Caroline closed her eyes with a sigh of relief. Then the feeling was swept away, overwhelmed by regret. She could not marry Jervais knowing he neither loved nor trusted her: but, oh, how it hurt to do the right thing and set him free, loving him as she did!

''Caroline, dear.'' It was her aunt, a note of indulgent chiding in her voice as she entered the room to find her niece unchaperoned with Lord Barnard.

''Flora!'' Caroline jumped, startled out of her intense preoccupation where only she and Jervais existed.

''You really should have waited to come down to breakfast with me, Caroline,'' Flora admonished her niece fondly, while sending Jervais a look which implied that her protest was merely a matter of form, that she trusted him implicitly.

''Yes, Flora, I am sorry.'' Caroline took a step towards her, but was halted in her tracks by Jervais's hand on her arm.

"My dear, allow me to tell your aunt of our happiness. Lady Grey, yesterday I asked Sir Vivian for the honour of addressing Miss Franklin, and I am overjoyed to tell you she has accepted my proposal."

Caroline's gasp of shock and horror was lost in her aunt's fervent embrace and shower of kisses. It was impossible to get a word in as Flora, bubbling over with excitement, gave vent to her feelings.

Finally she ran out of breath, gave Jervais a resounding kiss on the cheek which took them both by surprise, and fluttered out, calling over her shoulder, "I must tell Anthony... I mean, Major Gresham..."

"Jervais! Have you lost your mind?" Caroline exploded the moment her aunt was out of sight. "You have just released me from the engagement..."

"I told you that I believed you when you said you did not wish to marry me."

"Well, then?" Caroline stamped her foot in fury. She wanted to strike his complacent face, drive that superior, knowing expression from his features.

"What you want, Caroline, is not of first consequence here: there are greater considerations at stake."

"I fail to understand what other consideration there can be beyond my...our feelings."

"Our feelings are not at issue—and I was not aware that we had discussed mine in any case. No, your reputation and my honour, these are of paramount importance."

"I only want to do the right thing," she burst out, tears stinging the back of her throat. "And all you do, you self-righteous...prig, is prate about reputation and honour. If you had kept quiet, then neither would be at risk!" Almost blindly she stumbled to a chair and sat, her face averted. Surely her expression would betray how she felt, how much she loved him, her turmoil at having her sacrifice thrown back at her...

A long silence ensued. At length Caroline ventured a surreptitious peep through wet lashes at his calm, patient face. She was searching for some vestige of emotion, some sign of his true feelings, the slightest hint that he wished to marry her for herself, not for honour or duty... She opened her mouth, the words "But do you love me?" trembling on her lips.

Their eyes locked, he took a step towards her and the words were almost out when there was a rustle of gowns, an excited chattering and the library was suddenly filled with people.

Lady Shannon was kissing Caroline; Major Gresham was shaking hands with Jervais, whilst Sir Richard and Major Routh added their congratulations and Vivian, with Julia at his side, had the proprietorial expression of a man who has just seen his sister make a most eligible match.

It was almost a relief. Caroline found she was not required to do anything except smile and nod and accept graciously the good wishes which showered upon her.

Serena Shannon, noticing Caroline's damp lashes, stroked her arm maternally. "You are quite overset, my dear—tell me, when did my cousin propose?"

Caroline shot Jervais a glance inviting him to answer this pertinent question. Vivian, suddenly overcome by confusion, opened his mouth to speak but Jervais cut in urbanely.

"Oh, very early this morning." He tucked Caroline's hand firmly under his arm, ignoring her startled look. "We both found ourselves up—" he paused "—and about at an unconscionable hour—I seized the moment, and to my great joy Caroline accepted me."

Caroline, nettled by his ready manipulation of the facts, looked up at him and found herself transfixed and rattled by the intensity of his expression as he looked at her.

They could have been alone. Their eyes locked and held for what seemed like forever. She seemed to see a reflection of their past embraces in his eyes; his mouth curved, conjuring up the memory of its pressure on her own, the answering ardour of her response.

Caroline drew breath sharply. He was an excellent actor, there could be no doubt of that, but equally there could be no doubting his desire for her. And mine for him, she thought dumbly.

Breakfast seemed to have taken on the air of a betrothal party. Caroline was aware of a procession of servants sneaking glances round the screen which shielded the entrance to the butler's pantry and twice as many people than were necessary were serving, considering that the table and buffet were already laid for guests to help themselves.

Jervais held out a chair for her, enquiring solicitously what she would eat.

"Oh, nothing...perhaps a little bread and butter and some tea..."

When she looked at the plate he put before her she found it quite full with shaved ham, omelette and slices of warm bread. "I cannot eat all this," she protested.

Flora, overhearing, leaned across. "Now do eat

up, my dear Caroline. I think you look quite pale this morning. The excitement, I expect," she added smugly to Lady Shannon who nodded in agreement.

Jervais spoke low into her ear, his breath stirring her hair. "The after-effects of the rum more like," he murmured.

"I declare, I will never touch alcohol again," she murmured back, shuddering delicately. "And, just at this moment, I do not believe I will ever eat again either!"

In response Jervais cut off a morsel of the omelette and held it to her lips. "Eat it, trust me, if only in this."

Her startled eyes flew to his face, but there was nothing sardonic there. He smiled, coaxingly and she opened her mouth.

The food was warming and savoury and surprisingly good. "Oh, that is better!"

Caroline was aware of a sudden silence in the room and looked up to find most of the others gazing at the affianced couple with expressions of indulgent approval. Only Major Routh, not a man to neglect his food for the sake of sentiment, was addressing himself to a large sirloin.

Embarrassed and irked, Caroline spoke so that only Jervais could hear. "I have no trouble in trusting you in matters concerning the after-effects of strong drink, sir!"

"There are many things of which I have more experience than you, Caroline," he responded huskily. "It will be my pleasure to be your tutor."

Flora, observing, but not able to overhear this byplay, saw the hectic flush rise to her niece's cheeks and intervened. "What a beautiful crisp day it is," she announced brightly. "But the snow is too deep, I hear, for us to venture outside. What shall we do today, my dear Lady Shannon?"

"I shall be occupied all day with domestic tasks, I am afraid, Lady Grey—I must review the menus with Cook in case we are snowbound for long and cannot get fresh supplies from the village. And I must speak with Mrs Chawton: if the weather breaks sufficient for our guests to come for our New Year's Eve party, we must have rooms prepared in case they cannot return that night." She looked enquiringly at her guest. "Would you perhaps care to accompany me? Jervais has had one of the new cast iron ovens installed—you may be interested..."

"Indeed, yes!" Flora was all enthusiasm. "I have read of them, and I did think of having one put in at Brook Street, but our cook is sadly hidebound in her views and does not think it would be an improvement."

Vivian, overhearing, laughed. "What she actually said, Lady Shannon, was that it was flying in the face of nature, would blow up, burn us all in our beds and she would never be able to make a decent egg custard again."

The whole party laughed at Vivian's lively imitation of Cook's outraged Essex accents. Caroline, relieved to be no longer the centre of attraction, concentrated on finishing her breakfast.

"Is there anything I can do to assist you, Mama?" Lady Julia enquired. "Because if not..."

"I know," her mother said indulgently. "You wish to continue with your play. Well, I see no objections unless Lady Grey has any little tasks she would like you to perform."

Flora caught Vivian's eye and smiled. "No, you go and enjoy yourself, my dear. Vivian, how do you intend to occupy yourself?"

Vivian looked somewhat self-conscious, but replied easily enough. "If Lady Julia would care for my assistance, I would be happy to join her."

"Oh, please do," Lady Julia was positively glowing. "You are such a help!"

Caroline, reaching for the honey, stopped, arrested by the unlikely vision of her brother as literary muse. "Just how do you help, Vivian?" she enquired innocently.

Julia answered for him, all girlish enthusiasm. "He sharpens my quills for me, and stands by with Dr Johnson's *Dictionary* should I be at a loss for a word. And he is very encouraging when I read a scene to him. He always laughs at my jests."

Caroline managed to get her twitching lips under control and turned back to her breakfast, only to find that Jervais was cutting her honey soldiers from brown bread.

"I am not an invalid!" she said sharply as he handed her the plate.

"You must allow me the pleasure of looking after you, Caroline," he said mildly. "I intend to start as I mean to go on."

The look in her eyes was bleak as she said softly, "There is no escape now, is there?"

Equally quietly, he responded, "No, none at all for either of us." And his voice was grim.

Chapter Twelve

The two days before Christmas passed swiftly. Caroline moved as if in a dream, unable to believe the rapid changes that had occurred in such a short space of time. She was affianced to Jervais, mistress-to-be of Dunharrow and treated with due deference by the servants; and, embarrassingly, Lady Shannon showed the greatest alacrity in consulting her at every turn on household matters.

Caroline was used to managing her father's household when he was alive—both the town house and the country seat, Longford—but neither were on the scale of Dunharrow.

Indeed, the most modern wing where they were living presently, and where all the renovation had been done, was almost as large as Longford. On Christmas Eve, as she stood in the interior courtyard with her hostess gazing round, she marvelled out loud at the work still to be done.

"I quite agree, it will be many years before it will be complete. The old wing will be very fine once restored, but as to this—" Serena Shannon gestured at the dismal facade of the central, linking wing

"—the sooner Jervais's plan to demolish it is put in hand the better. It has neither architectural merit nor domestic convenience."

"How difficult it will be to manage whilst that work is being done," Caroline mused. "The kitchens are, after all, in the old wing!"

"I see you are already applying your thoughts to the matter," Lady Shannon remarked approvingly.

The remark brought home to Caroline her own involvement in Dunharrow. All that had occupied her since Jervais had announced their engagement was her feelings for him. But his cousin was forcing her to see that in a few weeks she would be the mistress of this estate with all that that entailed. She shivered, pulling her cloak more closely round her shoulders.

"Forgive me, my dear Caroline," Lady Shannon said with a concerned glance. "With my enthusiasm for architecture I have kept you out in the cold for an unconscionable time. Let us go back inside, there is something I particularly wanted to show you."

They hurried back into the house, their footsteps crunching loudly on the crisp snow. Still, foggy weather had set in after the snowstorm: Dunharrow seemed isolated in a silent white landscape, but the roads were passable and, provided no thaw set in to mire the roads with mud, the party was still expected for New Year's Eve.

Lady Shannon shook the snow off her hem and led Caroline up the great oak staircase.

"Is the floor safe?" Caroline asked anxiously, remembering her own accident in the Great Hall.

"The upper floors are still secure, and, of course, the kitchen and ground floor passages are all stone flagged. It is only the Great Hall floor which has dry rot. That will cost a pretty penny to put right,'' she added.

''Yes, indeed,'' Caroline said, with more meaning in her voice than she had intended.

She had been wondering for some time about the amount of money Jervais had obviously already spent on the house. The restrained opulence and good taste evident in every one of the restored rooms spoke of lavish resources: in the small hours of the morning the unworthy thought had crossed her mind that Jervais's insistence on marrying her despite all obstacles and her own resistance might be due to his need to marry an heiress.

Lady Shannon looked at her sharply. ''You need have no fear Jervais is marrying you for your money, my dear. Cousin Humphrey was always known to be a very warm man, but when he died the size of his fortune came as a surprise to us all. Besides,'' she added, patting Caroline on the cheek, ''you only have to look at Jervais to see he is deeply in love with you.''

Oh, no, he is not! Caroline thought bitterly, just a consummate actor. But she hastened to respond, ''Oh, Lady Shannon, forgive me—I had no intention of implying that Jervais was a fortune hunter...''

Her confused apology was cut short by her hostess throwing open the door into a darkened room. She gathered up her skirts from the dust with a moue of distaste and crossed to the window, throwing open the shutters to let in the bright snow-reflected light. Even under the patina of dirt and shrouding cobwebs, it was evident that the room had been a nursery.

''Cousin Humphrey was a man who believed in procreation outside wedlock,'' Serena observed tartly, finding a rag and flapping dust off a charming carved cradle, "and therefore never had need for this room. Which, when one thinks of it, was a most fortunate circumstance for you and Jervais! I am sure it will not be long before this pretty cradle will be filled."

Caroline, who had been amusing herself pushing a wooden baby walker across the floor, looked up, shocked. Her face flamed as she took in the thought of being the mother of Jervais's children. "I never thought..." Her voice trailed off.

Serena was indulgent. "Well, you may be sure your husband-to-be will have considered the matter! It is about time Jervais was setting up his nursery..."

She was prevented from elaborating further by a voice called along the corridor. "My lady! My lady!"

Lady Shannon bustled onto the landing. "What is it?"

At the bottom of the staircase a scrawny lad in a baize apron stood panting. "Cook says, can you come quick, my lady! The copper has burst all over the scullery and flooded the floor and Mrs Chawton says she don't know how she's going to get the washing done..."

"Oh dear, I suppose I had better see what can be done!" She turned to Caroline. "Excuse me, my dear, if I leave you: if it isn't one thing it's another in a house this size, as you will soon discover!"

Caroline wandered back into the nursery, attempting to come to terms with the thought of motherhood. She stood, one finger gently rocking the cradle, trying to imagine what her children would look like. Would they favour her or Jervais?

"What a charming sight you make," Jervais remarked from the doorway.

Caroline whipped round, her heart thudding with the shock of seeing him.

"What have I said to make you colour up so?" he asked in an amused tone, strolling into the room. He was dressed for riding in buckskins and top boots, his greatcoat unbuttoned, his gloves still in his hands. It seemed he had newly returned from riding, for the cold had raised the colour in his cheeks and his eyes were sparkling.

Caroline looked at him, suddenly helpless in her love for him. The harsh cold light reflected off his hair and sharpened the bones of his face and she wanted nothing more than to throw herself into his embrace and kiss the snow-chill off his skin. She took an involuntary step towards him, then checked herself.

"Lady Shannon was showing me around...but she has had to go to the kitchens, there has been some crisis with the copper..."

"Tell me why you are blushing." He caught her confused glance at the cradle and laughed. "Ah, I understand, Serena has been talking of nurseries in her forthright way. And that alarms you?" The question was not a simple one to answer, involving as it did emotions she did not really wish to examine. Jervais was watching her carefully, but to her surprise made no move to touch her.

"No...not alarm. Of course I want children..."

"But not mine." The statement was hard and flat.

Tears stung the back of her eyes. Caroline felt trapped, aware she had hurt him, but unable to make things right. She gathered up her skirts and, before he could stop her, ran from the room, down the stairs and along the cold corridors back to the others in the new wing.

Caroline took care not to be alone with Jervais for the rest of the day, firmly putting all thoughts of babies out of her mind. In the event, this proved easier than she might have hoped for the household was in turmoil with preparations for the Christmas meal.

The disaster with the copper had not affected Cook's ability to produce a magnificent repast and the table was groaning with delicious accompaniments to the goose, a noble bird borne in with much ceremony by Chawton. Jervais sent for Cook, who arrived red-faced and resplendent in her best apron to receive the congratulations of the party.

"Your very good health, Mrs Burke. Chawton, take six of the best burgundy and see that the staff sit down to their own dinner now." He turned to Caroline, seated at his right hand. "I trust you do not disapprove of our family tradition of serving ourselves at our Christmas table?"

"Of course not," she said warmly. "It has always seemed to me unjust that the servants should have to wait until they return from church. Will you carve the goose, my lord?"

After the meal was consumed they exchanged gifts with much laughter and exclamations, leaving a sea of silver paper and abandoned ribbons.

Caroline's gift of *The Natural History of Selborne* was a great success and she glowed as Jervais passed it round the table for all to admire. "You must inscribe it," he insisted, once it was back in his hands.

She had finished opening all the packages before her, smiling and thanking her friends for their gifts.

But there was nothing from Jervais: surely he would not have forgotten her when he had made presents to everyone else?

Serena Shannon was regarding them both with an arch smile, which turned to one of satisfaction when she saw the blue Morocco case Jervais lifted from the sideboard.

"This was my mother's, Caroline, I would like you to have it now," he said gravely, placing the large flat case before her.

Hesitantly she opened the catch and put back the lid. A gasp escaped her lips as a blaze of white fire dazzled her eyes. A parure of diamonds lay on a bed of blue velvet, their myriad fires dancing in the candlelight.

"Oh, but I cannot wear these!" she gasped.

"Magnificent!" Flora declared, coming round from her seat to admire the jewels. "But, yes, you can wear them. Coloured stones, of course, would be quite ineligible until you were married, but diamonds, especially now you are betrothed, are most suitable."

Caroline stared dumbly into the box, at the tiara, necklace, earrings, bracelets and pins, which sparkled back at her. She had never seen anything so fine, but it was not the splendour and the worth of the gift that had overwhelmed her. These were Jervais's mother's jewels, the mark of how her life was about to be turned upside down within a few weeks. They were the jewels of Lady Barnard, not of Miss Franklin.

"Will you permit me, Caroline?" Jervais asked softly and before she could respond he was unfastening the modest pearl necklace at her throat and clasping the cold diamonds in their place. His fingers were warm at her nape as he disentangled a few fine hairs from the setting and she shivered responsively. His hands settled possessively on her bare shoulders as he bent to kiss her cheek. On impulse Caroline turned her face to him and his lips met hers.

The caress could only have lasted a few brief seconds, but everyone watched them silently until Sir Richard broke the mood by clearing his throat noisily.

Flora, whose cheeks were quite pink, turned to her hostess. "Should we not get our cloaks and prayer-books? I think the clock just struck the hour."

The party broke up, to reassemble on the steps where the carriages were already drawn up to take them to the parish church. Jervais, Serena, Julia, Caroline, Flora and Vivian travelled together in the large carriage while Sir Richard and Major Routh followed in a curricle.

"Do you intend to have the chapel at Dunharrow put into repair for your wedding, Jervais?" Serena asked her cousin as the carriage made its cautious way down the drive.

"It will take too long: I swear every woodworm in Hampshire has taken up residence there. Besides, I have not yet discussed with Caroline where she wishes to be married."

"Well, properly I suppose it should be from Longford," said Flora dubiously when Caroline made no reply.

"Lord, no!" Vivian groaned. "Not with that prosy bore of a parson. I want to enjoy the wedding, not spend two hours listening to a bad sermon."

"Well, dear, your father installed him in the living, so presumably you can dismiss him,'' Flora remarked. ''But I have to agree, the man is a complete bore.'' She turned to Lady Shannon. ''A good sermon I do enjoy, but Mr Colwell...''

Jervais spoke low to Caroline in the gloom. ''Well, your family has made their feelings plain—but what do you want?''

''You know what I want!'' she hissed back vehemently. ''I do not want this marriage to take place at all!''

''But given that it will, do you have any preference?'' His gloved hand closed over the fine kid of her own and he began rubbing one finger gently down the back of her hand. Her breath tightened in her throat and she could hardly speak, the diamond necklace cold and heavy round her neck.

''I do not care...'' she began as the carriage drew up at the lych gate and they entered the parish church, thus ending all conversation.

They arrived back at the house soon after midnight with the sound of the church bells still echoing across the frosty valley. Glad to be back inside, they shed their cloaks before entering the drawing room for a glass of warming punch.

''That was a splendid sermon,'' Flora observed. ''And such an attractive church. Much nicer than St Godric's at Longford. Why not hold the wedding here?''

''Have you settled on a date yet?'' Serena asked.

''Not yet,'' Caroline, compelled by a direct question, replied. ''But surely there is no need for haste? Let us consider it after the Christmas season.''

''There is no need for haste, indeed,'' Flora agreed, ''but equally there is no cause for delay.''

"Quite," observed Major Gresham, *sotto voce*, with a speaking glance at his beloved, who blushed rosily. Caroline caught the exchange and reproached herself for her selfishness. Flora had sacrificed much to provide a home for her orphaned nephew and niece and every day Caroline postponed her own wedding put off Flora's own match with her patient major.

Her glance fell on her brother as he sat shoulder to shoulder with Lady Julia, turning over an album of prints she had given him, their two heads dark and blonde almost touching. It was early days yet, but Caroline sensed that they could make a match of it, and her position as Jervais's wife would help the courtship along, making it more acceptable to the Earl of Shannon.

Lady Shannon, perhaps feeling that this public debate was a little unseemly, rose, saying to her daughter, "Come, Julia, it is time we were both to bed. My friends, the season's blessings on you! Good night."

The departure of their hostess signalled a general retirement, although Major Routh attempted to press the men to a game of billiards. Caroline had just set foot on the bottom stair when Jervais reached her side. He caught up her hand, detaining her as the others mounted the staircase.

"I will have a decision before the week is out," he said softly, his head bent over the hand he held. Caroline gasped as his lips grazed the sensitive skin of the inside of her wrist in a possessive caress: her other hand closed over his trapping it as if she wanted the kiss to last for ever. Perhaps, she thought shakily, he really does love me.

"I... I... Jervais, all I want..."

"And all I want, madam," he said, looking up with hard, dark eyes, "is to get you respectably married. I warned you before, I will not be fobbed off: I expect a date from you by the end of this week."

Caroline, who had been on the verge of telling him she loved him, snatched back her hand as if stung and ran upstairs, sick with reaction. She flung herself down on the bed and pummelled the defenceless pillow. He did not love her, that was abundantly clear: and how humiliating it would be if he guessed her own feelings for him!

This evening had proved to her the futility of trying to escape this marriage. Too many people knew of it and too many people had a stake in it: Flora and Anthony Gresham, Julia and Vivian—and Jervais himself, with his wretched concepts of honour and duty.

Caroline undressed slowly, her mind twisting and turning futilely. Very well, then, tomorrow—no, today, for the clock was chiming one o'clock—she would tell Jervais to have the banns read. Today was Monday, so it would be almost a week before the first banns were called, with another two weeks' grace after that: it would be almost the end of January before any ceremony could take place.

Christmas Day dawned crisp and sunny and Jervais took Caroline to matins in his curricle. As they passed between the snowy hedgerows with the barouche following more sedately behind, Caroline found her spirits rising in the frosty, invigorating air.

Jervais glanced sideways at her. "Are you warm

enough? It is good to see the colour back in your cheeks—you have been too pale of late."

She bit back the retort that had risen to her lips that he was the cause of her pallor. She was going to marry this man, the man she loved when all was said and done, and nothing was to be gained by endless bickering and sparring. It was a beautiful morning, everyone else was happy; she was determined, suddenly, to make the best of things.

Caroline twisted on the seat to look at him better and smiled, her face alive and vital. "Oh yes, I am quite warm enough! This is such a beautiful day after all that lowering fog. Can we not drive on a little after church?" She saw the fleeting look of surprise on his face and dropped her eyes. "There is something I wish to discuss with you."

"Very well," Jervais agreed, as they drew up at the church. The groom who had ridden with the barouche jumped down to take the horses' heads and the whole party entered the church.

Caroline tried hard to keep her thoughts from wandering during the service, but felt guiltily that her Christmas devotions had been somewhat distracted. Lady Shannon, on hearing of their plans, said, "A good idea, we are all fusty from so much time indoors. What do you think, Lady Grey? Shall we take a turn around the park before returning?"

It was agreed and Jervais reined back his team until he saw what direction the coachman was taking, then turned their heads down the opposite road. They drove in silence for a space, then Jervais drew up on top of a slight rise with a view over a fine burst of country below. The sun was red and low in the sky casting a roseate glow over the snow-clad fields.

"Do you hunt?" he asked.

"Always, at Longford," Caroline replied. "I have missed it in London."

"Will you come out for the Boxing Day meet?"

"I would if I had my mare with me, but she is at Longford," Caroline said absently, her eyes assessing the fine hunting terrain with the clipped hedges and neat banks.

"You must let me mount you, there is a bay gelding in my stables which would just suit you."

"Then I will hunt, with pleasure," she agreed.

Silence fell between them again. Jervais seemed content to survey his land, but Caroline struggled to find the words to introduce the subject of their wedding day.

"Jervais…" she began, just as he said,

"There was something you wished to say to me…"

They both broke off, then he prompted, "Go on."

"Our wedding date—let us have the banns called soon. Next Sunday, if you wish, then we can be married on, say, the twentieth of next month."

"As you wish," he said with cool politeness. "But what of your bride clothes? Does that allow you sufficient time to order them up?"

"Oh, that is not important!" Really, he was the most exasperating man! Here she was, finally agreeing a date with him and all he could do was demur about bride clothes…

"Not important?" He raised an amused eyebrow. "Why, I thought the bride clothes were an overriding consideration in a bride's mind—in the ordinary scheme of things."

"Well, this is not the ordinary scheme of things,

is it?'' Caroline responded tartly, then remembered her resolution to remain pleasant and not spoil the day. ''Fortunately, my wardrobe is well furnished at present,'' she added in a more conciliatory tone.

''You are being surprisingly matter of fact about this, all at once, Caroline,'' Jervais remarked, eyeing her closely. ''Why?''

The directness of his question startled the truth out of her. ''As you yourself pointed out to me, there is no escape from this marriage, so I have resolved to shift as best I can. And it occurs to me I am being selfish to those I love best.''

''What do you mean by that?'' he demanded.

''I overheard Flora tell Major Gresham she could not marry him until I was safely settled: now they can be married. And Vivian is showing a marked partiality for Lady Julia...if I am married to you, perhaps the earl will look more favourably on his suit.''

''How very flattering,'' Jervais said frostily. ''I had no idea you were of such a romantic disposition: how noble of you to force yourself to marry me for their sake! I trust they will be grateful for your sacrifice.''

''Oh, get down from your high horse, my lord!'' Caroline said, half laughing at the thought he might be wounded by her words. ''You know you are forcing me to marry you—would you have me be such a hypocrite as pretend I am marrying you for any other reason?''

There was a pregnant pause. Caroline stole a sideways glance at his set profile, wondering if she had perhaps gone a little too far this time. But when Jervais finally spoke there was no trace of the chagrin she thought she had detected.

"I commend your honesty. Between ourselves then, let us not pretend we are marrying for any other reason save necessity. But that should not preclude us behaving civilly each to the other, I trust?"

"Indeed not," Caroline agreed warmly. "After all, marriages of convenience have existed for centuries: I am sure we can reach an accommodation and learn to deal agreeably together."

The horses shifted uneasily as though his hands had tightened on the reins. "Your horses are becoming restive in the cold," Caroline observed.

"Indeed." He shook the reins and the team walked on. "Would you care to expand a little on what you mean by 'an accommodation'?"

"Surely you do not imagine I am consenting to anything other than a marriage of convenience?" she stammered. "There is no question of..."

"Let me assure you, Caroline, that there is every question that I require an heir," he declared bluntly.

"Oh!" Caroline reddened. "But that means you... I mean, I must...oh, dear!"

"You must have realised what it would entail." His irritation seemed to be dissolving into amusement.

"But you are only marrying me because you have to," she wailed.

"And I fully intend making the best of it! Come now, Caroline, nothing in our past dealings has led me to believe you would find our lovemaking so repugnant."

Even the memory of the encounters between them made her tingle from top to toe, but she could not, would not, give herself to a man who did not love her! Unable to answer him, she averted her burning face, biting her lip as she stared unseeingly at a cock pheasant stalking over the nearby field.

"Are you frightened?" he asked, his voice suddenly gentle. "There is no need, you know—I will be very gentle." Receiving only a muffled sound in response, he added, "You should speak to your aunt, she will set your mind at rest."

Still, she could not look at him, only shake her head mutely. She felt the cool soft leather of his gloved finger tracing down the line of her cheekbone. "We will say no more of this now, Caro. Come, luncheon will be awaiting us."

The rest of the day passed quietly. Caroline felt chilled and could not get warm, although Flora, noticing her shivering, insisted she sat by the fire, and scolded Jervais roundly for keeping her out in the cold.

When bedtime came at last, Caroline was still feeling very subdued. As her maid unpinned her hair and unfastened her dress, Caroline's eyes fastened on the big bed. She had pushed to the back of her mind the outcome of accepting Jervais as her husband. She knew he only had to touch her for her senses to be on fire, but she had thought little beyond kisses and caresses since that moment when she had almost gone to his bed in Belgium.

Of course she knew what marriage entailed—in theory! But the practice was shadowy and not something it had occurred to her—until now—to fear.

Flora came in with a warming cup of chocolate and, when the maid had gone and Caroline was sitting against the pillows sipping it, said, "What is wrong, my dear? You have been very subdued ever since you returned from your drive this morning."

Caroline blushed rosily. "It is nothing, Flora. Jervais... I mean, he..." Her voice trailed away.

"Ah," said Flora knowingly, settling herself on the edge of the bed. "So Jervais has been making love to you and it has alarmed you. You must make allowance for the ardour gentlemen feel on these occasions. I am sure he would not have overstepped the mark."

It was almost a question and Caroline said feebly, "No, no, of course not."

"Then what is it, Caro? You can talk to me, my dear, I have been a married woman!"

"It is just that I had not considered..." Caroline searched for the words "...the wedding night."

"Well, that is something a young lady has no need to consider," Flora said briskly, then relenting, added, "It will be all right, my dear, especially after the first time." Rather pink herself after that pronouncement, she gathered up her skirts and hurried out. "Good night, dear Caro. Sleep well."

Sleep well! After that helpful intervention, she doubted she could sleep at all! As she pulled the sheets up around her shoulders, Caroline found herself viewing quite starkly the intimacy that marriage would entail. How would she ever conceal from Jervais that she loved him? And when he found out, how would he react? Which would be worse—that he pity her or that he despise her?

Chapter Thirteen

Only Flora remained behind the next morning as the party set off for the first meet on the village green in Harrowbridge.

Julia and Lady Shannon had their own horses with them, fine Irish hunters, which showed off both ladies as accomplished horsewomen. Julia looked particularly fetching in a bronze-green habit which moulded itself to her slender figure and, to Caroline's hidden amusement, Vivian could hardly take his eyes off her.

Caroline was well satisfied with the bay gelding Jervais had ordered saddled for her. Although it was several months since she had last been in the saddle, she was pleased to find herself coping easily with the fresh young animal's playful cavortings. She was heavy eyed after a restless night but, somehow, in this morning's sunlight and crisp air, her fears of yesterday seemed exaggerated.

She glanced over at Jervais, caught his eye, and they both smiled spontaneously. Caroline was delighted to see that Caesar, now recovered from his injury, had been hacked down from London by a groom and was now jumping out of his skin with fitness and oats.

Jervais, immaculately dressed, seemed to control the big horse by the pressure of his thighs alone, one hand only holding the reins lightly as the cavalry charger tossed his head and mumbled the bit impatiently. Seeing him brought back all her memories of Jervais in uniform astride Caesar on the battlefield, of herself sitting up behind him as they rode back to Brussels, the feel of his muscular torso under her encircling arms...

"A penny for your thoughts?" Jervais asked, riding close beside her.

"I was thinking of Belgium," she replied honestly. "Seeing Caesar called it all to mind again: the battlefield, riding back to Brussels..."

There was a slight pause while Jervais smiled reminiscently. "I must say, Caroline, you are more suitably dressed for riding than you were on that occasion."

That remark was too near the knuckle for comfort: Caroline was not going to dwell on what had passed between them then and had no intention of allowing him to do so either.

"So you approve of my new riding habit?" Caroline enquired lightly, gesturing at the garment which was in the very height of fashion.

Garnet red cloth had been tailored in a dashing military cut. Black frogging laced the close-fitting jacket and reached from the cuffs to the elbow. The skirts, in contrast, flowed lavishly from the tight waist to show the occasional glimpse of matching half-boots and the entire ensemble was crowned by a black veiled hat tilted pertly over one eye.

"Very fetching, Caroline, but then, I have always thought red becomes you." The words were cool, but the look in his eyes scorched her, leaving her in no doubt that his thoughts were of removing the outfit rather than admiring it!

She was saved from having to reply by their arrival at the village green where the Master, a local squire by the name of Stacpoole, was shouting at the hunt servants who were unleashing the hounds.

"My lord!" He hailed Jervais bluffly, riding across to be introduced to the house party. "It is good to see a Barnard hunting with us once more. May we hope to meet at Dunharrow again as my father told me we used to?"

"Next year, perhaps," Jervais agreed, bending to accept a stirrup cup from one of the waiters scurrying to and from the inn with loaded trays.

The entire gentry of the surrounding areas seemed to have converged on the meet. Caroline was introduced to local farmers, clergymen astride cobs, young ladies showing off new habits under the doting eye of approving papas and a host of people who Jervais told her would be among the guests at the New Year party.

The hounds wove in and out of the horses, sterns waving in excitement as they stole as many of the savory pasties as the waiters let drop in the crush.

At last the Master gestured to the whippers-in, the hunting horns blew and the entire hunt streamed off the green and down the lane towards the first covert.

Caroline's horse kept trying to break into a canter and she was forced to rein it in. The side-saddle was either new or very well polished and she found it took all her skill to keep her seat.

"Is he too fresh for you?" Jervais enquired, coming up beside her, and bringing Caesar close, protectively.

Caroline laughed. "No, indeed not! He is full of the fidgets, but as soon as we draw this covert and I can let him have his head, he will calm down."

"Yes, you are right, the snow will make heavy going," Jervais agreed.

The field reined in at the first covert and stood around in small knots exchanging gossip and news. A tenant farmer stopped to ask Jervais's opinion of the wisdom of diverting a small stream and he listened with half an ear, his attention on Caroline.

Seeing him engaged, she walked the bay over to talk to Major Routh and Sir Richard. Jervais's eyes followed her intently. He had never seen her looking so beautiful and vital, glowing in the red habit against the snowy backdrop.

Nor had he ever found her so mystifying. Yesterday, she had seemed apprehensive, as though he were a stranger to her, not a man who had held her quivering with passion in his arms. And she was capable of great passion, of that he had no doubt. Despite the angry accusations he had made he had never really doubted that she was a virgin, yet there was that secret she would not reveal even though they were about to be man and wife.

He shook his head at the turn his thoughts were taking and the tenant farmer, misinterpreting the gesture, said in a disappointed tone, "I am sorry you feel like that, my lord, but, of course, if you do not wish it…"

"Forgive me, Johnson, I was wool-gathering. It sounds a capital scheme: come up to the house the day after next when Hambledon will be going over the leases with me.''

''Very well, my lord. I will attend you and your steward as you suggest.'' The man tipped his hat and moved aside as the hounds gave tongue and the field swung round to see the flash of russet as the fox broke cover and ran for the distant woods.

Horns were sounding the ''gone away'' and the riders fell in behind the Master as he began the pursuit. The snow cloaked the fields, making it difficult to distinguish stubble from plough and at first the riders were cautious.

At the first hedge they were still bunched close together and there was much jostling and milling around as the more confident took the jump whilst the more prudent went through the gate or crashed through gaps in the quickthorn.

Caroline used the gate, nodding her thanks to the curate, who was holding it open with the handle of his riding crop. Once through, she let the gelding have its head and found herself towards the front of the field, now strung out across the white downland.

At first she was too concerned with controlling the strange horse to notice where Jervais was. Her eyes were stinging in the cold as the air whipped past her face, her ears were full of the drum of hooves on the hard ground and the snorting breath of her mount.

Then, after a few minutes, she began to feel more confident. Her horse settled into his stride and responded to her signals and Caroline glanced round to see where everyone else was. In front, the Master and hunt servants led the field, the pack well in sight. The young bloods in the party were also in front of her, ''view hallooing'' with noisy enthusiasm and she saw that the curate on a particularly fine hunter was up with them.

Lady Shannon was a hundred yards to her right, in her element, the raw-boned Irish hunter well in hand. Julia and Vivian must be somewhere behind and she was just wondering where Jervais had got to when Caesar came up on her off side.

"I thought you must have fallen off!" she shouted, her words snatched by the breeze.

There was a flash of white teeth as Jervais laughed at her jibe. Caroline thought how brown his face still was, in contrast to the white faces of the other gentlemen, and what a raffish air it lent him. She laughed back at him, totally at ease, as though nothing existed except the excitement of this moment and the pleasure of being together.

"I didn't fall," he shouted back, "but you did well to take the gate back there: the ditch on the far side of the hedge caught several people by surprise—I think Caesar thought himself back in a cavalry charge!"

A flock of sheep which had been sheltering in the lee of a hedge now scattered in bleating panic at the approach of the horses. Before she had time to think the bay had taken the scrubby hedge, soaring over the dense thorn and easily clearing the ditch beyond. Her blood sang in her veins with the exhilaration of it all, the speed, the stinging air, her rapport with her mount and Jervais's dominant presence by her side.

"This way!" he shouted, pulling Caesar to the right, up the slope and towards a patch of woodland. "We can cut through here."

The horses dropped to a trot as they wove through the trees. Caroline realised Jervais was following the contour round at a higher level than the fox, and its pursuers, had taken. After a few moments they reached the edge of the woodland again, emerging to look down on the slope of the valley.

"Lost the scent, by the look of it," Jervais observed, gesturing with his whip at the pack which was milling round, casting for the scent. The Master and the whippers-in were shouting encouragement to the hounds and the front of the field was reining in to allow them to work.

"Look," Jervais pointed again, and Caroline saw a flash of red beyond a frozen pond. "Reynard's got the best of us this time." The fox trotted off almost contemptuously, ignoring the tumult behind it.

"He's outwitted the Master—who does not seem best pleased!" Caroline observed. Even at a distance the rubicund face of Squire Stacpoole glowed like a beacon. "What will he do now?"

"Curse and swear for a while, then draw Hangman's Covert, I would guess," Jervais answered almost lazily. His eyes were no longer on the Squire and the hounds. Caesar had dropped his head and cocked one hoof in the attitude of a horse which had learned to take a rest when one was offered, and Caroline's bay moved closer to the big grey in a companionable manner.

Finding herself almost knee to knee with Jervais, Caroline was very aware of him, and of how she must look, flushed and panting in the clinging habit. Her bosom was rising and falling, constrained by the close fitting garnet cloth, and underneath the veil her eyes sparkled.

"Caroline." It was all he said before he reached out and with one arm pulled her against him. The

horses stood like statues and Caroline found herself
supported by her one foot in the stirrup, the rest of
her weight held easily against Jervais's hard body.

"My lord!" she managed to squeak, knowing she
should resist and equally knowing she could not. His
mouth came down on hers through the coarse veiling.
She gave a little gasp at the strangeness of the sensation, then yielded to the heat and urgency of the
kiss. She dropped the reins to encircle his neck and
he lifted her bodily onto the saddle in front of him.

The bay snorted and moved aside, but the two of
them were oblivious, locked together. Jervais's
gloved hands were cold where they touched her body
at waist and throat, his cheek against hers was cold
also, but his lips were burning on her chilled skin.
His heart beat against her breast, he was holding her
so tightly, and Caroline was startlingly aware that the
two of them were on equal terms in their mutual
desire.

This man was going to be her husband very soon
and all the fears she had been experiencing the previous day had evaporated in the heat of their embrace. She wanted him...now. If he pulled her to the
frozen earth, claimed her as his wife now, she would
offer no resistance, would go to him eagerly.

Caesar proved an unexpected chaperon. Growing
bored with the inexplicable behaviour of his master,
he lifted his head and began to amble forwards to
where the bay was cropping a bedraggled patch of
grass.

Jervais swore under his breath, snatched up the
reins one-handed and snarled, "Stand!" Caesar
obeyed immediately.

"My lord... Jervais...we should not..." Caroline

stammered. Through the pounding of her pulse she was conscious that her hat was awry, her stock almost under one ear and a mere hundred yards away the entire hunt were gathered. "...not here," she added, then blushed furiously, scarcely crediting she could have said anything so bold.

"You are quite right," Jervais said huskily, gently letting her slide to the ground before dismounting himself. He caught the bay's reins over his arm and lifted her, hands firm at her waist, into the saddle.

He swung back onto Caesar, and turned the horse around. "This is not the place. Come back with me to Dunharrow: I want you...now."

Caroline stared at him, her lips parted to protest, but no words came.

"And you want me," he stated. "Come."

She gathered up the reins and kicked the bay to follow Caesar. It was outrageous, it was shocking and given the depths of misunderstanding between them, it was unwise, but she did not care. She loved him, she wanted to be with him, part of him—and when she was in his bed, in his arms, she could at last show him that love and he would know he could trust her.

They took the most direct route back to the house, cantering across the fields wordlessly, oblivious to the fading clamour of the hunt behind them as the hounds picked up the scent once more. At the outskirts of Harrowbridge they reined in and looked at each other. Jervais's lips twitched. "I think you should do something about your hat and your stock, or onlookers will believe you have fallen from your horse."

"And you, too," Caroline murmured with a sideways glance. "You are uncharacteristically dishevelled, my lord."

He straightened his stock and tugged at his jacket. "Not as dishevelled as I intend to be shortly, madam," he remarked, casting her into total confusion.

They rode sedately along the village street, outwardly composed. Caroline could hardly believe she was doing such a thing, going unmarried to a man's bed, even if he were her affianced and the man she loved.

"Lord Barnard! A word if I may!" It was the rector, striding down the churchyard path.

Jervais reined in with a glance at Caroline. "I had better see what he wants. Ride ahead and I will catch up with you."

"Will he not think me rude?"

"Not at all, and you are a little discomposed, you know. We would not have him wondering at the cause…"

Indeed not! Caroline waved to the rector and urged the bay on down the street. As she passed the inn a voice called, "Miss…miss!" and Fanny came out, almost tumbling in her haste, pulling on a cloak.

"How are you? Did you get back home safe the other night?" The young woman stood with one hand on the horse's neck looking up, real concern on her pretty face. "Oh, I have been all agog to know how things go—but I can't ask Simon—Major Routh, I should say."

"I got back safely," Caroline assured her. "But what an adventure! I was quite tiddly with that punch, you know, it led me into a terrible scrape!"

Fanny's eyes shone with glee. "Ooh, er! But everything is right and tight now, isn't it?" she asked shrewdly, nodding to herself at Caroline's ready blush. "That's the party all the excitement's about, isn't it?" she asked, nodding towards Jervais, who was still being detained by the rector.

"Well, yes," Caroline admitted. "Lord Barnard and I are to be married."

"Well, if that don't beat all," Fanny exclaimed delightedly. "A big London wedding?"

"No, that is, it is not yet decided," Caroline began, then glancing down the street, added quickly, "You had better go, here he comes!"

Fanny whisked inside. For a moment Caroline believed Jervais had seen nothing, but as he reached her side she saw his eyes were narrowed and his expression far from pleased.

"You should not be seen talking to persons of that kind," he said firmly.

"What kind?" Caroline asked innocently, although her heart was thudding.

Jervais was not deceived. "You know perfectly well what kind, madam!"

"No, I do not," she said stubbornly.

"One of the muslin company, if I am not mistaken."

"Well, you would know better than I if that were the case, sir." Her cheeks were red, her temper rising.

"And just what do you mean by that?" he enquired dangerously.

"You leapt to that conclusion very readily, Jervais," Caroline riposted. "Did you not make the same judgement of me when we first met?"

Jervais laughed without humour. "It is the normal conclusion one reaches when confronted by a young woman in an indecent gown and with paint on her face.''

"There is nothing indecent about Fanny's gown!"

There was a long silence. "So you are on first name terms with that little ladybird? Tell me, just how do you come to know Major Routh's whore so well?"

Caroline drew breath sharply. "How dare you use such language to me! Sir, you are offensive and you have no right to speak of Fanny so..."

"I have every right to guard my wife against unsuitable company."

"I am not your wife yet, sir, and you have no rights over me that I do not chose to give you!"

He leaned over and snatched her rein from her hand, pulling both horses to a standstill. The bay snorted and tossed its head in alarm.

"Have a care, Jervais!" Caroline cried, afraid she was about to be unseated.

"No, you have a care, Caroline. You are going to be my wife—perhaps sooner than you think—and that gives me every right I choose to claim! I insist you tell me what you are about with that woman."

"Or what?" Caroline glared back at him. "What sanctions do you threaten me with? Do you intend to beat your disobedient wife? Confine me to my room, perhaps?" He made an exclamation of impatience, but she pressed on. "If you cannot decide, perhaps you should yield to the inevitable: we can always say we have decided we do not suit."

"You will marry me, Caroline." His voice was harsh, commanding. "You will receive no help from me in whatever tarradiddle you choose to peddle to your friends: I will merely say you are suffering from pre-wedding nerves. No one will pay you any attention.''

For the first time that day she used her blunted spur on the gelding, sending the startled animal galloping up the drive towards the big house, Caesar thundering behind them.

At the front steps she reined in hard and slid hastily from the plunging animal. As Jervais reached her side, she threw the reins to him, forcing him to control both horses while she ran into the house.

Caroline flung the front door open in the startled face of the butler, who jumped backwards in alarm. ''Miss Franklin! I beg your pardon, I was not expecting...''

''No, indeed, Chawton, I beg your pardon for startling you so.'' Caroline tried to calm her breathing. She peeled off her gloves and smoothed down the jacket of her riding habit, forcing a smile to her lips. It would never do to give Jervais's servants cause to gossip about their master. She walked briskly across the hallway to the stairs, her hearing straining to catch any sound of Jervais beyond the heavy door.

''Shall I send your maid up, Miss Franklin?'' the butler asked, hurrying in her wake.

''No, no, thank you, Chawton. I have had rather a tiring ride and I am going to lie down. Please say I am not to be disturbed.''

Caroline gained the passage outside her room, surprised there was no sound of footsteps in pursuit. She glanced nervously over her shoulder as she put her hand on the doorknob, but there was no sign of Jervais.

Safely inside she leaned back against the panelling and closed her eyes with a sigh. Her heart was still thudding in her chest, but it was nothing to do with her flight from Jervais. No, her agitation stemmed from his words, and the way he had looked at her as he had declared his intention to marry her and do as he wished, come what may.

A frisson of apprehension tinged with excitement ran through her. Had she not encountered Fanny she would even now be in his bed, irrevocably bound to him. But that meeting in the village had once more demonstrated the vast gulf of misunderstanding and distrust that lay at the heart of their relations.

A faint click from the other side of the room made her open her eyes. Jervais stood in the doorway of her dressing room.

"Jervais! How did you...?" The housekeeper had assured her that the connecting door between her dressing room and the master dressing-room was always locked.

He smiled lazily and held up the key. "No doors are locked to me in my own house." The smile was deceptive: as he strolled towards her, she realised that it masked a tightly reined anger. "You are provocative, rebellious, devious and difficult, Caroline. I have decided that the sooner you are my wife, the sooner I can curb these unfortunate tendencies in you."

Caroline's sharp intake of breath was clearly audible. "This is not the Middle Ages, my lord! You cannot coerce me into marriage and you can control neither my behaviour nor my thoughts!"

"Coerce is an unfortunate word," he said silkily. "However, I do hold all the cards in this game. Your aunt earnestly desires this match—not only for your sake, but for hers also. Your brother knows you are so compromised he has no choice but to insist that you marry me. And, of course, you realise that if you make a scandal, any chance he has of an alliance with Julia is at an end.''

Caroline stared at him as he stood before her, implacable. ''All you give me, Jervais, is a catalogue of reasons why I cannot escape marriage to you. Now, give me a reason why I should want to marry you.'' Her chin came up and she met his hard gaze defiantly, willing him to speak of love.

''Considerations of your honour and mine...''

''To hell with honour!'' she retorted angrily. ''My own is my concern, and as to yours, I suggest it would be better served by not forcing an unwilling woman into marriage.''

''Unwilling?'' he murmured softly, moving towards her. ''Oh, I think not. And if you are asking me for a reason why you should want to marry me, I will give you this one...'' He reached out a hand and gently trailed his fingers down the line of her cheek, down her throat, across the swell of her breast.

Caroline gasped, unable to conceal her response to the thrill of his touch, even through the fabric. She grasped his hand to remove it, but instead her betraying body pressed more insistently against the warmth of his palm.

''Well?'' he enquired huskily. ''There is your reason for you.''

''It's...it is not enough,'' she managed to say in a scarcely audible whisper. ''I cannot give myself in marriage where there is not love.''

She saw his face darken and she was suddenly afraid. Mercifully, there was a tap on the panels at her back and Flora's voice came clearly. "Caroline, my dear! May I come in?"

Jervais gave her an unfathomable look and stalked back across the room, pulling the dressing-room door shut softly behind him. Caroline stood looking after him until Flora called again, more insistently this time. "Caroline! Are you unwell?"

Caroline reached behind her and turned the knob, stepping aside to admit her aunt. Flora bustled in, peering anxiously at her niece. "Chawton informs me that you appeared somewhat discommoded when you returned from the hunt, and that you came back alone. Is anything wrong?" Her eyes surveyed the subtle disorder of Caroline's habit. "Have you had a fall?"

"I cannot marry him!" Caroline burst out, ignoring Flora's questions. She moved agitatedly to stare out over the snowy park. "I cannot—I will not—do it!"

Flora bit back a sharp response with an effort, telling herself this was only pre-wedding nerves. "Now then, Caroline, do not be gooseish! It is natural that you should feel some apprehension, but this is mere foolishness. Why cannot you marry Lord Barnard?"

"He does not love me!"

"Young women of our class do not expect to marry for love," said Flora firmly. "There are higher considerations: family, propriety, the alliance of equals to continue family lineage..."

"You are marrying Anthony for love!" Caroline burst out rebelliously.

"I am a widow. Anthony is my choice." She flushed. "Lord Grey was my father's choice, and a most suitable one, of course. Naturally, he knew what was best for me..."

"Oh, I see. I must marry Jervais and hope to be widowed so I may find a second husband who will love me!" Seeing the shock and pain on her aunt's face, she instantly regretted her bitter words. "Oh, I am sorry, Flora, I did not mean that... I know you would never have thought like that when you were married..."

But she had gone too far for Flora's patience and forbearance. "You are beside yourself, Caroline," she said icily. "What do you want? You have a man who is eligible, intelligent, handsome to a fault. He is indulgent towards you, totally acceptable to your friends... You will never receive a comparable offer. If you were much younger, just out, I could understand these vapours, but I remind you, you have been out some time. If you cannot consider your own best interests, then think of others—your brother, for example."

Looking at her aunt's angry face, Caroline knew she deserved the tirade. Upbringing and duty to her family must make this match acceptable to her. Even if she explained everything that had happened in Belgium to Flora, that would only serve to add greater weight to the need to marry Jervais. Love was something women of her class found as a happy accident, not something she had any right or expectation of finding in marriage.

"I suggest you stay in your room until you have regained your composure and have come to your senses," Flora continued, her tone frigid.

Caroline sighed, turning her eyes once more to the frosty landscape. "I have come to my senses. I will marry Lord Barnard: do not concern yourself, aunt, there will be no further scenes.''

''I sincerely hope not,'' Flora remarked, gathering up her skirts. ''I will have some luncheon sent up. You should rest until this evening, by which time you might have regained your composure.''

Caroline spent the afternoon in intense thought, scarcely noticing the short day swiftly drawing into darkness. Too intelligent to suppose she had any realistic alternative now but to marry Jervais, she resolved to make the best of it. And she did love him.

Balancing the scales, that love weighed heavily. Added to it were the happiness of both her brother and her aunt. On the other side of the balance was the knowledge that Jervais did not love her, although undoubtedly he desired her passionately. Nor did he trust her. Well, she must live with that, hope that with marriage the trust would grow.

When Katy came to dress her for dinner she found her mistress composed and cheerful. To her own surprise, Caroline found that now she had made her decision a great weight had lifted from her. She knew what she faced and what she had to do. She must make Jervais trust her first, unconditionally: then would be the time for explanations. To tell him all, to set his suspicions to rest, would only serve until the next time they had a misunderstanding and they could not build love on such shaky foundations.

Jervais was crossing the hall as she began to descend the staircase for dinner. He glanced up at the sound of her skirts, then stopped, his eyes following her every step. He took in the frosty drift of silver spider gauze over aquamarine silk, the burnished sheen of her hair confined in a silver filet and the ice fire of his diamonds at her throat and on her arms.

"Caroline." He looked at her, unsmiling, and she braced herself to meet coldness. "You look ravishing: an ice princess."

It seemed she was forgiven. Letting her relief show in the warmth of her smile she responded, "I would rather be a baroness, my lord."

There was no mistaking the pleasure that lit his face as he handed her down the last two steps. "You are reconciled then, to our marriage?"

"Perfectly," she said, demurely, fighting down all her fears as she spoke.

"You make me very happy," he replied. The calm formality of his words were belied by the heat of his kiss as he brushed her fingertips with his lips. "Shall we join our guests?"

Chapter Fourteen

The weather broke overnight. The twenty-seventh of December dawned sodden and dank, depressing everyone's spirits at breakfast that morning.

"Well, that puts paid to hunting today," Major Routh remarked, regarding the slushy lake which had been the front lawn. "The scent will never hold up even if I was prepared to take my animals out in this heavy going. Which I am not," he added, sitting down to a plate of kedgeree.

"We must find some other occupation," Lady Shannon remarked bracingly.

"But, Mama, what of the play?" Julia broke in earnestly. "We only have four days to learn our parts and rehearse if we are to perform it on New Year's Eve for Jervais's guests."

"You have finished writing it, then?" Lady Shannon queried, slicing a little thin bread and butter. "I must confess I thought you would tire of it before it was complete."

Julia looked shyly across at Vivian. "Sir Vivian was such a help, Mama."

"I'll be bound," Major Routh muttered into his coffee.

"I think it is a splendid idea," Caroline encouraged. "It will keep us from getting dull until we can venture out again. I do not know the weather in Hampshire, but at Longford we have found that once a thaw sets in at this time of year it will be days before the weather lifts."

Flora smiled round the table, seeing nods and looks of interest from the assembled party. "Shall we all meet in the library after breakfast? We can decide the parts." She looked at her beloved Major Gresham with sparkling eyes, "I will confess I did not quite approve at first, but now I find I am quite excited."

"For myself, I consider play-acting, within reason, a most rational entertainment," Sir Richard declared.

Caroline caught Jervais's eye and smothered her smile with her napkin. Jervais obviously found Sir Richard as pompous as she did on occasion.

In the library they found Julia fussing over piles of paper. "I have written out all the parts," she explained. "Now, we must decide who will take which rôle."

Caroline could see that once Julia grew out of her girlish uncertainties she had the potential to be as decisive as her mama. Just what Vivian needed, in fact!

"We need a heroine, a hero, a villain, a heartless father, a clergyman, a faithful retainer and a lady's maid," Julia explained shyly. "There is a part for everyone except, of course, Mama and Lady Grey, who said they did not wish to act."

"I will take charge of the costumes," Flora offered.

"And I will be prompter," added Serena.

"I think Julia should be the heroine," Vivian announced, his eyes warm on her blushing face.

"Then you must be the hero Sir Ambrose," she responded.

"I think not," Serena said firmly. "It would be more seemly if Caroline were to act the heroine's part."

There was general agreement and Caroline found herself cast as Rosalyne, an innocent heiress.

"May I be the villain? It really is a capital part!" Major Routh looked up from his reading of the script. He twirled his moustache and read, in throbbing tones, "There is no escape from me now, my proud beauty!"

"I shall take the part of the clergyman, if you all agree," Sir Richard announced. This seemed so appropriate, there was no dissent.

"That would seem to leave you and I with the faithful old retainer or the harsh father," Major Gresham remarked to Jervais. "I think I can dodder better than I can rant, so if you are agreeable, old chap, that leaves you as Papa."

Jervais grinned. "I shall just have to remember how I dealt with headstrong subalterns and act accordingly! Julia, does that leave you a part?"

"Only that of Dorcas, the maidservant," Julia said primly, managing to look both noble and disappointed simultaneously.

"But you have a truly dramatic speech in the second scene when you throw yourself at the feet of the cruel father, pleading for your mistress," Vivian said consolingly.

Jervais's eyebrows shot up. "Good grief! What have I taken on? I shall go and look out a horse whip and start practising at once."

There was general laughter and even Julia smiled. Serena bent towards Flora as they sat together on the sofa and murmured, "I really do not feel it suitable that Julia and Vivian should be seen swooning in each other's arms, do you, Flora? At least, not until they are officially engaged to be married."

"You would have no objection to an engagement, then?" Flora queried, low-voiced.

"Indeed not. A most eligible young man, and so kind and charming. I know the Earl would concur. But they are young yet: I would wish Julia to have her first Season before anything is said."

"I do so agree with you, Serena." Flora clapped her hands to gather the attention of the players. "If I am to be in charge of costumes, I must know when the play is set. Julia dear, does it take place in this day and age, or is it an historical play?"

The author of the piece appeared unsure and a general debate broke out. Sir Richard wanted to perform the play in Roman togas but was voted down on the grounds of unseemliness and warmth. Major Routh urged Elizabethan dress, apparently feeling he would appear to best advantage in a ruff, but Sir Anthony drew the line at wearing tights.

At length Jervais held up a hand to still the hubbub. "I believe there are several trunks of old clothes and hangings—silks and brocades—in the attics. Could not something of no particular period be contrived from those?" He looked round for agreement.

"Good, then I will order them fetched down for Lady Grey's approval. You must summon us for costume fittings, ma'am, when you are ready."

The cast took their scripts and dispersed to con their lines, each in their own way. Major Routh rendered the breakfast room uninhabitable by striding about it, twirling his moustache and declaiming loudly. Sir Richard took to his room, requesting that he was not disturbed while he thought himself into his character; Major Gresham reduced Flora to fits of giggles by doddering in the drawing room, and despite Lady Shannon's best intentions, Julia and Vivian sat, heads together, helping each other with their lines.

Later that afternoon, Caroline found herself a quiet, book-lined alcove in the library and tried to memorise her first speech. This was an uncomfortable experience as most of her lines called for her to protest against a marriage of convenience.

"No, no, Papa!" she declaimed. "Although I am a dutiful daughter, you cannot ask this of me! To marry a man against my heart..."

From behind her, Jervais said softly, "I see the part has been written for you."

Caroline jumped, then felt the hot colour flood her cheeks. This was a little too near the mark for comfort. "I did not hear you come in... I thought I was alone."

"I am sorry I startled you. It occurred to me you might like someone to read through your lines with—but I can go away if you prefer." Jervais turned on his heel.

Caroline reached out and touched his sleeve. "No, Jervais, please do not go. I would like someone... I would like you to help me learn my part.'' She stood up and tentatively kissed his cheek. ''The theme of the play is unfortunate, but I hope we can put that to one side, now you and I have reached an agreement.'' She looked up into his unreadable face and her heart contracted with love for him. Taking a deep breath she plucked up all her courage. She would tell him how she felt, however unwise that was. ''Jervais, I...''

''You are quite right,'' he said pleasantly. ''We must not be over-sensitive and spoil the others' pleasure in the entertainment. Now, shall we read through the scenes we play together or would you prefer to read all of your part and I will listen?''

''I... I will read mine through.'' Caroline managed to disguise her disappointment; perhaps, after all, he had saved her from making a very unwise declaration.

By the twenty-ninth the party were almost fluent in their parts. The continuing wet weather was ignored by all, so absorbed were they in Julia's melodrama. Small groups could be found in every room holding spontaneous rehearsals, much to the well-hidden annoyance of the servants hampered in their household duties.

In the kitchen Mrs Chawton grumbled to Cook. ''I don't know what they think they're about, spanielling all over my nice clean carpets with those filthy old trunks. They fetched so much dust and cobwebs down, I'll have to get the girl to go over the floor with damp tea-leaves after!''

''And no interest in their food, do what I may,'' Cook opined. ''Mr Chawton tells me they spend so much time talking they're letting it go cold! I just hope my lady comes down to talk to me about the big party on New Year's Day: we've got to get the poultry soon and I still don't know how many we're expecting.''

The two women fell silent, musing on the strange ways of the gentry. Then Lady Shannon appeared as if she had been summoned by their complaints and paused inside the kitchen door regarding the long faces. ''Now then, Mrs Chawton, Cook—why so gloomy? We have no time to mope about! There is much to do. Now, as to the poultry...'' The two women exchanged speaking glances before listening attentively to their mistress.

Upstairs Jervais and Caroline had commandeered the hall to rehearse their big scene. Caroline cowered on her knees, hands raised imploringly while Jervais struck an attitude of implacable sternness.

''Father, do not cast me out, I implore you! It is snowing!''

''Thankless child! Ingrate! Will you obey me, then?''

''Never! I will die in the snow sooner than marry that monster!''

''To your room, then! You shall have bread and water until you submit to my will!'' He broke off with a snort of laughter. ''I swear that Julia has used every old chestnut from every ghastly novel she has ever read. I am not sure how the bishop will react.''

''Is he to be amongst the guests, then?'' Caroline sat back on her heels and looked up at him. Once she had got over the unfortunate subject matter, she had started to enjoy the play-acting. Or rather, if she was honest with herself, she was enjoying being with Jervais when he was in such a light-hearted mood.

"Yes, along with all my neighbours! I must have been mad to agree to make such an exhibition of myself." He reached down a hand to help her to her feet. "Come, it must be nearly time for luncheon. Let us find the others."

He tucked her hand snugly under his arm and they strolled companionably into the library together. The well-oiled door opened soundlessly and they stood on the threshold without Julia and Vivian realising they were there. The young lovers were sitting close on a window-seat, gazing deeply into each other's eyes. Vivian was holding Julia's hand and was obviously in the act of raising it to his lips.

Caroline tugged Jervais's sleeve gently and they backed out unseen. Closing the door with care, she said, "I am so thankful Vivian has found a girl like Julia. They are deeply in love: I am so pleased for him."

Jervais was silent, although she felt the muscles of his arm tense under her hand. "I had feared that what he encountered under my father's roof would make him hard and cynical about marriage," she continued.

"You never speak of your father. Why not?"

Caroline hesitated, then said frankly, "I should not say such things of a parent, I know, but after the death of my mother he knew no restraint. He drank too much, kept a string of mistresses…"

"My God, Caroline! I had no idea! And this happened when you were at home?"

"Oh, yes. It was not so much the mistresses in London who were such a trial, although, of course, they were very expensive. No, it was rather the occasional young women who turned up on our doorstep. What you would call 'bits of muslin', no doubt.''

''But you would have had nothing to do with them!'' There was shock in Jervais's tone.

''I had to buy one of them off, once. Poor thing, he was very thoughtless and, after all, it is men like him who make women like that what they are. I could not see her suffer by his negligence.''

A short silence ensued, then Jervais exclaimed, ''So that is how you come to be acquainted with Major Routh's...er, friend!''

Caroline recognised the relief in his voice at having found an acceptable reason for her scandalous acquaintance. It would have been very easy to allow him to continue thinking that, but she would not lie to him. ''No. To my knowledge she had no dealings with my father, although she is very much in his style.'' She met his eyes frankly, unprepared to elaborate further, challenging him to persist in his questioning.

For a second, she thought Jervais was going to demand she tell him about Fanny, but the moment passed, leaving a feeling of constraint between them. Caroline was painfully aware that the feeling of trust had vanished.

New Year's Eve being a Sunday, the normal revels were to be held on New Year's Day, but despite attendance at church, morning and afternoon, the house-party and the servants all found themselves busier than usual for a Sabbath.

Flora was being driven almost to distraction by

Major Routh's inability to stand still while she finished his costume. As the villain, Earl Dastardly, he was suitably sinister in his own dark coat and breeches, but Flora had decided to put the finishing touch with a swirling black cloak fashioned out of some old velvet curtains. She had persuaded the Major to stand on the library steps whilst she pinned up the hem, but compelling him to stop posturing was quite beyond her powers.

Sir Richard found her gazing despairingly up at Simon Routh, her mouth full of pins, and took charge. "Stand still, man!" he barked. "Cannot you see her ladyship is in difficulties!"

He earned a feeling look of gratitude from Flora, and startled obedience from the Major who goggled at his friend's costume.

"By jove, old chap, the clerical get up becomes you well!" Simon Routh said somewhat slyly. "Didn't realise you carried a dog collar and gaiters around in your luggage...?"

"I borrowed them from the rector," Sir Richard replied loftily. "Fortunately, he has no conscientious objection to play-acting and being much of my size was able to oblige me."

Meanwhile, Caroline was practising controlling her long skirts in the passage outside her room. Flora had found a heavy silk gown of the fashion of perhaps forty years before and had removed the heavy petticoats. It now flowed and swept around Caroline's feet producing a most Romantic effect, but used as she was to the shorter, slimmer skirts of the day she was finding it difficult to manage without tripping.

Jervais's door opened as she passed and he stepped

out, stopping immediately at the sight of her. Caroline struck an attitude, one hand pressed to her forehead, the other resting on the swell of her breast exposed by the *décolleté* of the gown. "Oh, Papa!" she quavered, "Do not send me to the nunnery!"

Jervais caught both her hands in his and stared down at her. "When I see you like this, the last thing I feel is paternal!" he said huskily.

"You like my costume?" she enquired, her voice not quite steady.

He stepped back regarding her, still with her hands trapped in his. "You look ravishing. There is something not quite right, however... I know!" He released her hands and began to unpin her hair, freeing the black curls from their confining ribbon and fanning the soft hair with his fingers until it stood out like a halo around her face.

Caroline shivered with pleasure as his cool fingers ran through her hair, closing her eyes in anticipation of the kiss that must surely follow as Jervais's hands dropped to her shoulders, pulling her tight into his embrace.

A discreet cough broke the moment and Caroline stepped back hastily, patting her hair into some sort of order. Jervais turned to face his cousin and said drily, "Your sense of timing, Serena, is, as always, superb."

"It needs to be, cousin," Lady Shannon retorted with good humour. "You two may be engaged, Jervais, but Caroline still requires chaperonage."

"But not for long," Jervais remarked, with a glance at Caroline.

"Ah, yes, I was going to enquire about that." Serena took Caroline's arm and steered her towards the head of the stairs. "Let us go down to tea, my dear. No, never mind the dress, it will be good practice in managing those skirts. Now, Jervais, the wedding. We must make some arrangements; I was saying as much to Lady Grey only this morning."

"I had assumed we would call the banns next Sunday," Caroline said. "Then we would be married at the end of the month. That is what we agreed, is it not, Jervais?"

"I was not aware that we had come to an agreement on that," Jervais said smoothly, holding out his hand to steady her as she gathered up her long skirts. "We will not have banns called: I prefer to be married by licence. We will speak to the bishop tomorrow."

They were entering the library as he spoke. Lady Grey waited until the footman who had just brought in the tea tray left before adding her approval to the scheme. "Are you discussing marriage by licence rather than by banns? I do so agree, it seems so much more discreet than having one's affairs bruited about in public."

Caroline was beginning to feel that events were sweeping her along. "But...when do you intend us to be married then, my lord?"

"Why, next Saturday, to be sure." Jervais seemed surprised at her confusion.

"Next Saturday!" Caroline was aghast. With all her heart and body she yearned to be his wife, yet her mind was still not accustomed to the idea, to the reality of tying herself to a man from whom she still had secrets, a man who did not love her or completely trust her.

"You had not intended to invite a larger party than

are already gathered here, had you?'' Lady Shannon asked gently as she began to pour the tea. ''And you and Lady Grey agreed it was unnecessary for you to return to London to obtain bride clothes before the ceremony. And the weather, of course, you must allow to be a consideration. For the party to disperse, only to reassemble at the end of the month would be quite impractical.''

Jervais, seeing Caroline's agitation, secured two cups of tea and steered her towards a window-seat at the far end of the room. Serena and Flora, already settled to a comfortable discussion of wedding breakfasts, and the difficulty of decorating the church at this time of year, scarcely noticed their absence.

''Do you regret your decision, then, Caroline?'' he asked her gently.

''I...no...no, of course not! It is just so soon...''

''Yes, I imagine the prospect and the actuality of marriage are somewhat different things,'' Jervais said drily, causing her to blush deeply. ''I do not wish to frighten you, Caroline. And I do not believe you are frightened of me and of what marriage will entail—when I hold you in my arms you respond to me so warmly...''

''Oh, hush!'' Caroline pleaded, glancing nervously down the room towards the tea party. ''It is not that I am afraid of you or of...what marriage will bring. It is just...'' She broke off, her hands trembling so much she had to put her cup down.

''Then what is it? Caroline, you must tell me!''

''I cannot convince myself that marriage without love is right!'' she burst out in a desperate whisper.

Before he could respond she jumped to her feet and hurried down the room to sit beside Flora, who gave her a warm smile and drew her into the discussion of wedding preparations.

Caroline could only regret her outburst, but as she had no occasion to be alone with Jervais for the remainder of that day, or the next morning, she had no opportunity to set things right.

The entire household was a hive of activity the next morning. Servants Caroline had not set eyes on before were to be seen scurrying up and down the staircases and in and out of rooms, and most of the village women appeared to have been pressed into service in the kitchen and scullery.

Julia was in a high state of nerves about her play and drove Chawton almost to distraction by redirecting the footmen from their duties about the house in order to rearrange the library furniture and the makeshift stage at what seemed like hourly intervals. Even Lady Shannon was relieved when Vivian persuaded her to leave well enough alone and help him polish his lines in the small parlour.

On the occasions when Caroline came across Jervais, he seemed quite as normal and made no reference to her outburst the day before. If she could have been alone with him, Caroline would have tried to explain, but there was never a suitable moment and as time passed it seemed more and more difficult to say anything.

The guests began to arrive in the early afternoon while there was still some light remaining. The front hall grew quite chilly as the front doors were opened and closed incessantly, and Caroline struggled to remember names as Jervais introduced her to one party of neighbours after another.

It was obvious that the reopening of the refurbished Dunharrow and the opportunity to meet the future Lady Barnard had overcome any qualms about making a journey on such a drear winter's day and the gathering seemed set to become the social event of the local season.

The bishop arrived with his wife and an attendant curate just as the daylight was finally fading. He greeted Jervais warmly, then turned to Caroline with evident approval. "My dear! Let me join my congratulations to those of your friends on this most happy occasion! Mrs Browning!" His wife, a rather sharp-nosed, mousy woman, scurried obediently to his side. "This is Miss Franklin, who is shortly to become Lady Barnard."

Caroline curtsied to the Bishop's wife and thanked his lordship for his good wishes with suitable modesty. He seemed most taken with her and demanded of Jervais who would be conducting the ceremony.

"Our rector, Mr Colwell."

"Indeed? Excuse me a moment, Barnard." The bishop, his ecclesiastical purple a startling patch of colour amongst the more soberly clad male guests, forged across the room to where his curate and Sir Richard were deep in conversation with the rector.

When he returned he had the rector, looking somewhat bemused by this descent of authority, in tow. "Well, Barnard, that is decided. I will personally perform the ceremony with the able assistance of Colwell here. No, no," he dismissed Jervais's thanks with a wave of his hand. "It is the least I can do. And it is many years since I conducted a wedding in a parish church."

Caroline guided him towards the cold collation,

encouraging him to reminisce about his earlier career and the many marriages he had presided over in the past.

As the hour struck she noticed Chawton move discreetly to Julia's side and address her low voiced. In turn she went to speak to her mother, than began to circulate amongst the rest of the cast, reminding them it was time to change into costume.

"My lord!" Lady Shannon's voice rang out over the babble of conversation. "Ladies and gentlemen! Members of the house-party have prepared a light entertainment for your amusement: I crave your indulgence if they leave you to ready themselves."

"Are you participating in this mysterious diversion, my dear?" the bishop asked Caroline.

"Indeed, my lord. It is nothing but a short and very frivolous play, but one which we hope you will find amusing."

The Bishop's wife gave a disapproving sniff, but her husband hurried to disagree with her unspoken views. "Now, now, Mrs Browning. It is not the Sabbath, and this is a private party. I am sure Lady Shannon would permit nothing unseemly..."

Caroline slipped away while he was still debating the point. The rest of the cast were already in the hall. The ladies were to change in the Blue Parlour, the gentlemen in a rather draughty anteroom.

Sir Richard, looking uncommonly pale, was being chafed by Major Routh. "I do declare you are nervous, old chap! Come, come, you know your lines better than all of us!"

"I have to confess I find the idea of playing a clergyman in front of the bishop somewhat daunting."

"Nonsense! Get a grip, man! It's not as if you have to perform a ceremony..." The door closed cutting off the remainder of the Major's attempts at reassurance.

Caroline was surprised to discover that she, too, was suffering from nerves, but forgot her own feelings when she saw Julia's white face. "There is nothing to worry about," she began as their maids helped them out of their dresses.

"When it was just for us, it was such fun," Julia wailed, her voice muffled by the plain skirts of the maid's costume which were being lowered over her head. "But all these guests...and I wrote it..." Her face emerged, looking more worried than ever.

"Nonsense!" Caroline declared in tones as bracing as she could manage, considering the tight lacing her gown necessitated. "Just think how proud Vivian will be of you..." She was interrupted by a small sob and added rashly, "Come, come. Is this any way for the future wife of a soldier to behave?"

That did the trick. Julia regarded her wide-eyed with hope. "You would not object? Oh, if only Papa and Mama will agree..."

"I will be delighted to have you as my sister, and to see Vivian so happy," Caroline assured her warmly. "And you may rely on Lady Shannon to persuade your papa, I am sure of it. Now, no more vapours, you are first on the stage!"

An hour later, sweeping a curtsy at the end of the performance, Caroline could not believe how well it had gone or how much she had enjoyed it. And there was no doubt the audience had enjoyed it, too: they had laughed in all the right places, had booed the villain roundly and there had even been a stifled sob at the end when father and daughter were reconciled.

The cast spilled out into the hall, glowing with excitement. Caroline picked up her flowing skirts and ran lightly up the staircase to her room to change. The sooner she got out of the terrible tight-lacing of her bodice, the better. She could scarcely breathe! As she opened the door her maid scurried past her, dropped a small curtsy and was gone.

"Katy? Come back…"

"I told her to go," a low, husky voice spoke from the shadowed corner.

"Jervais!" Caroline protested as he strode across to close the door firmly behind her. "But I need her…my hair…"

"I like your hair as it is." He ran his fingertips through it, fanning it into even greater disarray. "I told you before, Caroline, acting those scenes with you makes me feel anything but paternal." He did not wait for any response, drawing her hard into his embrace, kissing her ruthlessly, making no effort to disguise his desire.

His mouth was hot and hard, sealing over hers, his tongue invading and claiming. Unaware of her tight lacing, Jervais held her closer, his arms bending her back into his embrace.

All Caroline was conscious of was a total inability to breathe, an overwhelming feeling of panic that she must surely suffocate in the intensity of his embrace. She struggled to free herself, desperate for air and, in doing so, fetched him a sharp blow across the ear with her flailing hand.

He released her instantly, his face suffused with anger. "There is no need to box my ears, madam! If my attentions are so repugnant to you, you merely have to say so.''

Caroline, appalled, and with an apology forming on her lips, gasped at the injustice of his anger. ''How dare you! You force your way into my chamber, dismiss my maid, maul me...''

''Maul you! I would have you know I have never in my life mauled a woman! Do you think me some yokel, forcing my attentions on a milkmaid?''

Caroline was suddenly as angry as he. ''If the cap fits, wear it, my lord! I am sure the many women you have bought—your 'bits of muslin'—always bent to your will. But I give you notice now: I have no intention of doing the same!''

Jervais smiled thinly. ''You may think so, madam. But as my wife you will do as you are told. Now, make haste and change; our guests are waiting.'' And he was gone.

Chapter Fifteen

How Caroline endured the rest of that evening she would never know. Somehow she managed to show a pleasant face to the guests, play-acting the part of the radiant bride-to-be. Jervais, to her eye, appeared constrained, but nobody else seemed to notice anything amiss.

When they found themselves alone briefly in the hall at one point, Caroline forced herself to ask, "When do you intend announcing that our engagement is broken?"

"Broken?" He raised an interrogative brow. "I have not broken the engagement: nothing has changed. We will be married as planned in a week's time. Now, come into dinner, our guests will be waiting."

She was still perplexed, and still angry with him, when Flora came into her chamber to bid her goodnight. Caroline sat up against her pillows and patted the edge of the bed. "Flora, may I ask you something? You have more experience than I in the way men's minds work."

Flora looked at her knowingly and sat down. "I thought so—you and Jervais have had a tiff."

"A tiff! A pretty understatement! He kissed me—very passionately—while I was wearing my costume for the play. I was laced so tightly I could not breathe, and when I tried to free myself and accidently hit him...he became most angry."

"Hit him?" Flora's eyebrows nearly disappeared. "My dear Caroline, what unladylike behaviour!"

"What should I have done," her indignant niece demanded. "Faint?"

"That would certainly have answered the purpose. Now listen to me, Caroline, men do not like to feel rejected, it hurts their pride. And for a man in love it would be particularly galling."

Flora looked severe. Caroline almost blurted out the truth, then recollected herself. This was not the time to tell her aunt she was marrying a man who did not love her.

A short silence followed, then Flora, obviously picking her words with care, said, "The, er...physical side of marriage is always a shock. But you will become accustomed and after you have presented your lord with an heir, you will find his attentions will be less pressing."

"Because he has taken them elsewhere, presumably!" Caroline riposted sharply, thinking of Fanny, of her father's dalliances.

"A well-bred wife does not think of such things, let alone speak of them," Flora reproved, equally sharp. "I think you are overtired, Caroline. You will feel better in the morning, with all the preparations to be made. Goodnight, dear," she added more gently, dropping a light kiss on Caroline's head.

* * *

The sun came out from behind scudding grey clouds to greet Lord and Lady Barnard as they emerged from the church porch six days later. Caroline blinked in amazement at the crowd of villagers who had gathered to wish them well; she had hardly spared a thought for the other changes that marriage would bring. Now she was lady of the manor, mistress to all these people who had become her responsibility the moment she had said "I do."

Caroline and Jervais walked slowly down the churchyard path, stopping frequently to exchange a few words with well-wishers, and she strove hard to remember names and faces.

As they reached the lych gate a woman pushed forward a shy little girl. Her face, emerging from a thick wool shawl, glowed from a recent scrubbing as she struggled to recall the words her mother had spent all morning teaching her. The child's memory failed her at the sight of such a beautiful lady and, speechlessly, she thrust a tiny fistful of snowdrops and ivy trails at Caroline.

"For me?" Caroline bent down and stroked the child's soft cheek with her gloved finger. "Thank you very much! Did you pick them yourself?"

The child, now totally overcome, hid her face in her mother's skirts. Caroline smiled at the woman and caught a look of satisfaction on Jervais's face. At least he seemed to be pleased with his new wife's demeanour with the tenants of Dunharrow.

She gathered up her skirts carefully, although the dry weather and strong wind of the past day and night had done much to dry paths and steps. The carriage awaited them at the lych gate and Caroline noticed for the first time how beautifully turned out

were the team of horses. Truth to tell, on the way to
the church with Vivian and Flora, she had been so
nervous she would not have noticed if the horses had
been winged.

Jervais took her hand to help her into the carriage
and she felt the strength of him, even through the
fine kid of her gloves. The fog which had seemed to
swirl through her mind for the past week was clearing, leaving her acutely aware of the man sitting beside her—her husband.

A little shiver ran through her, although wrapped
as she was in a blue velvet cloak she was snug
enough against outside chills.

"Caroline, you are cold, here, let me..." He
pulled a fur rug from the opposite seat and tucked it
carefully around her. "There should be some hot
bricks under the seat."

As he bent, Caroline touched his arm, "No, no. I
am quite warm enough, thank you, Jervais."

"If you say so." He looked doubtfully at the ivory
silk of her gown peeping over the wide collar of the
cloak. "That gown is very beautiful, but I fear it is
inappropriate for the season."

That exchange appeared to have exhausted conversation between husband and wife. After a tentative glance at Jervais's calm profile, Caroline turned
to the window just in time to catch sight of Fanny
waving from the steps of the inn.

Mercifully Jervais had not seen the other woman,
but the shock jolted Caroline into speech. "How fortunate, my lord, it did not snow again last night."

The feebleness of the words fell into the silence,
then Jervais said, almost conversationally, "Never
mind the weather, that bonnet is damnably in the

way." His fingers were already working on the ribbons under her chin; seconds later, her fine velvet hat was tossed carelessly aside and Jervais was kissing her with a conviction and thoroughness that brought home to her more forcibly than any wedding ceremony that they were indeed married!

Caroline swayed closer into his embrace, clutching his lapels as the coach swung between the gateposts of Dunharrow. Faintly in her ears came the muted cheers of the ground staff and keepers gathered round the lodge, but Caroline felt no embarrassment that the servants should see them embracing.

As the coach slowed Jervais released her, picked up her hat and gently placed it back on her head. His gloveless fingers worked deftly to retie the ribbons, then just as the coach came to a halt he touched and traced the delicate curve of her upper lip with a warm finger. "You are so very beautiful, Caroline," he murmured huskily.

Stepping down onto the gravel, Caroline felt a surge of hope that it was going to be all right, that Jervais had put behind him all their previous misunderstandings, the suspicions, now they were indeed married.

But there was no time for further reflection, for Chawton and Mrs Chawton were leading out the entire domestic staff to line the steps, the menservants on one side in their best livery, the maids on the other with new ribbons in their caps.

As the carriages conveying the guests drew up behind, Caroline walked slowly up the steps while Jervais formally introduced her to the staff as the new mistress of Dunharrow.

After a period of confusion, whilst fifty or so

guests shed pelisses and top coats, ladies were shown to bedchambers to tidy their hair and gentlemen warmed their coat tails before blazing fires, Chawton managed to seat everyone in the dining room.

The long table, augmented by all of its four extensions, was further enlarged by two end tables set crosswise. Caroline and Jervais sat at the centre, presiding over a quite magnificent wedding breakfast.

Caroline swallowed a moment of panic and realised that the bishop, seated on her right hand, was speaking to her. "...a most sumptuous collation. You are to be congratulated, my dear Lady Barnard, on such an achievement, especially considering the difficulties of the season."

"Oh, I can take no credit, my lord," Caroline demurred. "My aunt and Lady Shannon arranged all." As the servants began to pour wine and the gentlemen to carve the various dishes set before them, Caroline glanced round, seeking out the familiar faces of her friends amongst the throng.

Vivian was opposite her with Julia on his left hand. Beside Julia, Sir James Porteous, a neighbour she scarcely knew, was engaging Flora in conversation, apparently to the disapproval of his very plain wife seated further down the table.

Serena was out of sight beyond the bishop's wife on Jervais's left hand, but Caroline could hear her robust tones discussing the difficulties of obtaining pineapples in January.

A partnership further down the board caught Caroline's fancy and she put her head close to Jervais and said in low tones, "See Major Routh! I fear Serena's stratagem to separate him from the prettier guests has misfired."

Lady Shannon, having taken Simon Routh's measure early in their acquaintance, had intended to give him no opportunity for flirtation and so had seated him between a rather deaf dowager in her eighties and the bishop's drab little mouse of a daughter.

The Major, always one to relish a challenge, had evidently set out to fascinate Miss Lavinia, whose sallow cheeks were becomingly flushed as a result of his badinage.

Jervais laughed. "Simon is incorrigible," he responded softly. "I just hope he does not break her heart."

"She has more sense than that, I am sure. But a flirtation will give her some confidence—perhaps enough to discharge her dressmaker!"

They exchanged warm, intimate glances and Caroline felt her heart skip a beat. With an effort she turned from her husband and began to make conversation with her immediate neighbours.

Outside the light was dying as the afternoon wore on and the meal progressed. At last the servants brought in the sweetmeats and fruit, people were pushing back their chairs a little and several portly gentlemen looked as though they wished they could unbutton their waistcoats.

With a glance at Jervais, Vivian rose to commence the speechmaking, to be followed by the bridegroom himself. Sir Richard, who had acted as Jervais's supporter at the church, rose finally to deliver a charming and surprisingly witty address of thanks to the bridesmaids and to Lady Shannon for the magnificence of the wedding breakfast.

At last, Caroline, in her new role of lady of the house, rose, caught the eye of the other ladies present and bore them off to the various upstairs chambers set aside for their convenience.

She and Lady Shannon met on the landing after all the female guests had been accommodated. Serena smiled warmly at her new cousin. "Welcome to the family, my dear. I am so pleased Jervais has found a bride like you. No, no false modesty," she insisted as Caroline blushingly protested. "You have the style and presence Jervais needs in a wife but, more importantly, the spirit and intelligence to keep him interested! I speak frankly, I hope I do not give you offence, but he sets standards which are too high, both for himself and for others. You will be more than a match for him!"

Having succeeded in casting Caroline into considerable confusion, Serena swept off to her own chamber. Downstairs the servants cleared away the remnants of the feast and set out card tables in the small salons. Chawton surveyed the ballroom and noted with satisfaction that the hothouse flowers were at their peak, scenting the warm air. Musicians arrived and began to set up their scores and tune their instruments for the evening's dancing and in every bedchamber in the house guests loosened stays, unbuttoned waistcoats, eased off shoes and rested until ready to begin again.

In her chamber, Caroline was helped out of her wedding gown and into a loose wrapper by Katy, almost beside herself with the excitement of the day and the heady realisation that now, as the lady's maid to the mistress of the house, she had achieved a position in the household second only to that of Mrs Chawton.

"Shall I redress your hair now, my lady?"

Caroline, still accustoming herself to being addressed thus, looked at her flushed face in the glass before her and thought how unchanged she looked from the unmarried girl of the morning. Perhaps she would look different tomorrow morning...but the implications of that thought were too agitating to dwell on.

"No, just unpin it and brush it out, please, Katy. I will wait until I am ready to go down before we redress it. You may go now, I think I will lie down for a while."

Caroline had realised she was weary after the day's excitements, but she had not expected to fall so quickly into a light doze. She awakened with a start to the sound of a light knock on the dressing-room door. The room was in shadows: all but one branch of candles had gone out and the chamber was lit by the flickering fire.

The door swung open to reveal Jervais in shirt-sleeves and breeches, his shirt open at the neck. "Did I wake you? May I come in?"

"Of course you may." Caroline sat up hurriedly against the pillows, running her hands through her disordered hair. Somehow she had not expected him to come to her like this before the night and her heart was beating wildly.

Jervais crossed the room and settled himself at the foot of the bed. She had grown used to him, to the urbane and well-groomed Lord Barnard, but half-dressed in the flickering firelight he was once again the dangerous saturnine stranger of the battlefield.

Seeing her eyes widen, he asked her softly, "What are you thinking of?"

"Of the first time I met you...of waking up in the barn beside you."

"But now you have your memory back," he observed gently. "You know who you are, and who I am." His fingers ran lightly over the arch of her bare foot and Caroline started, but did not draw away.

"My husband," she replied, her eyes steady on his face as his fingers strayed higher, caressing her ankle.

"You must not be afraid, Caroline. I am not the ogre you sometimes believe me to be. No, let me speak," he insisted as she opened her mouth to protest. "I will not do anything to alarm you, you have my word as a gentleman."

Caroline wanted to cry out that nothing he could do would alarm her, that she welcomed his embraces and what would follow, but she still could not be absolutely open and trusting with him while he did not trust her. He was a man on his wedding day; he might well be putting to one side all the doubts and suspicions which he had of her, but they would surface again when this night was over.

Jervais watched the play of emotions on her face, marvelling that someone seemingly so open, so guileless, still held back secrets from him.

To her surprise he stood up. "I can see you still doubt me: but I promise you, Caroline, you will believe me tonight." Before she could reply he was gone, the door closing softly behind him.

Caroline danced the evening away in a dream, unable to concentrate on anything but Jervais's words to her, the way he had looked, the thought of the night to come.

She did her best to be a good hostess, but was unaware of the indulgent smiles of the guests who, noticing her high colour and abstracted manner, forgave it easily as only to be expected of a new bride.

As the clock struck ten, Jervais, who was waltzing with Caroline, manoeuvred her neatly out of the door into the hall. "Come, Caroline," he said, holding out his hand and leading her up the staircase.

Caroline felt her knees weakening until she feared they would hardly support her as the sound of the music diminished behind them. She was conscious of the swish of her gown on the wooden treads, of their shadows thrown on the walls by the sconces of candles as they passed, of the warmth and sureness of his hand as he led her inexorably towards her bedchamber door.

She was conscious of a slight feeling of surprise. She had not expected to slip off with him this way, had assumed they would retire at the same time as the guests and that he would come to her room later. And why, if they were retiring together now, why did they not go to the master bedchamber?

To her surprise Jervais turned not to the big, waiting bed, but to the chairs by the fireside. He seated her firmly in one and took the other, remaining at a distance. For a long moment he said nothing, his expression serious as he regarded her. Caroline thought she saw a nervous jump in his cheek, but perhaps it was only the firelight dancing on the planes of his face.

The silence was almost tangible. Caroline felt the pleasurable frisson of apprehension that had filled her since Jervais had taken her away from the celebrations become a leaden foreboding.

"Caroline...I have been giving much thought to what you have said...of love in marriage. I know it is not expected that people of our rank and station will necessarily make a love match, but I understand now how much it means to you. I am sorry I cannot give you that."

It was as though he had struck her to the heart: all her hopes that he might love her died. Caroline fought the pain with all her pride and training, masking it behind a façade of cold composure. Only her hands, tightly clasped in her lap, betrayed her, but Jervais's eyes were fixed implacably on her face.

"Under these circumstances," he continued relentlessly, "you need have no fear I shall force my attentions upon you." He stood up. "I will leave you now, you must be fatigued. Goodnight, Caroline."

For several minutes after the door clicked shut behind him, Caroline sat unmoving, gazing into the fire. The flames were blurred before her eyes as the tears coursed silently down her cheeks.

There could be no doubt he did not love her. Surely if he had any tender feelings towards her he would have coaxed her, wooed her into the marriage bed? She was not so innocent as to believe a man needed to be in love before he bedded a woman, especially his wife. But this cold formality could only mean he distrusted her so deeply that he could not bring himself to lie with her. The angry accusations he had thrown at her, his obduracy in refusing to believe there might be an innocent explanation for her presence on the battlefield meant he could not bring himself to trust her.

Eventually, overcome by emotion and exhaustion, she fell into a deep sleep in the chair.

She woke as dawn broke, stiff and cold before the ashes of the dead fire. For a moment she was confused, then it all came flooding back.

Katy must not see her like this! Caroline cringed at the thought of the gossip which would spread like wildfire below stairs if she were to be discovered still in her gown of the evening before on the morning after her wedding night.

She struggled out of her gown, dropping it and her stockings onto the chair. Her hair was already so tumbled that it only needed her to pull out the remaining pins for it all to come down. Crossing swiftly to the foot of the bed she pulled on her night-gown, leaving the ties at the neck undone.

Caroline scrambled into bed, disordering the pillows and covers on both sides. It was humiliating to have to undertake such a deception, but the alternative—having everyone know that the marriage had not been consummated—was worse!

She was only just in time; no sooner had she wriggled down under the covers than a soft knock heralded the arrival of Katy with her morning cup of hot chocolate.

Caroline feigned sleep whilst the maidservant cautiously approached the bed and set the cup down. "My lady?"

"Oh... Katy. Good morning." She sat up with a show of reluctance, rubbing her eyes.

"Good morning, my lady. Miss...madam, I should say, you're still wearing your earrings."

Caroline's hands flew to her ears. "How careless of me," she said lightly. "It is fortunate they did not catch in the lace." She knew she was blushing, but realised that, above everything, confirmed the picture of a new bride.

Despising herself for the deception, Caroline took up the hot chocolate and began to sip it while Katy gathered up her discarded garments. The girl was obviously agog but Caroline was not going to give her any encouragement to chatter.

Caroline dressed with care. When the maid had gone she crossed to the glass and schooled her face into an expression of calm serenity, far from what she felt inside.

When she reached the small salon Jervais was already breaking his fast, alone. "Oh, my lord…where are the other guests?" she stammered. She had been hoping for the protection of company.

"Good morning. You have just missed your brother who has gone out riding with some of the other men. I believe the ladies have had trays sent to their rooms."

Caroline sat at the opposite end of the table feeling gauche and awkward. "May I pour you coffee, my lord?"

"Thank you, I have some." Jervais paused, then said with a touch of impatience, "I thought I had made myself plain last night: there is no need for you to be so stiff in my company, I shall not force myself upon you. But," he added drily, "I am afraid you will have to accustom yourself to being alone with me from time to time."

Caroline rallied. "I understand that. However, you must agree that not everything was said last night that needed to be said!"

"Very well. When you have finished your breakfast perhaps we can meet in the study." Jervais pushed back his chair, made his wife a slight bow, and left.

Caroline toyed with a piece of bread and butter, then, realising she had no appetite, rose and followed him.

Jervais was sitting at his desk, but rose immediately she entered the room. Once again he led her to a chair by the fire, but this time he remained standing, one foot on the fender while he waited for her to speak.

Caroline took a deep breath. "Jervais, why did you marry me?"

"Because I had compromised you, of course." His brows drew together as he looked at her. "We have been into this before—I had compromised you, not once, but twice. We might have escaped the consequences of your battlefield escapade, but once your brother had discovered you in my bed, there was no alternative." She made an abrupt gesture with her hands which he interpreted as impatience. "You have no heed for your reputation, madam, but as a gentleman, I must." His voice was as hard as she had ever heard it.

"And as a gentleman, you will not force yourself upon me," she observed, equally cold. He nodded curtly. "But do you not expect an heir as part of the bargain? I can assure you the world will expect one."

Jervais removed his foot from the fender and faced her. "You are very frank, madam!"

"I am a married woman now—at least, in name."

Jervais appeared to choose his words with care. "In a few months, when we are more accustomed to one another, we will speak of this again. There is no need for you to concern yourself with it now."

If she had thought that by speaking so frankly she would pierce his armour, glimpse his true feelings, she was sorely disappointed. This morning her husband's cold implacability seemed impenetrable. Caroline stood, swept him a curtsy and left the study. She was mistress of Dunharrow now, with duties to perform and servants to order. Swallowing her pain and her anger, Caroline resolved to throw herself into her new rôle. At least she understood it, which was more than she did her husband.

Three nights later, Simon Routh pulled off his boots, unbuttoned his waistcoat and cast himself down on a low chair in front of the blazing fire in Fanny's bedchamber at the inn.

"By God, that's better! You know how to make a man comfortable, Fan, my girl." He reached out a hand and pulled her down to sit on his lap.

Fanny, snuggling down accommodatingly, remarked, "Not comfortable up at the big house, then?"

Simon took a deep draught of the hot punch Fanny had prepared before replying. "Oh, comfortable enough—as far as that goes. No, it's something else…the feel of the place. There's something very much amiss with our newlyweds: I tell you, Fan, if things don't cheer up soon, we're back to Town!"

Fanny sat up, her face concerned. "What's amiss, then?"

"No good asking me, I'm not a married man, so I don't understand wives. But, I tell you, if that marriage has been consummated, then I'm a Dutchman."

"But she is crazy in love with him!"

"And I would have said that if there was ever a

man in love it was Jervais Barnard,'' Simon added grimly. ''But there is something between them...if I didn't know better,'' he brooded, ''I'd say he was a man who had discovered some dark secret about his new wife, but was having to make the best of the bargain. But that must be nonsense, Caroline's a real lady if ever I... Here, Fan! Where are you going?''

Fanny had jumped off his lap and was pulling her cloak from its peg. ''Come on, get your boots on. You are going to take me up to the house now: I'm going to talk to his lordship, whether he wants to hear me or not. Men!''

At about the time that Fanny had been pushing the cloves into an orange to make Simon's mulled wine, Caroline had been sitting before her chamber fire, deep in meditation.

After three miserable days, and even more miserable, lonely, nights, she had come to the conclusion that if anything were to change, then she must initiate it. What was the point of having her pride intact, in insisting on some ideal relationship where Jervais trusted her implicitly, when her heart was breaking? What had she to look forward to, but years of loneliness with the occasional cold coupling when dynastic considerations demanded it? Perhaps she would find comfort in her children, but they seemed very remote now.

The clock struck midnight and she reached a decision. Testing his trust no longer seemed of any importance: she needed Jervais. If he knew her presence on the battlefield and those indecent and compromising clothes had all been an innocent accident of fate, then at least he could trust her and might show her affection. She would have to settle for that.

The connecting door between her room and his dressing-room was locked, and had been since their wedding night. Caroline did not even trouble to try it. She pulled on her thin wrapper and emerged gingerly into the corridor outside her room. To reach Jervais's door she had to creep along one passage and round a corner and she had no intention of being discovered. The house was very silent; all she could hear was the blood pounding in her ears as she tip-toed over the boards and eased open his door.

The room was empty, lit only by a branch of candles on the dresser. Jervais had been there: his jacket and neckcloth lay discarded. Puzzled, Caroline looked round the room and saw a splash of red cast across the bed.

Her hand flew to her throat. Blood! Then she realised it was not blood, but vivid cloth. The carmine dress she had last seen in Belgium lay on the covers, startling, incongruous in this masculine room. As if drawn to it, Caroline crossed the room and picked it up, feeling the flimsy silk, remembering how it felt to wear it, remembering Jervais's face as he looked at her dressed in it.

A latch clicked and she looked up, unconsciously holding the dress to her bosom, as Jervais walked in from his dressing-room.

"You kept it," she whispered.

"Of course. It was all I had of you," he replied as directly. "When you ran away in Brussels, I had to have something to remind me of you."

"But why did it matter?" But, looking into his

face, she thought she knew—if only she dared believe it. "You thought I was a…"

"I was a fool. I am a fool." He walked slowly across the room towards her. "I told myself I was right to marry you because I had compromised you. But then I realised how you felt, and that it would be wrong to ask for more when you did not love me. But I don't care. I love you, Caroline, and I will make you love me if you will only give me the chance."

Caroline was struck speechless, her throat tight with tears of happiness. Jervais took her by the shoulders, looking down into her face with eyes dark with passion and tenderness. "I know you do not love me, Caroline, but I also know you are not indifferent to me. Trust me, let me show you how much I love you, my darling…"

The kiss he claimed was dizzying in its intensity. For a moment, Caroline was so stunned by all that she had seen in his face she did not respond, then she was kissing him in return with equal passion, her arms twining round his body, seeking to lose herself, melt into him.

He released her, gazing down in disbelief. "Caroline, do you…?"

"Yes, I love you, Jervais! I loved you from the beginning, even when I did not know who I was, I loved you. But I thought you did not trust me, and I did not think there was any future for us if you could not trust me."

He kissed her again, then asked, "Then what are you doing here?"

"I could not bear it any longer. I had to tell you I loved you, tell you what had happened. Even if I would never know if you trusted me, at least I knew I was keeping no secrets from you. But where were you?''

"On the same errand. I had to tell you that I did not care why you were on the battlefield wearing this—'' he touched the dress "—that I loved you, and we had to make a fresh start together.''

At that moment the door opened without a knock and Fanny marched in, followed by a protesting Major Routh.

"Damn it all, Fanny, you can't walk into a man's bedchamber in the middle of the night!'' He caught sight of Caroline and stopped dead, his face crimson with embarrassment. "Oh, my God! My apologies, ma'am! Fan, get out of there!''

"No, I will not, not until I've said my piece! Now look here, my lord, I know you're a gentleman and I'm just a working girl, but I'm an honest girl and I stand by my friends. And I won't see you make Caroline unhappy, just because of some silly accident!'' She wagged a warning finger at Jervais. "Now don't you go interrupting me now!''

He leaned back against the bedpost, one arm still round Caroline. "I would not dream of it, my dear lady,'' he said solemnly.

"Good! She was looking for her brother after the battle and she took a tumble off her horse and banged her head. We—the girls and I in our wagon—we picked her up and lent her a dress 'cause hers was all muddy. Well, we couldn't leave her there, could we, with those nasty Frenchies about? We shouldn't have painted her face like that, but it passed the time and she looked so pale. Then we all fell asleep and she must have tumbled out when the wagon went over a bump. That's when she hit her head again and you found her. And all I can say is, if you think the worse of such a nice young lady just because of a bit of face paint and a skirt—well, you're not fit to be her husband!''

Fanny, having run out of breath and indignation, came to a full stop. Simon Routh had dropped into a chair, his head in his hands and was moaning gently.

Caroline crossed to the girl and gave her a big hug. ''It is all right, Fanny. He does trust me, and he loves me and everything is going to be wonderful. But it was so brave of you to come to my rescue. Thank you.''

''You sure?'' Fanny shot Jervais a dubious glance.

''She can be quite sure, miss…?'' Jervais was holding out his hand.

''Masterman,'' said Fanny stoutly, taking it. ''Well, you look after her—she deserves it. Come along, Simon.''

Jervais's straight face lasted until a spluttering Major Routh was bundled firmly out by Fanny. Then he turned the key in the lock and gave a great shout of laughter.

Caroline found herself caught up in his arms and whirled round. Jervais deposited her on the bed, caught her against his chest and bent to kiss her.

''Oh, Jervais, I am so sorry! Poor Major Routh! But was Fanny not magnificent? We must do something for her…a little shop, perhaps?''

''Not now, Caroline.'' Jervais slowly, and with infinite promise, began to trail kisses down her throat, and across the swell of her breast. He tugged gently at the ties of her nightgown and Caroline caught her breath in a little gasp of anticipation. "We have more important things to do tonight. I have waited quite long enough to show you that you are indeed my much loved wife."

"And you are my much loved husband," she murmured as she drew his head down to her breast again.

* * * * *

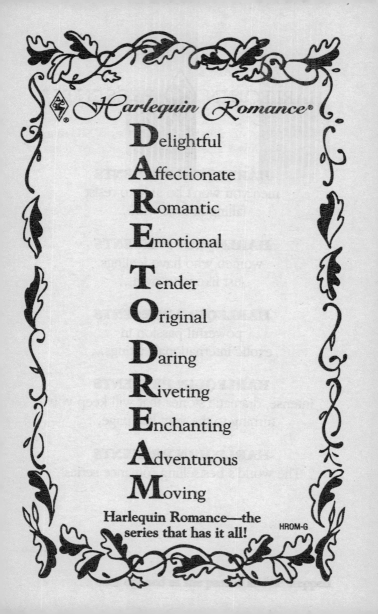

Harlequin Romance®

Delightful

Affectionate

Romantic

Emotional

Tender

Original

Daring

Riveting

Enchanting

Adventurous

Moving

Harlequin Romance—the
series that has it all!

HROM-G

HARLEQUIN PRESENTS®

HARLEQUIN PRESENTS
men you won't be able to resist
falling in love with...

HARLEQUIN PRESENTS
women who have feelings
just like your own...

HARLEQUIN PRESENTS
powerful passion in
exotic international settings...

HARLEQUIN PRESENTS
intense, dramatic stories that will keep you
turning to the very last page...

HARLEQUIN PRESENTS
The world's bestselling romance series!

Harlequin® Historical

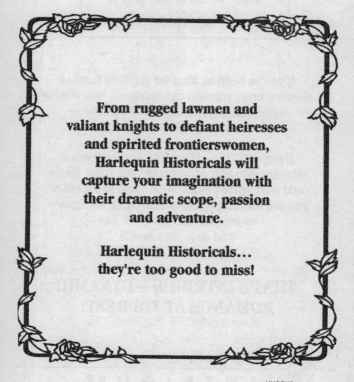

From rugged lawmen and
valiant knights to defiant heiresses
and spirited frontierswomen,
Harlequin Historicals will
capture your imagination with
their dramatic scope, passion
and adventure.

Harlequin Historicals…
they're too good to miss!

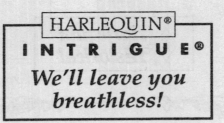

LOOK FOR OUR FOUR FABULOUS MEN!

Each month some of today's bestselling authors bring
four new fabulous men to Harlequin American Romance.
Whether they're rebel ranchers, millionaire power brokers
or sexy single dads, they're all gallant princes—and
they're all ready to sweep you into lighthearted fantasies
and contemporary fairy tales where anything is possible
and where all your dreams come true!

You don't even have to make a wish…
Harlequin American Romance will grant your every desire!

Look for Harlequin American Romance
wherever Harlequin books are sold!

S HARLEQUIN SUPERROMANCE®

...there's more to the story!

Superromance. A *big* satisfying read about unforget-
table characters. Each month we offer
four very different stories that range from family
drama to adventure and mystery, from highly emo-
tional stories to romantic comedies—and
much more! Stories about people you'll
believe in and care about. Stories too
compelling to put down....

Our authors are among today's *best* romance writ-
ers. You'll find familiar names and
talented newcomers. Many of them are
award winners—and you'll see why!

If you want the biggest and best
in romance fiction, you'll get it
from Superromance!

Available wherever Harlequin books are sold.

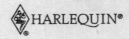 **HARLEQUIN®**

Not The Same Old Story!

 **PRESENTS®**

Exciting, glamorous romance stories that take readers around the world.

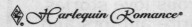 *Harlequin Romance®*

Sparkling, fresh and tender love stories that bring you pure romance.

 **HARLEQUIN®** *Temptation.*

Bold and adventurous— Temptation is strong women, bad boys, great sex!

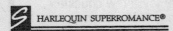 **HARLEQUIN SUPERROMANCE®**

Provocative and realistic stories that celebrate life and love.

 **HARLEQUIN®** **AMERICAN ROMANCE®**

Contemporary fairy tales—where anything is possible and where dreams come true.

 **HARLEQUIN®** **INTRIGUE®**

Heart-stopping, suspenseful adventures that combine the best of romance and mystery.

 **LOVE & LAUGHTER™**

Humorous and romantic stories that capture the lighter side of love.